CONFESSION OF AN ENGLISH SLAVE

My Mistress sprawled at her ease, inspecting me with half an eye while she sipped her drink and dangled the leash emerging between my parted thighs as I faced her. My erection throbbed mercilessly. She ordered me to lift my left foot and then locked a short silver chain around my ankle – my slave bracelet, never to be removed.

'Do you usually get stiff when you are tethered – and know a thrashing awaits?' she murmured.

'I – I am to be thrashed?' I swallowed and gasped as she tugged on the leash and my balls were squeezed.

'Of course you are to be thrashed. Answer the question.'

'Yes, Mistress. O, yes –'

CONFESSION OF AN ENGLISH SLAVE

Yolanda Celbridge

This book is a work of fiction.
In real life, make sure you practise safe sex.

First published in 1999 by
Nexus
Thames Wharf Studios
Rainville Road
London W6 9HT

Typeset by TW Typesetting, Plymouth, Devon

Printed and bound by
Cox & Wyman Ltd, Reading, Berks

ISBN 0 352 33433 9

Contents

Prologue

It is with trembling hand and shameful heart that I pen these memoirs, for I cannot boast of great deeds, only of abject humiliance. Yet I have pride and joy in daring to confess the truth of my submissive nature.

I hope that my story will inspire other males to look into their own hearts and admit their own truth: that they, too, desire nothing so much as to be the slave of a cruel, capricious and selfish lady; that they long to be the slave of a Mistress, and feel her whip on bare flesh at her slightest, sacred whim.

No joy equals that of serving a lady; of living wreathed in the scent of her furs and silks, her robes and intimate things, her boots ever ready to crush her worthless servitor!

No beauty can equal the pain of her instrument of discipline, be it cane, whip or supreme birch, as it descends on her slave's helpless and squirming bare buttocks, without respite and without mercy. No comfort can equal the thongs that bind her slave's limbs as his bare body writhes in his merited agony.

So I trust my story will help the reader understand that shame in one's true submissive nature is overcome a thousandfold by the joy of its fulfilment. For a male to worship and obey a lady, to bathe in her aura of cruel disdain, and kiss her boots in abject humiliation as she crushes him underfoot – this is the true manly joy.

1

Whipped in Disgrace

'In Russia, we are a large family.'

I think I shall never forget those words, for they have taught me so much truth. The sentence continues:

'The ladies of a family must be strong and not afraid to discipline their menfolk.'

Those words, too, stay with me and make me shiver with fear and delight . . .

But I must begin my curious tale with a short explanation. How did a young Englishman find himself on the Trans-Siberian Express, travelling across the steppes and tundra of vast Russia?

That part is simple. My glittering future as a Royal Naval cadet lay in ruins – I shall explain how in due course – and disgraced in the eyes of the Royal Navy, I found the only position open to me was in the merchant marine: I was to join a Norwegian shipping line, my vessel based in the Far East, in the Russian port of Vladivostok. My training at Shoeburyness Naval College stood me in good stead despite my disgrace, and I was to have an officer's grade, even at my tender eighteen years of age. The cachet of a Royal Naval cadet, whether in disgrace or out of it, wields considerable power among foreigners. So I embarked for Vladivostok, looking somewhat uneasily forward to being Third Officer Philip Demesne, of the Royal Norwegian Stavanger Line.

Uneasy, because a merchant seaman, however senior in rank, does not progress to His Majesty's ship of the line –

yet excited, as it was, after all, to be my first ship, and I was to be a proper ship's officer.

If the reader will forgive me a little philosophical musing – we become accustomed to such un-English ways in Russia – a ship is like a woman, a womb protecting her menfolk from harm, as they sail the vast mystery of the ocean (which is also a woman). And in my nineteenth year I knew as much of women as I did of the sea and ships, despite three years' schooling at Shoeburyness: a little, and a mysterious little at that.

Schooling is never the same as the real thing, and my schooling in the mystery of the female had been mere fumbling or vainglorious imagination – until I was unfortunate, or fortunate, enough to be ignominiously expelled from the college.

I was a foundling, probably abandoned by an unhappy serving wench. Perhaps that is why serving girls were kind to me, as I was sympathetic and (I hope) kind to them. I have learnt that however cruel or spiteful a lady may be, and whatever her situation in life, one must always be kind to her: a man is a fool to begrudge the ocean.

I was to take the train to Vladivostok simply because the maritime brokers who got my position for me (at the fee of half my first six months' stipend), Messrs Rundle and Rodd of Limehouse, deemed it cheaper than the sea passage via Singapore and Tokyo, and shorter, too. Also, at that time there was some trouble at the Suez Canal, which meant that ships were cautiously travelling east via Cape Town, thus lengthening the journey considerably.

My journey therefore took me from London to Dover, across to Calais, then to Paris, where I should take the Moscow Express, and in Moscow join the Trans-Siberian. Messrs Rundle and Rodd laughed heartily at my mortified expression as I explained my expulsion and said it was a trifle, and that east of Suez no one gave a fig for such scandals. This cheered me up.

Sea captains do not like waiting for their crew: if I had to rough it on board some barbarous Russian train in 'hard class', then so be it. I had never left England before,

4

but what of that? As a seaman I should spend most of my life out of England; as an orphan and foundling I had nothing to keep me there. I must admit that after the rigours of Shoeburyness, hard class on the Trans-Siberian proved not uncomfortable. And chance arranged that I did not spend too much time in hard class . . .

When I embarked at Dover in the November of 1909, not yet having seen my nineteenth birthday, I was as inexperienced in love as my tender years would suggest, but nevertheless not a virgin. I was proud in my crisp new officer's uniform of navy-blue wool (but without gold stripes as yet), my peaked cap worn jauntily; I imagined my tall person attracted admiring looks from ladies, who love a sailor, as popular wisdom has it. For a sailor is experienced with ladies and has a girl in every port.

Youthful imaginings!

Much is made of the drama of losing one's virgin status; ladies pretend it is a matter of wild passion, swooning, crashing waves and lightning followed by dazzling sunlight and the blossom of beautiful flowers; males prefer the more martial image of a conquering hero howling his triumph amid thunderbolts.

The truth is humbler and more prosaic in almost every case, as in my own. However, it was nice – I think that if one can look back on the occasion of one's defloration and remember it as nice, that is no small satisfaction. And, looking back, I see now what a powerful and sweet influence my first loving had on my subsequent happiness with ladies.

There were three sisters who lived in a cottage by the shore, not far from the college, and who served in the establishment as maids or 'skivvies' (an ungallant and ungracious term to describe any lady). We were nearly fifty young males, all accommodated in a draughty and uncomfortable dormitory, where we slept in hammocks, as though on board an old-fashioned square-rigger.

Most of the tasks attended to by Becky, Jessie and Jane were those, such as cooking, which involved too much delicacy to be left to coarse males. For cleaning and polishing, swabbing the deck (as we had to call the stone floors) and other muscular tasks, we cadets were required to acquit ourselves properly on pain of punishment. Yet, however much we strove to acquit ourselves, punishment was never tardy in visiting our young persons.

Punishment meant corporal punishment: the most severe, brutal and ruthless torment I thought I could ever imagine, delivered with implacable frequency and with rod, whip or even cat-o'-nine-tails on the naked flesh of the alleged miscreant for the most trivial of offences, whether a tarnished button, a loose bootlace or even an insufficiently docile expression on parade. It was as though the various Acts of Parliament mollifying the discipline of seamen had never been passed at all, or their passage had not been communicated to Shoeburyness.

Most floggings were delivered in public, before the other cadets, and sometimes before the officers and their wives and daughters. All beatings were delivered on the bare buttocks, except for the occasions when a cadet was strapped to the mainmast (a sort of flagpole in the middle of the parade ground) and whipped on the naked shoulders and back, with never fewer than thirty strokes. Afterwards he was left strapped, to stand with his wounds visible under rain or sun, until third bell. This punishment was meted to me on two occasions. It was not done to cry out, even as the lash wealed bare skin; nor, I pride myself, did I.

The punishment most severe and most dreaded was to 'kiss the gunner's daughter'. Beyond the mainmast stood a five-pound cannon of the Napoleonic Wars, about twelve feet in length and pointing defiantly out to the North Sea as though to warn off an imagined enemy.

A cadet who kissed the gunner's daughter was led in a nightshirt to the cannon, with the college band playing a funereal march, and watched by the entire company of the establishment, the officers in their dress uniforms and their wives and daughters in their best finery, eyes fluttering with excited mischief behind fans and parasols. Once arrived at the gun, the victim was stretched and strapped to its barrel, ankles and wrists pinioned, and his nightshirt lifted to his neck, but leaving his face exposed so that his expression of agony might be witnessed and relished – not least by the ladies.

His punishment was thirty strokes of a five-foot cane on the bare buttocks, and thirty lashes with the cat on the bare back delivered at the same time. I received this punishment once, and once only, on the occasion of my disgrace and expulsion from the college. My offence was to have acted recklessly in defence of a lady's honour.

If I might digress somewhat – though it is germane to my story – there is a popular legend that ships and naval establishments are infested by the vice of what I must frankly call buggery, that is, the practice of sodomic or anal penetration between young males bereft of the company of ladies. I have no harsh feelings against those whose bent is to indulge themselves thus, although I do find it rather unseemly, and in fact quite stupid: what sane man would desire intimacy with a hairy, smelly male just like himself when there are fragrant ladies to help us overcome our hairiness and smelliness?

However, it is indeed a legend, for the life of a seaman, and especially an officer cadet, is so exhausting that one scarcely has energy enough to sleep, let alone to bugger.

On only one occasion did I encounter, and resist, such advances. It was a boy called Tarker, an arrogant and rather thuggish fellow slightly my senior, and slightly my better in muscular development, though his prowess did not match mine in the boxing ring.

Tarker returned to the dormitory very late one night, much the worse for drink. He stripped entirely naked and did not don his nightshirt, and sang bawdy songs; no one dared tell the fellow to shut up. He lurched from side to side, and his bawdy songs grew to bawdy talk directed at the persons of his fellow cadets. In the wan light it was evident that his manly organ stood menacing and stiff.

Like many drunks, and especially those of the bugger persuasion, he simply would not be ignored. He stopped at my hammock and lewdly lifted my nightshirt to expose my own organ, which he attempted to touch. I pushed his hand away; he slid it towards my manly orbs. I pushed him away more forcibly with a gentle punch to the stomach, and he tottered and fell. I must admit my rage was kindled and I was tempted to punch him in those very orbs, his balls, but this is a measure so dire that any gentleman shrinks from it even in the fiercest combat.

Tarker lay squirming on the floor, unable to get up, he was so drunk. His ramblings brought the duty officer, who shone his torch. Quickly, I threw my shirt over Tarker's erect member to save him from suspicion of buggery or the attempting of it, so he was punished simply for drunkenness.

The next day he received twelve strokes of the rattan cane, on the bare, in front of the whole company of cadets. Thereafter he bore me a grudge, though my timely throwing of my shirt had rescued him from far more severe punishment.

I was sweet on each of the three sisters in turn! They were delicious coquettes, minxes worshipped by the whole corps of lusty and lonely young males. They flirted outrageously with each of us, causing burning jealousies and hatreds as only a lady knows how. We should all have died for one kiss, one flutter of an eyelash!

Rumours abounded that they would entertain gentlemen and go the whole way in love – or lust – in return for ten shillings, or perhaps a guinea. But no one admitted actually to having achieved this ecstasy. We had to content ourselves with walking out or holding hands; perhaps a decorous tea at Babington's Tea Rooms in Southend.

Becky was the eldest sister, I think about four or five years my senior, with a lush mane of corn-blonde tresses, which she liked to toss in the breeze and brush from her mouth, licking her lips as she mischievously eyed a young man. I was her slave – or wished to be – and would have followed her anywhere or done the greatest of manly deeds for one kiss or one glimpse of her shapely ankle sheathed in white silk above shoes shiny as the brightest mirror, with heels as sharp as daggers. In drowsy reverie I longed for her to trample me with those shoes – to show she cared for me . . .

One day she invited me to her cottage for tea! I was sleepless, overjoyed, terrified, proud . . . my organ stood ramrod stiff as I sat at her table and drank in her sweet voice, though I was oblivious of her words. She wore a lovely dress of white satin with a pink bodice, and underneath there were pink petticoats; white stockings and those devilish gleaming black shoes, mirrors like the sea itself. I grasped her waist, begged for a kiss – was granted a chaste peck on her cheek – tried for her lips – she disengaged, laughing with the adorable cruelty of a beautiful coquette.

'O, sir! If I let you go too far you will want to see my petticoats – you will have your hand on my stockings and try to touch me in my private place, on my very drawers. I know you males – you'll feel my breast and pretend it was an accident – my derrière, my thighs . . . your hand will be inside my garters. O, don't deny it!'

I did deny it – in vain, of course. A lady's lustful words inflame us quite as much as the scent and sight of her body. I could not hide my manly arousal.

She teased me and said that I should be whipped for my insolence if the officers found out. I responded that I was no stranger to whipping and would take the harshest flogging for her sake and smile under the lash. She invited me to prove my bold words; I asked in genuine confusion what she meant.

'Why, sir, you may lower your own drawers – in complete decorum, mind, and avoiding all offence – so that I may inspect your derrière and see if you are truthful and bear the marks of which you boast.'

My heart leapt. I was to show her my bare buttocks so that she could see my stripes. I had taken twelve with the cane only the day before, for smoking, and my bottom was still well raw, so, scarcely believing her command, I did as I was told.

She stood at a decorous distance from my exposed and well-striped nates, and I heard her gasp, and then, very

9

briefly, I felt her cool fingertips brush up and down my welts and across their ridges, and heard her gasp and sigh.

'So cruel . . .' she murmured, 'so brave . . .'

I replaced my clothing and grinned rather cheekily at her discomfiture then shrugged and said it was nothing. We were both flushed, and at last she consented to an embrace that was less than chaste, and a kiss, a long, lingering one, full on the lips. I felt her waist press against me, and her skirts billow round my straining uniform trousers; I felt hot, wet silk against my throbbing member!

Her protests grew fainter, and her palms gently stroked my buttocks, with little simpering sighs from the back of her throat. Her cheeks were moist, as though from tears.

At last, gasping, she forced me away and, not flirting now, said like the sweetest and most abashed schoolgirl that I was hurrying things; that she felt strongly for me; but I must respect her lady's confusion, and her need to ponder.

I composed myself and begged her for an assignation on my day off the following week, to which she blushingly assented. I left the cottage still stiff, and the proudest cadet in Shoeburyness. Unfortunately, I was spied on by Lemenson, one of Tarker's unpleasant toadies, and feared the worst. The worst duly came.

In the dormitory that night, Tarker made loud remarks about Miss Becky, seemingly to Lemenson but in reality directed at me. Of course, the whole company knew by now of my assignation; I could not tolerate Tarker's false bragging how he enjoyed Miss Becky's person on numerous occasions for the princely sum of two shillings, how she liked being buggered in the hayloft, and sucking his member to spurt, which she loved to swallow . . .

My blood boiled. I leapt from my hammock. Suffice it to say that I quite forgot myself and gave Tarker a veritable thrashing with fists and feet, continuing to kick and pummel him when he lay squirming in deserved agony on the floor, agony which I hoped was unfeigned. I rained kicks to his loathsome face and stomach, and, on reflection, I think it possible that the sodomite, in sodomites' mysterious ways, actually enjoyed his drubbing.

At any rate, the inevitable happened. I had just made Tarker howl with a vigorous kick to the stomach when the duty officer intervened. Tarker clutched his manly parts and writhed in an agony which was entirely feigned now, sobbing that I had kicked him in the privates.

Now, the code of honour of Shoeburyness was as strict as the discipline for its infringement. Fighting was forbidden, but a Nelsonian blind eye was turned provided it took place ostensibly in secret and according to Marquess of Queensberry rules. To kick a man in the privates was heinousness exceeded only by the crime of taking a lady's name in vain or lewdly.

If I had truthfully accused Tarker of the latter offence, agreed by my fellows, then my rage and alleged mistreatment of his manly parts should have been viewed quite leniently; it would have been Tarker who kissed the gunner's daughter for insulting a lady. But to blab or sneak was the most heinous crime in our cadets' unwritten rules, and so I did not blab. It was I who was condemned to kiss the gunner's daughter and be expelled in disgrace at once after my punishment.

The whole college, womenfolk and all, witnessed my humiliation. On the parade ground, an officer ripped my cadet's uniform to shreds with the point of his sword while I stood trembling to attention trying to hold back my tears. Then I donned my nightshirt, to the ladies' smirks and titters, and removed my underthings so that I was naked underneath it.

As I was led in my nightshirt to my flogging, I saw a pair of blue, wide eyes blink from the kitchen window: Miss Becky's! I felt cruel thongs strap me tightly to the cold metal; my nightshirt was raised, the wind chill on my bare body – my thighs were wide apart, exposing my privates quite shamelessly (or so I imagined) – yet the thought that *she* might witness my shame had the effect of hardening both my resolve and my manly organ!

I took full thirty with cat and thirty with rattan on

naked back and naked bottom without crying out once, though my shudders of pain heated the gunmetal to roasting under my squirming belly. Only when the torment eased, and I was unbound, did I permit myself a long, sobbing wail of agony.

In my civilian clothing I was cast out of Shoeburyness, with only my suitcase, my savings – enough to get me to London and to live on for a few weeks, I thought – and without a word of farewell from officers or fellows. I felt the most wretched creature on earth, and the smarting of my weals, which I thought I had borne manfully, now tormented me as evidence of my wretched shame. Tears coursed down my cheeks; I wandered aimlessly in the streets of Shoeburyness until it grew dark.

Suddenly I felt strong fingers grasp my arm and pull me towards a brightly lit doorway. It was Miss Becky, as bright-eyed, flushed and fragrant as I could have wished to imagine her. I had unconsciously directed my steps to her cottage, and now she pulled me inside.

I spent that night in Miss Becky's bed. It was the time of my defloration, and the sweetest, kindest night I had ever experienced. I felt I dreamt . . .

She made me strip and bathed me, naked, in her own bath; she anointed my wounds with soothing unguents, fed me and kissed me and begged me to tell her my story, which I blurted to her in every detail. I saw in her eyes, and by her moistened cheeks, that her heart melted for me.

My own heart melted when she led me to her chamber, lit only a single dim candle, and in its flickering light disrobed – the first time my eyes had drunk in the beauty of a willing, smiling lady, eyes misted heavy with love.

With the purring grace of a cat, she dropped her skirts to the floor, then her petticoats, and I saw her white silk stockings held by gleaming straps to a tight jarretière of pale white satin which bit adorably into her smooth belly-flesh. She wore no drawers and whispered shyly that I must think her a proper slut. I fell to her feet and kissed her toes, then her ankles, licking her stockinged feet until they were quite wet. She laughed and told me to rise.

12

'To your feet, I mean,' she said, tenderly pressing my engorgement, 'for I see you are well risen already, sir.'

I babbled that her beauty could provoke no less in me, and she drew me to the bed. Soon, we were both naked and underneath the cover; then the cover was thrown off and we clutched each other in the sweetest of embraces. I pleasured her with eager fingers, then, at her gentle insistence, with tongue and lips, which drank the love-juices that flowed from the swollen lips of her haven.

Her practised thighs straddled mine and showed me how to enter and how to pleasure her wet, silky temple of Venus, and reach the little button of delight that she called her 'boatman'.

I plunged inside her as her pumping, muscled thighs straddled me; how can words express the glory of her pale creamy teats as they swayed above me, the nipples stiff and serene like proud young plums – the swell of her mound as its fleecy hillock danced over my belly – the ecstasy as I gave my seed to the sucking wet embrace of her naked womb?

We made love until daybreak, and Miss Becky whispered that she had watched my punishment and had been wet between her thighs as she saw my naked body flogged, just as her cheeks had been wet with tears of sympathy. Then she coyly confessed that she loved to see a male's croup dance under her lady's lash, to prove his devotion, and had planned to beat me herself, to test my bold promise; a birch was already fashioned for my bare buttocks. I was astounded, but my heart beat madly in a strange new dance.

My member stiffened at her words! She said that I must not think her a blushing virgin, yet no trollop either. She had beaten males and got a curious satisfaction from it, I sensed as a kind of revenge for her low situation in life and the taunts a 'skivvy' must endure from louts.

Before I could make my manly assurances and protests, she put a finger to my lips, writhed on my stiff member until I was breathless and thought I should faint with pleasure, and said this disparity in our situations meant we should never meet again. I was to venture forth and make a name for myself in the world – it was Miss Becky who directed me to the maritime brokers – while she was to stay in Essex and hope to find 'a good man, an obedient man' . . .

Women's wisdom is not to be disputed. I begged only for a parting favour to remember her by.

'A lock of my hair?' she teased as she brought me to a gasping, shuddering spend, the like of which my own feeble stimulations had never approached.

'That, too, if you please, miss,' I panted, 'and a lock from the forest that adorns you so thick and wet *down there* . . .'

'Granted, my brave flogged officer – but what else?'

'The birching you had planned, to test me.'

'What? –' she rubbed the welts that ridged my bottom '– why, I think you have passed your test, sir.'

'No, Miss Becky,' I cried fiercely. 'I beg you, test me – make me worthy of *you*.'

She smiled, almost sadly despite her flushed and happy face.

'You poor boy. It will hurt very much,' she murmured.

'As hard as you can, miss,' I said.

'A birching of thirty strokes . . .'

'Twice that, miss! Three times that! From your rods, on my bare bottom,' I pleaded. 'It shall be my honour.'

'Well . . . before breakfast, then, before my sisters rise,' she said finally.

Her sisters! I had quite forgotten them!

'Won't they hear the crack of the birch?' I said, anxious for her own modesty.

She grinned with a lovely impish sparkle in her eyes and placed my hand on the lips of her temple, which gushed with new love-oil.

'O, they'll hear all right . . . every lash and every squirm you make. That's part of the fun. You see? I'm wet just thinking about birching your bare bum . . . sir.'

I slept fitfully. In the morning she birched me for an hour and laid forty strokes on my naked, squirming buttocks before it was time for breakfast. I took my

14

beating bent over and touching my toes, like a humble schoolboy, and my legs wide apart so that my balls, tight under my stiff member, hung clearly visible. The thought that her birch twigs might brush my balls by accident, or even by design, made me stiffen to bursting in my excitement at this test of shame ... the joyful shame of being in a lady's thrall and possession.

I had never felt such agony, not even when kissing the gunner's daughter; nor such joy, even inside her silken wet slit. She flogged me naked, and was naked herself.

Every person, I think, remembers the moment of defloration; a lover of a lady's discipline always remembers his first whipping from a female hand – more specially his first birching. I have taken many and far more severe birchings from far crueller ladies, until my naked buttocks were wealed raw to the bone, but still I recall with shivering fondness the implacable and practised severity of Miss Becky's birch on my bare bottom. She knew how to make a male squirm – she was expert! And her expertise thrilled me.

I know now that true ladies are born to take whip to the male; that their expertise is as perfect and natural as their breasts, or their croups, or their sweet quims ... I have always dreaded, and never sought, corporal discipline from a lady. Yet if a lady desires to impose her will by this fearful means, a male must submit to her, always.

My fesses are no stranger to punishment from a lady's hand – from tawse and cane, from the cat, or the heaviest bullwhip, to the fearful knout itself – yet the birch is always the cruellest and most sensuous of disciplinary instruments, for the birch is most truly alive: she is a woman. Her twigs crack and cling and claw at a man's buttocks, embracing them with darting tongues of white-hot fire, as though reluctant to leave his skin even in preparation for the next and crueller stroke.

Miss Becky's first cut was truly fire; the second more than fire; the third – O, how can I describe my sobbings and wrigglings, my pleas for mercy as my foolhardy challenge was visited on my naked person, and her sweet, soft voice intoned, counting:

'Ten . . . eleven . . . twelve . . . my, that made you jump, sir! . . . twenty-three, twenty-four . . . only two dozen yet, and you are bucking like a stallion! You were so brave when you took your flogging on the gun, sir. I think Mistress Birch shall have to tickle your soft bare bum that bit harder, for its impudence in squirming so. And the impudence of your manly organ – I gave no permission for John Thomas to stand so insolently.'

How I regretted my foolish boasts – and yet, under the steady stroking of her birch, how I longed for it never to stop, and for her to reduce me to the most abject and utter humiliance! It was as though I were alone with my Mistress and the sweet agony of her birching, and all cares and troubles had fled from me. There was only the stinging and smarting and burning of my wealed bare flesh, both our panting breaths and the perfume of her body, scented with the proud sweat of flogging.

On and on the birch hissed and crackled, while my lashed buttocks danced in spasms of trembling, helpless surrender, and she halted only when it was quite denuded of twigs.

I fell to my knees, clutching her heaving calves and thighs, and kissed the birch's stump, then Miss Becky's bare, sweating feet, her belly and sodden hairy mound, the lips of her temple, and the stiff plums of her breasts.

After my birching, my member was rock, and she obliged me to enter her once more, this time from behind, with her bending over and touching her toes, in imitation of my own schoolboy's flogging posture. I plunged my member into her silken wet purse of treasure and spurted almost at once, hearing her cry, 'O! O! O!' as I felt her belly flutter and her hand directing my fingers to caress her stiff little boatman. I slowly disengaged, rubbing my helmet against her engorged fount-lips, and sobbing with pain and joy.

'There!' she said brightly, tapping my softened organ. 'We've both spent, so now you'll be decent for breakfast, sir, and won't be embarrassed on the train to London . . .'

* * *

Her sisters giggled as I squatted stiffly to eat my bacon and eggs. They knew! They had listened to my agony, and I loved them for it. At the station I showered them all with kisses of gratitude before I boarded the train.

I bore Miss Becky's weals! And that is why my walk was jaunty, if a little stiff, as I embarked on the ferry to France, as proud as if I were master of the ship myself.

2

Bondage

A gentleman who has newly known the love of a lady finds his thoughts filled with her, and his whole being becomes alive and bright; yet her beauty also awakens him to the beauty of all ladies . . .

My journey was a joy: there were so many ladies to – I must not say ogle or inspect – to gaze on with adoration. I did not feel guilty towards Miss Becky's memory in my new-found lustful curiosity. Had she not ordered me to go out into the world and make myself a man?

One lady in particular drew my attention, and everyone else's. The travelled reader may be familiar with the Dover Marine station, where the passengers disembark from the London train and proceed through a labyrinth of dank corridors directly to the ship. All the passengers were obliged unaccountably to wait for a good five minutes. As we chafed, the reason for our discomfort became apparent. From the first-class train carriage emerged a female figure of the grandest and most mysterious beauty, swathed in dark sable fur and white silk, and glittering with gold and diamonds.

Her face was delicately veiled, under a mane of blonde tresses, lustrous as gemstones, and a discreet hat of tiered black silk. She was tall, I estimated nearly six feet, and under her furs a lithe tiger's agility was sensuously and irresistibly apparent. Oblivious of our angry or envious glances, she stepped over the cobbles with sure foot, and I noticed that her feet were encased in boots with the sharpest of toes and highest of spiked heels, gleaming brighter than Miss Becky's, yet the piercing click of her steps did not falter.

Beside her gleaming feet tapped another implement – she carried a walking-stick. On close examination it was thin and springy, and I guessed it to be of whalebone encased in black leather, with the suppleness and strength of a corset's rib.

This was no ordinary walking-stick but a powerful cane, and with my new and practised eye I saw that its only use was not support but chastisement. This made the lady even more beautiful and mysterious to me. I looked into her piercing, luminous green eyes and for a second I was *sure* – youthful vanity! – that she met my gaze, stabbing me with her eyes and making me tremble.

She was accompanied by a servant, I assumed. A veritable man-monster, well over six feet, and with a completely shaven head gleaming in the pale gaslight, which gave his darkly handsome and slightly oriental features a sinister look. He was not much older than myself but looked as though his muscles were whipcord toughened beyond his years.

He carried her trunk, an enormous thing of brass and mahogany, over his shoulder, as though it weighed no more than a feather. Under his tunic, his muscles rippled clearly, for the tunic was a uniform of tight, almost skin-tight shiny leather in battleship grey. I was filled with an unreasoning hatred of this man!

She and her servant embarked first; the officers and crew bowed to her; only then were we mortals permitted to go up the gangplank, by which time the supply of bowing and scraping had been used up. The ship was not very crowded, and I scoured it in search of her, not quite knowing why, but she had disappeared. When I gave up my search, I chose the fresh air and found a wooden bench on the deck.

The beauty of the English Channel is often ignored by ferry passengers too intent on the stuffy pleasures of the hamper of victuals and the brandy bottle. I was privileged to enjoy a magnificent winter's day, a pale sun in a watery blue sky illuminating the entire expanse of grey choppy water, the churning wake of our ship accompanied by the caws and swoops of handsome seagulls. This winter's day seemed almost spring to my joyful heart.

I discovered on this crossing that there is no point at which land is not visible: when the white cliffs of Dover have gone from view, there is the reassuring lump of Cap Gris Nez to take their place, and there is a magical moment in the middle of the Strait of Dover when both lands are visible at once. This is strangely comforting. I also discovered that my sea legs, learnt at Shoeburyness, had not deserted me. I felt as right as rain while all around me passengers groaned their way to the guard rail in various stages of distress, and as the ship heaved, so did they.

This gave me a rather mean sense of superiority, not least when the place beside me was taken by none other than the hulking figure in grey leather, who moaned and rolled his eyes, his tanned features suffused with greenish pallor, and made the noises of voiding himself over the white-capped Channel while I looked politely away.

He rested for a time, recovering some of his tan, and after casting me a baleful look for the crime of witnessing his distress he lurched unsteadily towards the lower deck, after stumbling against me in an involuntary embrace. We disengaged. I said 'sorry', like a proper Englishman, for *his* clumsiness – and without hesitation I followed him, intent on discovering my lady's hiding place: certainly, in one of the half-dozen day cabins reserved for first-class passengers who did not desire two hours' mingling with the common folk.

We descended two decks before entering a cosy passageway of apartments, into one of which the giant disappeared. There was no one else around. I heard her voice, sharply addressing him in some foreign language. I was uncertain what to do; the discovery of her presence seemed to lead nowhere else. Then, as the ship lurched there was a creak, and the beaten oak door of her stateroom fell open to a depth of about six inches. It was banged shut; the ship lurched again, and again the door opened. This time the lady laughed, a melodious peal of softness as beautiful as a waterfall, and she said, rather loudly and in curiously accented English: 'O, let it stay open. There is no one to peek.'

Like a booby, I did not ponder her use of my own language, despite her address to the servant in a foreign tongue. Needless to say, on hearing her words I positioned myself athwart the bulwark so that I *could* peek . . . the use of that word suggesting to my lustful intelligence that there should be something worth peeking at.

I looked into her stateroom. The mahogany trunk lay on the floor beside a leather sofa and all the accoutrements of a plush first-class cabin. From it extruded an array of ladies' clothing, both bodices and skirts, and flouncy, frilly pastel shades of more intimate and delicious apparel. I was shocked at this display of intimate things before a mere manservant.

The brute was standing rigidly to attention, while his Mistress placed a cigarette in a long, diamond-studded holder, lit it, then blew a plume of blue smoke disdainfully over him.

'My, you are a mess, Paul,' she said, again in her fluting, sensuous English. 'We are leaving England for *la belle France*, so you had better change into something more sumptuous. And you stink of sweat. You *are* an ugly brute. I scarcely know why I keep you on.'

She giggled, a sweet peal of bells.

'But you can't understand a word I say, you poor stupid Tatar. Perhaps that is why . . . and you haven't paid your bondsman's debt, have you? Nor shall you ever, my poor dumb *robotnik*.'

At this, she rapped a flurry of words at him in the strange foreign language, which might have been French, or anything, for all I knew . . . although her high-cheeked, aquiline beauty did not seem to have the dark grace of the Mediterranean people. There was something of the north in her, of the proud cold mountains and plains, and the icy ocean. I did know her to be beauty, wherever she hailed from. And I longed to find out.

Abruptly, she bent over, revealing a croup of swelling, magnificent ripeness pressed so firmly against the thin silken sheath of her skirts that I audibly gasped, and I felt my organ tremble into helpless stiffness at the sight.

She retrieved another servant's uniform, this one of bright crimson leather, from her trunk and threw it at Paul's feet. Then she selected garments for herself, pulling out one delicious silken shift or petticoat after another, and drawers, not the normal billowing silks, but tight little thongs that would scarcely seem to cover a lady's modesty, and be all the more beguiling for their teasing. She gazed into the mirror, cooing softly with girlish pleasure as she held them up. She rapped again in the foreign language and Paul obediently unbuttoned the back of her dress.

She shrugged off the billowing robe and stood in bodice and petticoat of the palest pink silk. I was taken aback by such immodesty, even though the pair were evidently foreigners; enraged more at the obvious intimacy between Mistress and servant. Now the brute moved his fingers to her breast and calmly undid the buttons of her chemise, which fell, too, leaving her bare-shouldered and corseted. I was furious with jealousy. Yet at the sight of her tight satin corselet, the whalebone stays clamping her slender, muscled back like a vice, my organ grew to full stiffness.

She turned slightly, with a coquettish grin, to the mirror, and then to the doorway, as if she knew I were peeking. And I saw that her corselet was in fact a waspie that covered her waist and lower back, but left her bubbies bare and thrust high. I was speechless.

Those breasts were mountains of delight, pale, creamy orbs of silky-smooth alabaster skin jutting proudly like two alps, and topped with big hillocks for nipples, with wide saucers of pink flesh spread tenderly around their quivering, hard little peaks, which seemed, in my obscured vision, to glisten or sparkle with some mysterious force.

As she turned, the silk of her petticoat flounced deliciously, trapping her buttocks in a clinging embrace. One fold of silk managed, coquettish as a sheaf of birch twigs, to trap itself in the furrow of her orbs, so that it lodged there, revealing her fesses in every splendour, as though they had been entirely naked. She turned again; the silk clung to her lady's place, the wet firm hillock nestling atop her swelling thighs, and I saw the outline of a magnificent curly bush that seemed to crawl like a forest beast all the way up her belly to her button; I marvelled, for it was obvious she wore no drawers at all under her pink silk petticoat!

I had never heard, nor dreamt, of such a thing, my experience with Miss Becky aside. Even the most shameless of public ladies will make a fetish of her drawers or knickers – it is her one sanction of privacy and modesty. What freedom and majesty must reign in this lady's breast, I imagined, to have no need of such things; to walk with the air swirling around her naked privates, serene in the knowledge of her secret power over men's desiring eyes. This regal disdain made her all the more precious, all the more unattainable, hence infinitely desirable – by my heart, and by my rampantly immodest organ that perched stiff in her honour between my own thighs.

I wondered that her *robotnik* had no such reaction and supposed, jealously, that familiarity with her charm had made him indifferent. This was unexpectedly proved when she barked another command and he obediently, and without expression, peeled off his tight leathers and stood before his Mistress entirely naked.

My eyes widened in genuine astonishment. His flaccid organ hung placidly like a tame wild beast, dangling across the meaty slabs of his thighs to over a foot in length. I was quite giddy at this spectacle and, I suppose, jealous of the man: fifteen inches, I thought wildly, and with a fist's girth. Yet even faced with its Mistress's body, it slept!

And to my further astonishment, his entire muscled body, the slabs swelling like bricks under taut skin, was completely hairless, like his head. This included his manly area: the huge organ and balls shone pink and menacing, their denudation robbing them of the mink's curly friendliness. Yet they were not entirely nude, for a large tattoo covered the manly area – balls and right up to the

23

helmet of the member – in dark green; it seemed to represent a pine tree or some dangerous foreign flower with spiky leaves that seemed to swallow up the bulge of the helmet while the roots clutched the balls as though holding them prisoner.

The lady gave him no more than a fleeting glance, then smiled and ordered her *robotnik* to go into the tiny bathroom and fetch her a jug of water, which he did, afterwards proceeding to splash and gurgle as he bathed himself. He had his back to me, the muscles of back and buttocks rippling in perfect terrifying harmony, like a well-oiled machine, and I thought him a suitable servant for such a precious lady, for he could surely crush any assailant. His back and buttocks also seemed tattooed, with long fronds like tendrils of another plant. When I peered more closely, I saw to my horror that they were the ridges of savage whipmarks.

My lady took a sponge and decorously daubed her face and under her arms, then slowly unfastened her corset, playing with each hole as though teasing an unseen audience, and revealing inch after tantalising inch of firm white skin. Finally, she sat on the stool quite naked but for her pink petticoat, her full peach spread like swelling ripe moons over the pink cushion. I do not think any gentleman can fail to melt at the sight of a lady's back and croup, with her hair cascading on her spine – in full or only in half-nudity. It is the loveliest view in nature.

I saw now that she, too, bore a tattoo! This was something I had never imagined in a lady, although of course I was familiar with tattoos at my naval school and had toyed with the idea of proving my virility by having one done. I never did – something in me revolted at the idea of one of the grubby male 'artists' of Shoeburyness or Southend applying his needle to my naked skin. And I realise now that while I wanted to suffer the adornment of a tattoo, I wanted the needle and inks to be a *lady*'s.

Her tattoo was thin and delicate, in a dark mauve shade that was almost purple. It snaked like a vine across her belly and up to her breasts, and its mysterious root delved into the pink petticoat, at her very lady's place. But it was no vine: with chilling clarity, the tattoo represented a cat-o'-nine-tails. Yet her back, where such a fearsome engine might reasonably be depicted, was bare of adornment.

Each thong spread delicately across her porcelain flesh, and each tip was adorned with a single diamond, which I saw was pierced into her skin by a pin like an earring's. The two longest thongs of the whip curled around her breasts, and their tips melded with the tips of her nipples, on each of whose jutting pink bulbs a diamond sparkled. How I longed to see the handle of the fearsome tattooed whip – the lady's place where it began and had its power . . .

The servant Paul emerged from his toilette, dripping, and she curtly ordered him to stand to attention once more. He did so, shivering as the rivulets of cold water showered the carpet, rolling in time with the ship's heave, and the lady smiled thinly at his discomfort.

Very slowly, she swivelled on her chair and, still with that thin, distant smile, lifted her petticoats to her knee; then above her thigh, until the pink silk was bundled across her belly and both of us males saw the wondrous flowering of her pubic thatch, a fleecy mink so bounteous that it seemed a veritable jungle of golden curls swallowing her belly and descending between thighs and furrow. And into that fleece descended the handle of her tattooed whip, a thick stave of leather, artfully braided in depiction, that from a distance looked like a massive male organ with its home between her sacred lips.

Then she lowered one dainty hand and placed the long fingers at the top of her fount, where I could just see the pink swollen lips of her gash shining moist through their hairy adornment. Gently, she began to rub herself there, moving her thighs in sinuous rhythm to squeeze her fingers into her slit, where they delved deeper and deeper.

All the time she stared her servant in the eye, and I saw the male swallow, then briefly close his eyes – to open them again at her barked command – as his member began to

25

tremble and stiffen. It was an awesome sight. The engine made little jerking movements, like a beast awakening from slumber, and gradually inched up towards its full erection, a towering, giant thing, which made me almost sorry for its owner, as I imagined it would frighten any but the most brazen of ladies.

The foreskin was drawn fully back, revealing a dark puce helmet shining and quivering as its owner shivered, watching the voluptuous frotting of his Mistress, who caressed her boatman more and more ardently. Her thighs writhed in a squeezing dance, and she began to breathe in short gasps; I saw that juices of her lust ran thickly through her thatch and trickled on the sweet soft thigh-skin, gleaming like the deep pools of her goddess's eyes.

'Such power, the sight of a lady frigging herself!' she murmured, in English, with surprising nonchalance. 'Did I give you permission to be excited, Paul?'

Then the movements of her fingers became a blur as she flicked hard and fast at the swollen bud that peeped now quite prominently between her fleshy quim-lips, and her writhing grew intense, her bare buttocks shifting and slamming on the cushion as though to punish it. When she gasped aloud a dozen times and closed her eyes, I knew the lady had frigged herself to a spend.

The male's organ was ramrod stiff, as was my own. Despite the lurching of the ship, the door happily stayed open for my inspection, almost as though wedged. When the lady's gasping had subsided, she looked down at the cushion of her seat and wiped it with a finger, which she held up. It shone wetly from the soaking of her lady's fluid.

'Pooh!' she said gaily.

Then she rose and placed her wet finger on the servant's lips, and on his peehole.

'Stiff!' she murmured to the erect organ itself. 'Hard, like a brute. I must teach you manners, brute.'

With studied nonchalance, she lifted her cane.

'This will hurt me more than it hurts you, my boy,' she said in the accent of an English schoolmistress, and giggled almost shyly.

As the male stood, member still throbbing stiff, she lifted the cane to the full length of her arm, swished it through the air with a loud whistle, and brought it squarely and hard across his bare buttocks.

Vip!

The crack echoed through the cabin. Only the slightest trembling of his fesses indicated that he had taken a savage canestroke to the bare.

'One,' she murmured, licking her lips and with eyebrows innocently raised, as though surprised at the delicacy of some new sweetmeat.

The cane whistled again, and she brought it down on the same place with horrid force. When it was raised from his skin, a vivid raw welt was left.

'Two,' she breathed again, her lips curled in amusement.

The naked male merely quivered, but his face remained expressionless. The cane stroked his bare buttocks a third time with, it seemed, redoubled force, although his Mistress seemed scarcely to exert herself. I thought fondly of Miss Becky's expertise and knew I had found her sister in pain.

The caning continued to eight or nine strokes, each cracking louder than the last and making the male's bare buttocks into quivering flans of wealed raw flesh. He could not help but clench his fesses as each whistle of the cane signalled a new impact, and I saw that his lower lip was trembling slightly and that his eyes were moist.

'Ten!' she said. 'Mmm . . . you are an arrogant beast, aren't you, Paul?' She added a remark in his own language, to which he made no answer.

'I lied to you,' she continued coolly in English, 'when I said it would hurt me more than it hurts you. It does not hurt me at all, my dear slave, but I know it hurts you most dreadfully, and you must take it like the brute you are. I love to beat you on the bare, Paul: make those buttocks crimson in agony, and you forbidden to utter even a squeal. I love to flog all males on their squirming bare bums . . .'

Her voice tailed off, almost dreamily. She proceeded to

27

flog him another two dozen times, counting at first in English, but then lapsing into his own barbarous tongue and making him shut his eyes in distress.

The man's naked fesses were a livid and quivering patchwork of weals by the time she announced, in English again, that he had taken a good four dozen. The flogged male made no response, but his organ still throbbed in, it seemed to me, mightier erection than ever. I recalled my own response to the stimulus of Miss Becky's birch and wondered if there were not more – a multitude – of males like me, whose fesses longed for the whip of a cruel lady . . .

'Well!' she said in her smoky, sensuous lilt. 'There is a small advance on your wages. She smiled her thin smile.

She barked something else in the foreign language, then returned to her boudoir table and selected pots and tubes and brushes, for the maquillage of her face. But she did not resume her seat. Instead, she bent over the table with her face inches from the glass and spread her thighs: the thick tufts of her pubic mink were sumptuously visible, draped around her furrow and quim-lips and even the pink pucker of her anus bud, which was surprisingly wide and crinkled like a threepence.

At once, the servant padded towards her, slowly and mechanically. His Mistress began to apply rouge and powder, pausing to inspect herself and smile in satisfaction as the naked male impassively pushed his stiff member between her parted thighs, and with a practised and fluid motion sank its massive shaft into her open, wet quim, right to his balls.

She made no remark, or any physical response to his entry, not even as his buttocks began to thrust and the giant organ plunged repeatedly into the silky wet chamber of her fount, withdrawing to its full extent with little sucking noises, and revealing the shaft slippery with gleaming and copious love-oil.

With steady fingers, my lady continued to paint her face as she was vigorously poked from behind, like an animal. As the male performed his shameful duty, I heard the hard slaps as his belly struck the orbs of her naked peach with each thrust.

I saw that her thighs quivered as she squeezed or relaxed the pressure of her cavern on his helmet, and I sensed she was expertly gauging the moment when he should spend in her, and alternately urging and delaying his spurt. Calmly, she applied rouge to her diamond-studded nipples and reached below her belly, even as his organ swived her gash, to powder her mink hairs and rouge the already reddened lips of her filled slit.

Abruptly, she clicked her fingers, and the brute disengaged from her quim with a loud plopping sound. She reached behind her and grasped the cheeks of her peach, spreading them wide so that the pucker of her anus bud was stretched and the little dark hole clearly open, just like a male's peehole. With brutish obedience, the male now placed the tip of his erection at her anus and thrust slowly until his helmet was embedded in that tender orifice to a depth of perhaps an inch.

She grunted softly and shifted, spreading her thighs wider and thrusting her buttocks very high so that her chin was almost touching the boudoir table, and her pendulous bubbies flopped deliciously beneath it, dangling and wobbling and glinting with their diamond studs on fully stiff nipples. The male now thrust firmly into her anus so that his shaft was buried right to the hilt, and now his Mistress emitted a louder grunt, of amused satisfaction.

He began to buck her in the anal hole just as strongly as in her quim – in fact, I think even more fiercely – and his lady took this dreadful torment with every evidence, not of discomfort, but of sensuous delight. I saw her buttocks squeeze tightly, her thighs tremble as she milked the huge organ that must surely cause her the most extreme agony. The male applied himself vigorously to his task, as though in some small way to avenge himself for his cruel and unmerited flogging. And she urged him on, her voice now a low growl.

'Do me, slave, *do* me, fuck my bumhole raw, give me all your spunk in my bum, you dirty beast, you brute ... O!

O! I'll whip you for this! I'll whip you to the bone, your arse will be red meat under my cane, I promise . . . You dare to bugger your Mistress! O! O! Split me in two with your fucking, split my bum and my belly with that cock of yours, spunk in me till you drown my hole, slave . . .'

I had never heard such language from a lady! Yet its effect on me was electrifying, as it was on her brutal paramour or slave. His fucking (I must use her own beastly term) grew stronger and his thrusts into her poor squirming bumhole more violent, until I really did think he would split her writhing, sweat-dewed buttocks clean apart.

The ship's siren sounded, long and mournful.

'We are arriving in port! We mustn't miss the train for Paris,' she panted. 'Hurry and do me, you rough brute, spunk in my dirty hole. I want to feel your cream spurting right at my belly's root. Bugger me, bugger my bum hard . . . Yes – yes – O! O! O!'

A deep, gurgling sigh arose from Paul's throat, and he shook and trembled as his buttocks slammed frantically against my lady, and I could see he was in the throes of a massive spend, which lasted far longer than I would have thought possible.

'Yes . . .' she moaned, 'heavy cream, heavy cream . . .'

'Ahhh . . .' he grunted, as the ship's siren sounded anew.

Gradually his motions slowed, and I saw that her bumhole was dilated from a threepence to a crown, and far beyond. I thought, disagreeably, of Tarker and his sodomic practices and reflected that such love of discomfort was not confined to the male bugger classes. I was surprised that even in her moment of passion, her voice expressed itself in the flawless diction of a lady of noble breeding: normally, in such moments, we revert to our origins.

What, I wondered, *were* her origins?

They disengaged, and she ordered her slave to bathe, with a tap to his tight balls that I thought rather harsh, though it did not seem to hasten the gradual softening of his glistening organ. Her thighs shone sticky where his creamy secretions, just as copious as her quim's juices, flowed and mingled with her own.

'I shan't have time to bathe,' she panted gaily, 'so I shall smell of your filthy spunk, Paul. No knickers – my dress shall be all scented with chestnut blossoms! O, how I'll punish you for *that*!'

She spoke briefly in his own language. Stiffly, her slave bowed, then knelt and kissed her feet before a kick to his belly ordered him to his toilette. I thought I detected a smile on those thick brute lips and a faraway gleam in his eyes . . .

I made to creep away, for I was anxious not to miss the Paris train myself. I cast one longing look as I watched my lady don corset and petticoat, toss her hair and roll the smoothest, shiniest white silk stockings up over the pale satin skin of her thighs and calves. As she was fastening the eyehole laces of her left boot, she glanced up suddenly towards the door. Her eyes fell on its aperture for but a fleeting moment, before she looked away to attend to her delectable shiny footwear – footwear that with a sudden shiver I wanted to feel crush me, crush my straining cock and balls, for their impudence in stiffening for her, before her lady's cane descended in cold fury on my helpless naked bottom.

But for that moment I was sure those luminous green eyes pierced mine, electrifying me, and that a cruel, sardonic smile played on her full red lips, as though contemplating torments to come for my abject male body. Wishful thinking or youthful imaginings?

Youthful imaginings are not always wrong.

3

Tethered and Trussed

Travelling arrangements at that time were still quite civilised, and the voyager was not usually obliged to encumber himself with passports, photographs and the like, although the further one went from England, and civilisation, the more documents one required. I was well provided for my trip, thanks to Messrs Rundle and Rodd.

My laisser passer from HM Foreign Office was in my breast pocket, ready for extraction, with my cash wallet snug inside my coat. However, I was grandly welcomed to France by a uniformed fellow (in need of a Wilkinson Sword razor), after a desultory inspection of my single holdall case, and ushered on board the Paris train, which waited by the ship at the Calais Maritime rail halt.

This was my introduction to abroad! At first sight Calais, with its hulks and cranes and sluices, looked much like Liverpool or Tilbury or any other port. The train rolled out, past a pretty little town, although the buildings seemed to jostle with no apparent regularity – part of foreign charm, I supposed – and into a flat, rather mournful countryside which reminded me of East Anglia or the Fens. This soon became vast rolling cornfields with coppices and quaint villages nestling in their midst; I was pleased to find abroad quite agreeable and the people civil, although judging by the males there was obviously a fearful crisis of razor blades.

If I permitted myself a little smugness, it was because my meagre savings in English banknotes had been exchanged in London for an alarming pile of crinkly and none too clean paper, which I was assured were French francs, and that one English pound was good for ten across the Channel. I must admit that youthful venery made me think of the Continental ladies' favours that could be purchased or leased for £10 . . .

My third-class wooden seat was not too uncomfortable, and the train was only half full. All the males were enthusiastically smoking villainous yellow cigarettes, which perfumed the air with a curious acrid smell, while the ladies had not stinted themselves in their use of cloying fruity scents. I at once assumed this was how abroad, or at least France, must invariably smell, and I detected another, indelicate fragrance beneath the tobacco and the scent, which they seemed intended to mask. Suffice it to say that on the advice of Messrs Rundle and Rodd I had equipped myself with a supply of English 'Sanitas' toilet tissue . . .

But I suppressed ungallant thoughts about our allies in the Entente Cordiale! Did not our good King Edward spend his winters at Biarritz, and some of the time between in Paris? The trip to Paris was just over four hours, giving me time to enjoy dinner. It was already twilight and soon became quite dark, so I made my way to the dining car as soon as the steward rang the dinner bell.

The dining car was quite empty. It was sumptuous, with crystal and linen, like a grand hotel. A fawning waiter beckoned me to a table as though I myself were the King of England, and my smugness at being an Englishman abroad grew apace. On opening the menu, a book as large and heavy as a church Bible, I found to my horror that I had blundered into the first-class dining car (it was in fact the only one, my companions in third class preferring jugs of wine, bread and smelly cheese, which perfumed the smoky air still further). But when I translated the prices from thousands of francs into English pounds, it seemed I had got a bargain.

There was a soup, fish, and a grill, and salad and some creamy pudding, and I had a half-bottle of wine, as recommended by another, still grander waiter, with a key chain round his neck. It was agreeable, but having no taste for liquor I contented myself with a few sips and concentrated on my food. I had forgotten how hungry I was.

It was only when sated that I began to inspect my surroundings and saw, three tables away, my cruel shipboard Mistress, sitting alone with her back to me. She wore a bewitching dress of black silk, which left her entire back and shoulders bare, and clung around her bejewelled neck by the flimsiest of silken cords.

I saw why she bore no tattoos on her magnificent back, for showing its beauty was evidently part of her arsenal of beguilement. Her mink stole lay demurely folded on the chair beside her. Her plate tinkled delicately as she ate, her glass sparkled with clear yellow wine as she drank with decorous sips, her fingers gloved in black satin. I longed to approach her – but on what pretext?

When the bill came I reached lazily into my coat, ready to dispense a lordly tip. Imagine the cold stab of terror when I discovered my wallet had gone! A frantic, sweating scrabble in pocket after pocket revealed that my travel documents, too, had disappeared! Any traveller has had such moments of panic – alone in a foreign land, bereft of money, friends, even identity. The worst nightmares assailed me, and I began to babble excuses in English, with 'British ambassador' and 'His Majesty King Edward' and suchlike inanities.

The waiter grew angry. He was soon joined by a second and a third, their previous fawning now equalled by their Gallic rage and contempt. I heard the dreadful word 'police' (the same in every language . . .) and imagined myself at once locked in the Bastille, to be the Man in the Iron Mask or the Count of Monte Cristo. I felt like weeping!

Suddenly, a cool lady's voice said something in French. I heard the words 'Majesty . . . Edward . . .' and the Frenchmen laughed with new obsequiousness. I looked up and saw the delicious globes of a lady's black-sheathed bosom dancing voluptuously before my eyes. It was she!

I say her bosom was sheathed in black – her silk dress – and technically it was, but the cups that covered her swelling alabaster bubbies were so thin and skimpy and diaphanous that the studs of her nipple-diamonds, and her nipples themselves, were plain for me to see.

Even in my confusion, I felt jealous that anyone but I should see those beautiful teats, let alone a Frenchman. Then, to my astonishment, the Frenchmen bowed and scraped, and the lady crooked her finger. She beckoned me to join her at her table, and in a trance I did. The waiter at once brought two balloon glasses of a smoky brown liquid, which he announced was with the 'compliments of the railway to Madame la Comtesse', and she motioned me to join her in a toast. I did so – coughed as the brandy bit my throat – and she laughed, pearl teeth peeping like eyes between lips painted a dark, almost purple, crimson.

Her blonde tresses were piled high over her head in a tower, with little wisps dancing around the perfect shells of her ears and her graceful swan's neck, firm and scented and white. Her cane nestled snugly at her silken rope belt.

'I could not leave a fellow subject in distress,' she murmured.

'You are English, madame?' I blurted.

'In a manner of speaking,' she said. 'Yes, in spirit, I am an English lady. I espied you earlier, a passably handsome young man. I suppose you will do. I like handsome men – strong young men, and well formed – for I feel their youth and beauty may touch the fading aura of my own.'

Even at my young age, I knew when a lady was fishing for compliments and duly supplied them, stammering all sorts of foolishness about her charm and grace – and telling nothing but my lustful, helpless truth. My compliments seemed genuinely to please her, for she awarded me a tender smile of such radiance that I blushed.

'I am nearly twenty-five years old,' she sighed. 'To be a countess, and twenty-five, without a husband . . . in my country, it is social disaster.'

'I thought you were English, ma'am,' I said.

'I am English, young man,' she replied sharply. 'My

35

country is a different matter. It is all in the mind,' she added darkly. 'But what of you? You are without money, and papers. I have rescued you from certain imprisonment in a stinking French jail – I believe you owe me a debt.'

I babbled that I was infinitely indebted to her but had no means at present to repay her. She smiled. Then, on her prompting, I gave her all the details of my journey, of the events at Shoeburyness that led to it . . . I think in a few short minutes she gleaned half my life from me.

'Strange, that our precious inviolate lives should depend on nothing more than pieces of paper,' she mused, not ceasing to fix me with her green eyes. 'Banknotes, passports . . . without these things, our selves count for nothing. Especially when among strangers. You foolishly babbled of the King of England, and you are lucky – it so happens I have just spent an enchanting weekend with dear Bertie at his estate in Norfolk. I instructed the waiters to put your bill on his account, along with my own.'

I felt a discreet but firm pressure of her calf against my own and the point of her cane stroking my ankle. Suddenly the point of the cane stabbed me harshly on my instep, and I jumped, but did not cry out. She smiled and said teasingly that a virile male had sensitive feet.

'Now, please sign this, young man, and then we shall not be strangers to each other. I shall be your creditor, and you my debtor. Go on, sign – your signature shall be your bond.'

I was so grateful! I signed the foolscap page without reading it – it was in English and two other languages, one of them in a foreign script. She smiled then folded the paper carefully, and, in full view of the company, lifted the hem of her silk robe right to her thigh, where she revealed black stockings with lacy tops, and garter straps leading to a frilly garter belt that hung quite loose around her firm bare hips. She wore no knickers!

For a fleeting, lustful moment I glimpsed the white skin of her thigh in its full expanse, as she kept the hillock of her lady's place decorously hidden. She tucked the paper swiftly into her left stocking top and patted her thigh, making the firm alabaster skin quiver, before lowering her dress with a flounce.

Suddenly and without warning, I felt her hand dive between my thighs and grasp my manhood. I stifled a cry of shock as she stared fiercely and unsmiling into my eyes, but she clutched my cock and balls in a grip so tight that my eyes moistened and I gasped. She held me there for several seconds, squeezing my balls until she felt the full, painful stiffening of my member. Then she nodded and released me with a lopsided little curl of her lips.

'You leave a sweetheart behind you?' she said abruptly.

I blushed and told her about Miss Becky and her sisters, too, leaving out the more intimate details. But like all ladies she pounced precisely on these.

'Older than you, your lady?'

I agreed.

'Then I suppose she would stand no nonsense. A strict lady ... with a firm hand, for unruly and callow young men?'

Her green eyes seemed to grow to limpid pools of merriment and a teasing disdain. I blurted out that Miss Becky was indeed strict in her affection. I had to remind myself that this was the same Mistress I had seen flogging the bare croup of a naked slave – who had presented her own fesses for the most vicious buggery, and shown every sign of enjoyment. And I was *sure* she had known of my presence.

Though awed by her acquaintance with our own King, I began to recover some of my self-esteem. She had chosen to come to my aid, and surely (I did know *something* of ladies!) with a selfish motive. My heart beat hard – might her selfish motive satisfy my own longing?

'The English are known to be fond of corporal discipline for unruly males,' she mused. 'Which means all males, in my opinion. I may take it, therefore, that Miss Becky's *strictness* expressed itself thus?'

I feigned incomprehension.

'I mean, dear boy, did she spank your bottom for you?'

I blushed fierily again and said yes.

37

'Or even took the cane to your behind?'

'Yes, madame.'

'On the bare?'

I nodded, my heart thumping.

'Yes, madame,' I blurted. 'I was caned on the bare frequently at college, and . . . and by Miss Becky too. And I have taken a bare birching from her.'

'O, yes, a bare birching,' she said in faint amusement. 'In Russia, we are much like the English. We are a large family – the ladies of a family must be strong, and not afraid to discipline their menfolk. So, then! In England, your bare cheeks were used to a severe lady's whip.'

'But we are no longer in England, madame,' I retorted.

She did not become angry at my impudence, but smiled warmly and said we should soon be in Russia.

'I, too, am taking the train in Paris – for Berlin, and then Moscow,' she said. 'It seems that as you are now my bonded servant, and thus a member of my family, I am responsible for your passage.'

This took me aback, and I demanded to know exactly what she meant – what was in the paper I had signed.

'It is a declaration of serfdom, in recompense for debt,' she said airily. 'Quite a normal contract in Russia. It means that you must do my bidding until such – *unspecified* – time as I decide your debt has been cancelled. You are, in essence, my slave, young man.'

Now her icy-green eyes did not laugh but pierced me with their unspoken question.

'Of course,' she whispered, 'your contract has no validity outside Russia. You may walk cheerfully off this train, young man. I shall even give you some money, and a letter to His Excellency the British Ambassador in Paris. Or you may choose to honour your debt – as an English gentleman.'

She shifted very slightly, and I felt the shaft of her cane brush my flank.

'I – I shall honour my debt, madame,' I whispered. 'I am yours – your slave – to do with what you will, and if I fail to give satisfaction, I promise to accept gladly whatever discipline you choose to impose.'

38

As I spoke, my cock rose to full erection.

'Your first task shall be to carry my trunk the few hundred metres between the Gare du Nord, where we arrive, and the Gare de l'Est, whence the Moscow train departs. My manservant has failed me, by catching cold, and I had to leave him in Calais – and only the King of England himself could manage to get a porter in Paris at this hour.'

'May – may I know whose bonded servant – whose slave – I have the honour to be, madame?' I quavered.

'I am Madame the Countess Galena Volchuk,' she said, beckoning me with a crooked finger to rise and follow.

'And don't you wish to know your slave's name, madame?' I asked. 'Your manservant – I heard you call him Paul.'

At once, I regretted my loose tongue.

'Whatever for?' she said without looking round at me. 'Slave – *robotnik* – will do. And I do not care whether you accept punishment gladly or not, for you shall shortly receive it with no choice. You should know I never use a slave's name in public.'

Now she did turn round, and her smile was a tiger's.

'If I choose to know *your* name, I shall whip it from you, young man. It is more amusing that way.'

'Well, slave?' said the Countess. 'What are you waiting for? Not strong enough?'

The train was slowing as it chugged through the suburbs of Paris. She pointed at her trunk, which lay on the floor of her first-class compartment. I tugged it: the trunk seemed to weigh a ton. Eventually I managed to shoulder it, just as we lurched to a stop at the Gare du Nord. She nodded her approval and told me to put it down.

Opening it with the lid up towards me, she extracted a pair of boots and said I was to attend her. She slipped off her strapped slingback shoes and put them into the trunk, then snapped it shut again and sat on it, lifting her robe to reveal her stockinged legs right up to the suspender belt. I knelt, and slid the boots on to her long, slender feet, then rolled up the skin-tight leather until it clung halfway up her thigh and almost at the frilly stocking tops.

She yawned as I performed my task and made little noises of impatience, for I took my time, breathing in the leather's scent, imbued with the perfume of her legs and stockinged feet. Finally she rubbed her booted and silk-stockinged thighs together, making a swishing sound, and clicked her high spiked heels sharply; then, with a satisfied flounce, lowered her skirts again before allowing me to wrap her in her mantle of black sable.

I took my time about this task also, for there is scarcely anything more heavenly for a male slave than to smell the musk of his Mistress's bare shoulders and bosom, while caressing her with her own fur coat, already a treasure of her body's perfume. I imagined my Mistress quite naked under her fur – I was sure she must have worn it so – and shivered in ecstasy.

I shouldered the trunk again; she waited for me to open the compartment door, and the carriage door too, descending before her to assist her alighting. At once we were assailed by a legion of porters, all protesting that they had waited especially for madame. She drew her cane from her waistband and brushed them airily aside with little flicks, then flicked the cane quite severely across my buttocks, just once, but enough to make me take notice. This was her order to proceed to the Gare de l'Est.

A few hundred metres! Although the path was downhill, it seemed as many miles, and accompanied by as many flicks of my Mistress's cane to my bottom. The urging was unnecessary, but I knew – and welcomed – the demonstration of her power. I was sweating with the trunk's weight and my own small case by the time we arrived at the *Muscovy Express* which was waiting there, its imperial purple and gold livery wreathed in impatient steam.

At once a stationmaster approached the Countess and babbled obsequiously at her in, I supposed, French, in which language she answered him fluently. I had the

40

impression that the train had been held especially for my Mistress's arrival! And that thought made me savour for the first time the knowledge that I had a powerful Mistress.

We clambered into the first, and grandest, of the carriages, labelled MOCKBA, and I almost dropped my burden in surprise at the luxury that greeted us. We were alone in a palace on wheels. As though guessing my thoughts, she tersely informed me it was her private carriage, and she kept it in Paris, or Berlin, or Moscow, as it suited her.

There was a sitting room with chairs in gilt frames and leather cushions in white, scarlet and black. There was electric lighting, of course, and a telephone; a kitchen, a bathroom, and bedrooms, with other, smaller rooms giving off the corridor. At each end, the heavy door was done in gold and scarlet, and in baroque style, with white sugar-spun figures of naked nymphs wielding sensuously curling canes or whips. But for the slight vibration of the train, we might have been in the drawing room of her castle.

The ceiling, like the doorway, was in scarlet, with more detailed and explicit nude figures in vigorous flagellation. And on each side of the fireplace stood a statue in brass: each represented a nude figure, one male, one female, seen from the rear, and adopting the spread-eagled position for a naval flogging. The buttocks and back of each figure were wealed with finely etched whipmarks, and their arms were raised in torment or supplication. Above them, over the mantelpiece, the lush tendrils of a brass cat-o'-nine-tails cascaded over their two scarred backs, down to their furrows so that the buttocks – plump and muscled in each case – were the most prominent part of the sculptures. A peek revealed that the male's organ was massively erect.

My Mistress at once threw off her sable, without looking at me, and I caught it proudly. She sprawled on the sofa and yawned. I asked her if I should hang the coat in the wardrobe, and she rewarded me with a baleful stare.

'Did I command you to speak, wretch?' she hissed.

Trembling, I hung the coat amid a scented wealth of

coats, dresses and robes, beneath them a glistening forest of leather boots and dainty shoes all perfumed with the aroma of her flesh. I restrained my impulse to lick and suck every inch of that sacred leather and returned meekly to the stateroom, where I was ordered to remove madame's boots. This I did, savouring anew the ripe scent of her damp stockinged toes, giddy with pleasure. Through lazy eyes she saw my stiffening cock as she ordered me to make her a bedtime glass of brandy and soda.

When I had fetched it from the array of bottles on the mahogany sideboard, she casually ordered me to strip naked. At that coldly sensuous command, nothing could stop my heart from pounding nor my organ stretching to full hardness. I removed my clothing while she scrutinised me with lazy eyes, noting my erection with nothing more than a purse of her lips. Unconsciously, I stood to attention, as Paul had, and said I awaited her orders.

'You do speak improperly, slave,' she said with an amused glint in her eye. 'Of course you await my orders. It is your function – your only function, now.'

Suddenly she leant sharply forward and placed her face inches from my tight balls and the shaft of my cock and proceeded to breathe deeply, sniffing me like a dog.

'My, how you stink,' she said in disgust. 'You are filthy. I do not permit you to bathe. I like the stench of a male, to remind me what disgusting animal has the honour to take my whip.'

She opened a drawer and I heard a clank of metal. Then I was obliged to kneel on all fours. With expert fingers, she fastened a spiked leather collar around my neck, loosely, and its sister around my balls, tightly – these collars were linked by a tense chain that snaked through my furrow, painfully rubbing my bumhole, then up my back.

To the chain was fastened a looped leather thong, which she flicked, sending a jangling tremor through my balls, to signal me to rise. My hands were placed in front of me and locked to my restraining chain with a pair of steel cuffs that snapped loudly and alarmingly shut. I was trussed and tethered!

She sprawled at her ease, inspecting me with half an eye

while she sipped her drink and dangled the leash emerging between my parted thighs as I faced her. My erection throbbed mercilessly. She ordered me to lift my left foot and then locked a short silver chain around my ankle – my slave bracelet, never to be removed.

'Do you usually get stiff when you are tethered – and know a thrashing awaits?' she murmured.

'I – I am to be thrashed?' I swallowed and gasped as she tugged on the leash and my balls were squeezed.

'Of course you are to be thrashed. Answer the question.'

'Yes, Mistress. O, yes –'

She laughed deep in her throat, a peal of dainty, cruel music that made my cock throb harder.

'Mistress. Good! You are learning, you stinking creature. I always cane a slave at bedtime, to remind it how it disgusts me. You will bend over and touch your toes – just as when you were at your English public school. And, like a schoolboy, a slave is always flogged on the bare.'

I obeyed and, on her command, spread my thighs wide. I trembled as I heard her fetch a cane for my croup, and through my open thighs I saw her approach on stockinged feet, delectably damp with her toes' moisture, bearing a fearsome rod of four feet in length, very thick and dark.

'You will take rattan,' she said. 'Public school must have hardened your horrid bum.'

I begged to speak, and with an impatient nod she granted my request, flexing and swishing the heavy cane as she listened. I stammered that I had never been to a proper English school and was unfamiliar with rattan, though had been caned on bare as a cadet. My explanation ended in a shriek, for she lashed my bare buttocks without warning.

'Uneducated!' she cried. 'Disgusting! Well, we have a long trip to Moscow, so I shall attempt to teach you the rudiments of manners, *robotnik* mine.'

She stroked me again, harder, and in the same weal. This time I restrained my cry, though not my tears. The pain of the rattan was dreadful! My stretched legs trembled violently, and my buttocks clenched tight, awaiting further cruel welts. My slave bracelet jangled with my pain.

It is a fact that we cannot remember bodily states: that is, in summer heat we cannot recall the cold of winter; well fed, we cannot recall the pangs of hunger. So it is with the lash. Unwhipped, I long to be trussed, bound and helpless under a Mistress's merciless lash – but when the thongs bite, the gag stifles and the first cut of a cruel rod weals my naked fesses, I gasp and squirm and think it the worst horror and myself the most foolish brute!

My Mistress yawned again and said that she was tired, and that she would content me with a couple of dozen. *Content* me! I shuddered: two with that heavy engine seemed unbearable – a further twenty-two should reduce me to a quivering jelly! The merciless cane whistled, slicing the air; the third stroke kissed my bare, then, very quickly, the fourth. Now the tears coursed down my cheeks, and I bit my lip white to stop from crying, for I could not remember a more intense pain.

'The rattan is of course for minor infractions of discipline,' she said. 'For real insolence, the birch, or the many-thonged cat, or the knout itself is called for. My ancestors would have female serfs flogged naked with the knout, while they dined at high table. They called their wails of agony the "cream on the borscht".'

Somehow, trembling and shaking like a leaf in a gale, I took that dreadful beating without protest. My bare bum was a sea of liquid fire, and I scarcely heard her bid me rise, after the twenty-fourth stroke. I did so stiffly and not trying to conceal my tears, which she contemplated with a thin smile of satisfaction. She announced it was bedtime and tapped my still-hard member with the cane handle.

'You will want to make commode,' she said. 'If you make a mess in your shameless hard state, slave, it will be a further drubbing, on the spot.'

I followed her to the little bathroom, where, quite unconcernedly, she squatted on the commode and made her own evacuation. My ears drank the tinkling from her sacred fount as though it were the sweetest music. She did not even seem to notice my presence, save when she rose to present her fesses to me and handed me towel and sponge. My cuffed hands were supposed to wipe her clean, in her most intimate place, and, shivering with shameful joy, I did so.

She said nonchalantly that a properly tamed slave would lick her clean, in both orifices – but I was not sufficiently broken yet. She left me to make my own awkward evacuation, which I did with great difficulty, then at the tug of my leash followed her into the sleeping compartment, where she was already installed in a charming, miniature four-poster bed. Beside it on the polished wooden floor was a square of rope matting.

'Slave sleeps beside Mistress,' she said.

She leant forward, revealing her flimsy silk nightdress that allowed me a clear and agonising view of her proudly jutting white breasts, the cherries of her nipples standing full and stiff – then she deftly hung the end of my leash over a peg in the wall. This meant that I could not lie down but was obliged to kneel on the rope matting.

Then she reached down and touched my erect cock on the throbbing helmet, and I sighed in joy and surprise.

'You poor slave,' she said, 'all excited by your beating. I raised some pretty weals, didn't I? And you took it not half badly, for a whelp without education.'

Slowly and tenderly, she began to run her fingertips up and down the shaft of my erect cock, tickling my balls and squeezing the bulb playfully, then stroking the sensitive ridge beneath my mushroom and making me sigh deeply. Her touch grew stronger; she grasped the shaft in her curled palm and rubbed firmly, drawing my prepuce all the way back and tickling my peehole with her thumb.

I was panting now, with the honey welling in my balls, and knew she should soon bring me to a spend.

'Interesting,' she mused, 'that this cock and this bum should have received the glimmerings of training from three sisters. I, too, am one of three sisters. It is my younger sister Dushanka, the savant, who has the real knowledge of your English disciplinary traditions. She devotes herself to the training of gentlemen, but, unaccountably, many miles from the civilised delights of Moscow.'

I felt her fingers sliding cool and caressing on my straining helmet, and experienced the first stirrings of joy as she brought my cream to the brink of spurt.

'I expect you'd like to spend, cock,' she said, looking at my throbbing flesh. 'I suppose you'd like to spurt cream all over me – all over my hand, my bosom, my belly . . .'

'O, Mistress,' I gasped, and, abruptly, she ceased her massage and rolled over to sleep.

'There!' she laughed. 'You are primed for your night's rest, slave. If I awake and see your manhood has impudently wilted, then I shall beat you again at once.'

I quavered that I did not know what I had done to deserve such cruel punishment, so soon in her service.

'Punishment!' she laughed from her scented pillow. 'Why, you stupid slave, this is a *respite* from punishment! You are so green and silly that I am breaking you gently. Now rest, and look forward to your breakfast whipping.'

At once, I heard the gentle breathing of her sleep. I knelt alone to contemplate my future: smarting with welts, chained like a dog, erect and with balls aching to spend, my horrid discomfort imposed at the whim of this cruel, selfish Mistress from hell.

I was in heaven!

4

On Parade

My morning whipping was even more severe than my caning before retirement. She delivered it with insouciance, as though it were a simple and perhaps amusing routine, like painting her toenails. I was amazed at my easy acceptance, in such a short time, of brute degradation as this lady's plaything. I knew my humiliance to be just and ordained.

I awoke from a fitful doze to the sound of my Mistress's yawning and stretching; she began to sing softly, in a cross between a lullaby and a martial song. She flung off her bedcovers and leapt to the floor, which shivered to the steady rhythm of the rails. I had forgotten we were moving, so comfortably sprung were the wheels of my Mistress's carriage. Swiftly, she unleashed me from my bondage. That is to say, I was freed to stand and my hands were uncuffed, but my ball-chain remained in place, as did my tight slave bracelet.

She threw off her nightgown and dropped it on the floor. If my cock had not been hard, with my morning urge to pee, it should surely have become rock at the sight of my magnificent Mistress totally nude. Any man, I think, would have agreed to be the slave of such beauty; would long to groan in delight, squashed by those proud, jutting breasts! Her jewelled nipples already stood big and stiff, as though lustfully excited by the joy of her awakening.

The firm peach of her buttocks rippled with full taut muscle, over powerful thighs, sinewy yet deliciously ripe, and promising to crush utterly any male whose balls and cock ventured towards her dome of moist pink pleasure; the fleecy fount's glistening temple held her tattoo whip, symbol of her power. Her indifference to my gaze was a sign of her inviolate beauty and my own abject wretchedness; I shivered at her disdain for me.

Then, with only a flickering glance at my stiff penis, she passed into her bathroom, where she squatted to make commode. I obediently followed her and proudly abased myself, kneeling at her feet as she sat with her thighs parted and made her several evacuations. She rose, her private places well soiled, and to my joy casually spread her lady's places to be licked clean by my eager tongue!

I fervently applied myself to her cleansing, my ardour the greater since I knew that she was about to bathe, and this unnecessary operation was purely to humiliate me. I longed for permission to evacuate, too, but could not imagine my cock softening, as I felt her soft bare soles resting on the small of my back during my cleansing duty. She made little chuckling noises and murmured that we had four days in the train before arriving in Moscow, and with firm discipline I might do as a passable imitation of a proper slave.

When her cleansing was finished, she beckoned me into the stateroom, without permitting me any of my own toilette. I was motioned towards the bronze statue of the flogged female, then, roughly, she pressed the small of my back and slammed me against the metal weals of the nude supplicant's back and buttocks. My wrists were swiftly cuffed by little hinged flaps that opened from the metal lady's shoulders. My erect cock was painfully squashed into the statue's furrow. My Mistress laughed and grasped my shaft very tight, then made me gasp as she pushed it right between the buttocks and into the cold chamber of the statue's fount!

'My creation – cast by my best foundry,' she said.

My cock was inserted to the hilt into a metal quim, then my Mistress reached into the vulva of the statue and touched the boatman: it was a switch, and with a sinister metallic click the bronze woman's wealed buttocks flexed and writhed, snapped tightly together, with a hum of clockwork, and trapped my cock inside her cold metal slit.

I could not move or withdraw; the buttocks continued to writhe and squirm, rubbing my stiff penis in a tormenting, mocking embrace. I clutched the neck and shoulders of my bronze tormentress, my flogging position the same as her own. My Mistress laughed and said I was lucky this was only a routine chastisement – for punishment, I should be fastened in utter humiliation to the *male* statue.

I looked round with wide eyes, pleading for mercy, and saw her select a cat-o'-nine-tails from a closet that gleamed with an array of whips, restrainers, barbed clustered canes and other disciplinary tools, so horrid I wondered what imagination, what culture, could conceive such things – although I knew the answer.

My 'breakfast' was a brisk, savage flogging, delivered with all the merry insouciance of a young girl picking daisies. The cat descended mercilessly on my bare skin, with no pause between lashes, and I found myself clinging to the statue as though to melt my pain into hers, while the fearful writhing of the metal buttocks and quim pummelled my stiff cock.

The cat's handle was shaped into a handgrip, like a pistol, and the thongs were of thick but supple leather, made harder by a braiding of thin copper wire, which broadened at the tips into sharp nodules like marbles or eyeballs. A lashing on bare with an unbraided whip is painful enough. I can assure the reader that thongs braided in metal cause a man's eyes to bulge in pure agony.

She whipped me with alternate strokes on the bare back and buttocks, my croup already wealed and furrowed by my beating the night before. Four days of such torment! It was this thought, as much as the liquid fire that wreathed my naked body, which caused me to shudder and sob and burn with regret for my foolish desire to be a lady's slave.

I have tried to describe the cane and the birch: how each instrument of torment has her own sweet and vicious magic. (Instruments of supplice are always *she*.) The cat is less sensuous than birch, less subtle than cane: pure ritual and contemptuous, jarring force, disdaining any delicacy in her task of raising welts on her victim.

Miss Cane purses her lips studiously; Miss Birch wears a lustful and sensuous grin; Mistress Cat sneers in gleeful and raucous contempt, delighted at her brutality and the colouring of the wealed male flesh beneath her. That morning, as my bare writhed under my flogging, I knew my Mistress's power, that I must submit utterly to her – and by the tenth stroke, my flesh seared and burning with white-hot welts, I loved the whip that made me squirm.

I took thirty lashes to each place, hard and merciless stroking that slammed me against my imprisoning metal lady at each cut, for the cat knocks the breath from you: she is a heavy and remorseless Mistress.

When Madame the Countess Galena had announced thirty, she flicked the statue and released my cock from her imprisonment. She still stood stiff! (I must add that my Mistress referred scornfully to my proud member as 'she', and I have kept the habit: it causes a delicious frisson of shame.) At once I sank to my knees and knelt before her bare feet, washing her toes with my coursing tears.

'O . . . O . . .,' I sobbed, licking the female power in her bare, ripe-scented feet. 'I am sorry, Mistress.'

'Sorry?' she murmured. 'Tell me what for, slave.'

'For being an abject wretch unworthy of your whip.'

'Mmm,' she mused. 'Perhaps you'll do, English boy.'

She bade me rise and follow her once more to the bathroom, where I was obliged to help her bathe, sponging her nude body but without allowing my skin to touch hers. My cock wanted to burst, and I longed to evacuate; I knew she was aware, for her green eyes darted mischievously to my straining member.

I was not permitted to shave her, although, using a decorous sponge, I had to make and apply scented lather to her legs, armpits and all around the huge forest of her pubic curls, whose edges she trimmed and sculpted most delicately like the finest landscaped garden.

Then she passed the razor over her naked gash, with equal delicacy; round her bum-crack, and the anus bud, which I longed to see in all her wrinkled beauty. When the lather was wiped, every whorl and crevice of her furrow and smooth quim-lips gleamed proud and shiny as pink ice.

Only when her toilette was complete, her skin dried, powdered and scented, did she nod contemptuously towards commode, and indicate that I might squat, but with seat up, above the porcelain, and without letting my skin touch the place *she* touched.

This simple permission seemed the greatest privilege! As I relieved myself with a sigh of joy, even the throbbing welts on my shoulders and buttocks seemed warm and friendly, lulled by the rhythm of the rails. I was permitted to douche my body in cold water; then she beckoned me to her bedchamber to assist her robing.

My cock had softened a little after making commode and attracted a frown from my Mistress. I was happy that the prospect of robing her nude body stiffened my cock again. Her lips pursed in prim satisfaction.

'I feel *black* today,' she said.

I knelt and rolled each stocking over her silken smooth legs. The hose were not themselves silk, but a daring and gaudy design of fishnet, the diamond apertures laced with flowers and stars, like a courtesan's. With mocking haughtiness, this slut's adornment seemed to dare the onlooker to disapprove. As I carefully rolled the stockings up the smooth alabaster skin of calves and thighs, my head was inches from the powerful scent of her fount and from the ripeness between her long, slightly wiggling toes.

I thrilled at her supreme indifference! She was naked before me – I was no more to her than a pet kitten. Robing her, I must not let my fingers even brush her bare skin by accident; her person was inviolable to a mere brute slave. To approach her nudity, yet not touch her flesh, made my cock throb mercilessly.

I rolled the stockings up her thighs, almost to the thick red lips of her quim, and anchored them on the inside of the thighs, which in many ladies is soft and fleshy, with an adorable little swelling of plumpness. My Mistress's thighs were not plump, and her inner thigh flesh was as hard as an apple, the silk of her skin swelling firmly with powerful taut muscle.

I knew that I must avert my eyes from her person; yet I could not but glimpse the swollen red lips of that divine quim, the moist pink gash splitting the golden luxury of her mink, and fancied – headstrong! – that my rolling of the stockings caused a little droplet of excitement to glisten there and made her boatman peep from the folds of his mantle. Certainly, her breath was deep and rhythmic, and she swayed to the train's motion as I robed her legs.

After the stockings, I fastened a lace garter belt around her waist and saw it perch like a crown above the broad enlargement of her firm massive bum-globes. The straps hung limp on her flesh, and I reached for black panties in the same gaudy lace as her stockings, but airily she brushed them away and shook her head.

'No panties today, I think,' she said with a little yawn.

With trembling fingers I fastened the garter straps, two to each stocking, making several attempts before the wicked little studs slid securely into their moorings, causing her to cluck with impatience.

Next, I fastened a black waspie corset, silk with whalebone frame, above her garter belt, covering her belly button and leaving her bubbies naked. The teats were thrust up adorably, like the prows of twin battleships, so that their swollen, tensed nipples were pointed out like the cones of cannon shells. The waspie was laced to its tightest but caused only the smallest of wrinkles to her pencil-thin waist.

'I like my *waspieee*,' she drawled, stretching out the last syllable in a way I found enticing.

Her robing continued with a pair of slingback shoes, the height of daring modernity at that time, with very pointed toes and spiky heels, made of black, gleaming patent leather, and into which I had to carefully buckle her feet. Then she allowed me to pin a silk cape around her neck to cover her bosom and shoulders, its flimsiness drawing attention to her naked jewelled breasts by its mere pretence at concealing them.

She stood and surveyed herself in the mirror, twirling the curls of her fleece with two or three sensuous fingers; her mink was so large that from a distance it seemed like a little apron or skirt in itself. I wondered if she proposed to receive guests, or confront the railway servants, in this deliciously uncompromising attire.

Suddenly, she reached into her closet and withdrew a device of, I was sure, gleaming black rubber. It was in the shape of two male cocks – an extremely large one, and much like my own, with its twin a slightly smaller prong, both shafts being bent up at the angle of erect penises and fastened together on a clip from which four little straps dangled, like garter straps.

She stroked the rubber prongs, purring to herself, and then half-squatted, bending her knees to spread her thighs and buttocks. With a swift and practised motion, she drove both prongs into her intimate holes: the larger into her quim, the smaller into her bumhole.

Both shafts disappeared inside her right to the hilt, and she gave a little gasp, then fixed the four straps to her garter belt, to hold the device in place. She smiled at herself in the glass, a radiant beam of cruel and lustful satisfaction. She turned and faced me, pushing the device into her holes with teasing motions of her fingertips.

'I like to feel former slaves when flogging a new one,' she purred. 'I may honour you later by moulding *you* . . .'

She completed her robing by wrapping a knee-length skirt around her waist. It was made of thin and shiny black rubber, and it clung to her thighs like a glove. She fastened only one button, over her garter belt, so that the skirt cleaved open at the front, right to her waist; with every swirl of her haunches, an onlooker would be bewitched by a fleeting glimpse of thigh-skin, garters and the fleecy mink-hairs at her hillock.

Then she announced that it was time for me to be properly attired for the service of her breakfast.

'I hope you will prove an obedient maid,' she murmured with the same thin smile, and showed me what I was to wear.

It was a maid's outfit, with a little black skirt and thong panties, a white blouse and pinnie, and black stockings, with a garter belt and high shoes like her own. I blushed fiercely – she wished to robe me shamefully as a *girl*!

This new and unexpected humiliation made me thrill, but I feigned distress as she watched me don my maid's attire, a lovely sneer curling her lips and a giggle bubbling in her throat. When I was finished, she bade me inspect myself in the glass, and I blushed again, for my starched pinnie was pushed up high by the stiff cock straining my thong panties. My shoes pinched most uncomfortably, with teetering high heels on which I stood with difficulty.

The panties themselves had a thong that was scarcely bigger than a string and which nestled tight and uncomfortable right inside my furrow, after she had pulled the waistband high; I soon understood the purpose of this shameful garment. She told me I was proper for my feeding.

I was instructed to mash two raw eggs into a kind of cornmeal porridge, and this was covered in honey. I had to kneel, with my bum high and my skirt up, to eat like a dog, with a saucer of Vichy water to drink. The thong panties left my wealed buttocks quite bare; as I ate, she caned me on the bare, quite hard but with infrequent strokes, so that my lapping was accompanied by the vip! vip! of leather-sheathed whalebone. It smarted awfully, but I was not permitted to budge – despite spilling at every jolt – until my dish was licked clean.

She told me gravely that for every permission to soil her commode, like the filthy whelp nature had made me, I should receive six with cane on the bare before my evacuation and six afterwards – at full arm's length.

'Manly discipline for a pretty girl!' she sneered.

And in truth I blushed deeper: I *was* rather pretty. Unnamable fears assailed me. What if a – a Tarker should ask my Mistress's permission to use her slave's person? My fears deepened when she took rouge, lipstick and powder and painted my face with a few deft strokes, then clamped a full dark wig on my skull. She asked me if my girl's bottom smarted, and I said it stung awfully; she nodded and said I might prepare her breakfast.

I was to lay the rosewood dining-table with crystal and linen, and she barked commands, cracking her cane all the while across my stockinged thighs, until I had it correctly done. My stockings were ripped, but she did not seem to care, saying with grim satisfaction that I looked a proper slut. Next I had to make tea, toast and scrambled eggs with smoked salmon, a task thankfully within my cadet's skills. I expected her to find fault and deliver a further whipping to my already raw bum, but to my suprise she pronounced herself pleased and said she would reward me with an important errand.

'You are to take an invitation for luncheon to General Hochhuth, who has a compartment three first-class carriages along,' she said.

She wrote a dainty note, which she sealed in an envelope, leaving an imprint of her rouged lips.

'I – I must walk through three carriages – like this, Mistress?' I stammered.

'Of course,' she said coldly. 'And mind you curtsy properly to the general.'

My passage through the first-class carriages was only slightly mortifying, as a male eye winked or male lips mimed a kiss at my wiggling posterior. I did wiggle, in a lady's gait, and unconsciously, for ladies' high shoes make one sway and accentuate the rolling of the bum-cheeks – delicious to a male observer! I did not mind – I knew my embarrassment to be part of my Mistress's plan.

I dare advise the reader to flirt with the wearing of ladies' things – just for a laugh, of course, you fellow males – and he will discover wondrous things about the beauty of women: how every piece of clothing, every movement dictated by bodice, corset, panties or girdle or perilous high shoes is designed to enchant and enrapture. A lady dressed is a parcel of beauty, her wrapping a wealth of hints at the contents.

I arrived at the general's compartment and knocked timidly. A voice barked 'Come!' On entering, I curtsied as instructed, and with lowered eyes tended the letter, which was taken, opened and read while I awaited my dismissal with head bowed and hands demurely at my 'lady's place'.

'Such a pretty maid!' murmured the general. 'Where are you from, girl?'

I felt her fingers coolly and sensuously stroke my silken buttocks! First on my skirt, then below, on my panties. I blushed and shivered a little. *Her* fingers – the general was a lady!

She was surprisingly young to be a general, not more than my Mistress's twenty-five years. I supposed that the rules were different for lady generals, though I had never heard of such a thing. Her strong, high-boned face, imperiously handsome, was framed in lush russet curls that spilt over her bare shoulders, brown from the sun, and the big melons of her teats, whose nipples were clearly outlined like saucers under the tight silk of her nightie.

Her stern bearing, if not her accoutrements, was certainly military. She reclined on a chaise longue, still in her morning dishabille, smoking a pungent cigarette in an amethyst holder. In her repose, her crisp white negligee lay carelessly open to reveal a royal-blue chemise, flounced well over powerful brown thighs, and bare feet with one set of toenails carefully lacquered blue to match her nightie. Yet her carelessness was somehow planned: her dress precisely casual, as though for some military exercise. I had heard of ladies auxiliaries to the armed forces, but kept my humble silence.

'I am English,' I said in a whisper, to disguise my male gruffness – now willingly a part of my Mistress's scheme!

'And your name, English maid?'

'Philip – Philippa,' I stammered in the same whisper.

Her fingers still lazily stroked my croup, and now I felt the firm caress of her palm; the fingers began to delve deep into my furrow, and I wriggled a little, trying to stay standing at attention, as I felt her nails tweak my bumhole through my narrow string panties.

'Such delectable fesses, a lovely juicy bum, ripe for spanking. Does your Mistress spank her?' she drawled.

I was used to military directness and answered that my Mistress imposed stern discipline when I was wilful.

'So – a hard spanking for a naughty girl?'

'Yes, Madame General,' I stammered.

'On bare bum?'

'Why – why, of course, Madame General.'

She nodded approval; her hand continued its exploration, full on my bare, and fastened on the painful ridges of my weals from my morning's flogging. She ran her fingers impishly up and down my raw skin, making me squirm as my welts smarted anew. I gave a little gasp of discomfort and closed my eyes as she stabbed quite hard at a particularly sore place.

'I think she does more than just spank you, Philippa,' she said breathily. 'I find evidence of stronger chastisement.'

I replied that my Mistress was generous with cane and whip to her undeserving slave.

'And you must be a very naughty slave indeed, Philippa,' she said. 'Come and sit on my lap.'

Her hands were now stroking my thighs, and she had further raised the nightie over her powerful naked thighs, somewhat to my discomfiture. I obeyed, careful to keep my loins, and my trembling penis, a distance from her grasp. She tut-tutted, and said I was very modest – her hands slid down my furrow towards my balls – I squeaked, and slid to the edge of her bare knee, feeling the skin against my bum-cheeks. I mumbled that I should be flogged if I did not return without delay, and she laughed and said I deserved to be, for my prettiness.

'I have need of pretty, strong girls in the Kaiser's Nursing Corps,' she said. 'There is going to be a war soon, and there will be plenty of work for nurses. Imagine, Philippa, the thrill of having brute males suddenly tamed, under your lady's command, bandaged and in splints and receiving hot poultices, enemas – their bums squirming as you pump hot water – your groaning, willing slaves!'

I said I was not sure I should be among the German Kaiser's nurses if war was to come, and that I should rather join up and do my duty like a man. No sooner were these foolish words out of my mouth than I regretted them, but luckily she gave me a severe slap on the buttocks and said she liked the Joan of Arc spirit. She asked me if I liked my Mistress, and I whispered that it was not a slave's place to like her Mistress.

'You do not find her attractive – thrilling? Her lovely strong breasts, and her peach and thighs that could crush any foolish invading male? Her silken skin?'

Even this brief description of my Mistress was enough to make my cock tremble with desire, and I blushed, which pleased the lady general.

'She pleases you,' she drawled. 'Why, she pleases me, the teasing minx! I wish – I only wish – she would be a superb nurse, among loving sisters, who understand each other's female needs and desires.'

I rose awkwardly and smoothed my pinnie before bowing and asking to be dismissed. The general made a move and shifted on her chaise longue so that her nightie slipped up her thighs a few inches, and I saw almost the whole of her rippling bare legs. That, too, caused perturbation in my penis, for her steely beauty reminded me of my Mistress, and I felt guilty that my cock should rise for any other lady! She said that I had time to help her by lacquering the toenails of her left foot.

'A little task, dear Philippa, which my friend the Countess shall not begrudge me.'

With little protest, I knelt by her feet, and in truth I was excited by the prospect. Her feet, like my Mistress's, were strong and shapely, with long, tapering toes almost like fingers, and I shivered as I had a momentary vision of those toes caressing me most intimately, invading my mouth and probing my tongue, or at my balls and cock, crushing me breathless!

I took the pot of lacquer and began painting her toenails. After a while I felt her palm stroking my head, and noted that her feet were trembling slightly, as her calves shifted on the couch.

I looked up and saw that the general's nightie was now fully up, revealing her bare belly and fount: a ripe hillock completely shaven, and every whorl and detail of her swollen red quim-lips clearly outlined to my gaze, as was the fleshy wet pink within, for, as I painted her, the general was openly frigging herself.

Her fingers delved into her wet slit, the thumb caressing her boatman and making her give little mewls of pleasure as her belly shivered. Her other hand now ceased stroking my head and moved to her teats; she threw the nightie right to her neck and showed me two firm and quivering melons, topped with wide pink cherries standing stiff under harsh pinching and squashing from her thumb and forefinger. Her fierce white smile dazzled me.

'Come, Philippa,' she hissed, 'don't you diddle, like other girls? O, you would love it as a nurse: alone in barracks, we ladies know how to pleasure each other as no beastly male can. We frig each other all the time, you know – bum to bum, lips and fingers to quim and pucker, until we gush all wet. It is called nurses' parade.'

Trembling, I applied myself to my task, only to find that her lacquering was complete.

'Now, I want *you* to do me, Philippa. It is so much more fun when another girl diddles your clitty, don't you think? Don't be shy, my girl, we all do it – to spend at another girl's fingers or lips in gash is true pleasure.'

I could not resist. My cock was shamefully hard as I approached the writhing lady, keeping my back to her lest she spy my erection straining under my girl's clothing. I touched her gash and found her swimming in juices; quickly found the stiff, throbbing clitty and began to rub. My fingers slid easily into her clinging wet slit. I frigged her very vigorously, then she clasped my head once more and obliged me to kneel, my face against her bare hillock.

'O . . . O . . .' she moaned softly. 'O, Philippa, you bitch.'

Now my fingers were joined by my lips. My tongue began to flicker inside her slit, like a cock, and with my whole face – nose, lips and chin – I frotted her heaving fount until she gasped and shook, with little mewling squeals, and panted in the throes of her spend.

'O! O! Yes! Do me! Frig me hard! Frig my clitty! O! You slut! You dirty sweet bitch! O, I'm coming – O! O! *Ooo!*'

At last I rose, my face shining oily with her love-juices, and whispered that my Mistress would be cross if I were any later. The general beamed at me, her hand replacing my lips at her fount as she continued a gentle frottage. With a wave, she motioned me to go and whispered that she looked forward to my serving her luncheon.

I sped back to my Mistress's carriage, trying vainly to hide the evidence of my excitement. My cock was reduced, but still half-erect, when I returned; my Mistress noticed at once. She slapped me gently across the mouth, then sniffed and licked my fingers, which shone from the general's copious love-oils. Then she slapped me, harder, on the helmet of my protruding stiff cock. Her face was a sneer of utter, thrilling contempt, her eyes diamonds.

'Well, slave. You told me you had kissed the gunner's daughter – now it seems you have kissed the general's *chatte*, too. You really are quite a military girl. And since we have a good hour before luncheon, it is plenty of time for me to skin you. Prepare for punishment, slave. Skirt up high, and knickers off. I'll take you on bare, of course, and you may kiss bronze again. I'll give you rattan now. I want you too raw to even think of sitting down.'

My heart pounded in dread and longing for my fearsome humiliance. I removed my knickers and lifted my skirt and pinnie to stand stiffly over my back and bared my bottom for the cane. Her orbs trembled, and I felt goose pimples of cold fear. I stood in stockings and suspenders, my cock now insolently hard. With head bowed, I moved to take position on the female statue which was still warm from my morning's routine flogging. The thought flashed through my mind – how had my Mistress been so sure of my guilt? What had been in her note to the lady general, that the general had known to address me in English?

'No,' said my Mistress. 'For a *very* wicked girl, not that statue – the other one.'

5

Practical Nursing

I gasped in horror, unable to believe my ears. But I was
not mistaken; she pointed firmly to the statue of the erect
male, whose bronze cock stood as shiny, stiff and rampant
as my own. I had not previously paid this creation much
heed, not desiring to study the male in any way. Now that
I was obliged to, I saw that the body of the statue was
curiously sensuous and curved, the musculature smooth
and rippling like a woman's, and the face, twisted in agony,
had an elfin, girlish expression. In fact the croup was not
a male's hard, bony thing but gentle and fleshy, just like a
girl's; the breasts swollen with muscle, but nevertheless a
lady's small bosom; and only the erect cock indicated the
gender of the supplicant.

'My Joan of Arc,' said my Mistress. 'Pretty, isn't she?
And you'll feel just how pretty she is.'

I trembled in disgust and shame. I was to put my cock
in that bronze anus, a facsimile of a male – yet had my
Mistress not said the figure was Joan of Arc, female? What,
then, was a female doing with a huge male organ?

'You haven't heard of all the wonders of nature, slave,' she
continued. 'There are boys who are ladies, ladies who are boys
. . . one tribe in Siberia has nine different words, besides man
and woman, to denote the wonderful variety of the human
mind and body. St Joan had the prowess of a male, because
secretly she *was* one. Spread buttocks, slave, and mount.'

My horror grew. My Mistress's purpose was clear. I was
to be whipped while buggered by a lady-man!

We males are justly horrified of the crime of Sodom, threatened on our unwilling persons by those of the Tarker persuasion. Yet a slave must joyfully accept the worst shame from his Mistress – and to be buggered by a lady, with devices like the dildo my Mistress wore even now inside her own holes, is a giddy, horrid and ecstatic pleasure. It is the ultimate in humiliation, the tickling and filling of the bumhole a joy, as the male submits to the lady, and shivers at her contempt for his bottom which she buggers with such cruel delight.

It was Joan of Arc who was to take my bumhole's virginity! I swallowed, bowed my head to hide my blushes – ineffectually – and prepared to obey my Mistress. I parted my thighs, looked at the monstrous bronze cock of the lady, and straddled the engine, feeling the helmet brush my quivering bumhole.

I hesitated, felt my Mistress's arms around me, her hands squeezing my breasts most painfully, and her forearms locking me under the armpits. Then, with a snarl, she lifted me bodily over the engine and with a fierce thrust forced me down so that the bronze cock penetrated me to half its length. I could not help squealing at the dreadful pain, my legs flailing in anguish. Now she laughed grimly and applied another thrust, so that I was impaled right to my very root. I was filled with agony.

Yet in my pain was the knowledge of the sweetest humiliance, the more so as my Mistress began to lift me up and down, bouncing me rapidly so that the bronze organ slid in and out of my anus, as though in real buggery. Gradually, to my anguished delight, my bumhole relaxed to accommodate the savage deep thrusts of the shaft, and despite my groans I grew to relish my cruel buggery.

My sobs and groans made her thrust harder and harder, and having penetrated to my root she would twist my body, making the dildo swivel inside me as I squirmed. My arms clutched the statue as I whimpered in shame.

'O, Mistress,' I gasped, 'O . . . yes . . . please . . . bugger me, Mistress, bugger my hole, I beg you, don't stop.'

Now, with a cruel laugh, she left me abruptly and took a heavy cane from her closet. This was the rattan. My ankles and wrists were rapidly and securely cuffed, and with my bottom and hole well smarting from my buggery I dreaded the impact of that fearful cane.

The rattan is a hard wood from the east and makes the cruellest of flogging implements. There it is used on the bare buttocks of criminals; in the Royal Navy, on officer cadets. Its impact is loud, heavy and merciless, and even its dark brown colour is sullen and menacing.

She lifted and swished her cane, and it whistled, not with the bright, sharp whistle of an English cane, but with a dry, crashing sound, as though even the air had the breath whipped from it. The impact on my naked fesses slammed me against the bronze, and my teeth fastened on the statue's shoulder to stifle my squeal of agony.

As that bright hot pain seared my bare bum, again I regretted my foolish pride in thinking myself strong enough for a lady's slave! The second stroke took me, harder than the first, and then the third, each seeming to seek out a tender weal from my previous floggings, and fastening sharp teeth of agony on my raw ridged flesh.

'O . . . O . . .,' I heard my sobs, as my tethered bottom squirmed in a frenzy of remorse, and at each movement my anus smarted with the cruel filling of the lady's cock. My Mistress counted sternly: '*And* four! *And* five! *And* six!'

Her flogging took a harsh and sensuous rhythm, and the wriggles of my wealed bottom followed it, so that each thudding impact drove my anus hard on to the dildo that buggered me. Yet as the dildo and cane both maddened me with pain, my cock throbbed harder than I could imagine. The tip of the buggering shaft seemed to touch a new, raw nerve of pleasure somewhere deep above my writhing balls.

'This is what an impudent slave gets,' she panted at about the twelfth or thirteenth stroke. 'Forcing yourself on my friend the general! *And* fourteen!'

'Mistress, she –' I began, then screamed as the rattan took me twice in hard succession, a cruel whap!, whap! that echoed above the roaring of the train.

'Do not *dare* speak to me of a lady!' she hissed in real fury. And now my caning became faster and even harder.

She bounced me on the dildo like a doll, until I thought my anus should burst, and my buttocks turn to molten jelly.

'I shall deal appropriately with my impudent friend the general,' she panted between gleeful strokes to my bare.

I began to feel I deserved punishment – perhaps I *had* been guilty of inciting the lady general to impudence! But such thoughts faded as my whole being was suffused with the excruciating pain of the rattan. And I may assure the reader that of all canes, the rattan *is* the most excruciating.

It was not until the fortieth stroke that my Mistress declared my beating complete; she left me a sobbing, shuddering rag, impaled on the cruel dildo, and yet my balls tickled strangely, my cock still throbbed rampant, and with that delicious, agonising pressure in my bumhole, I felt as though I could spurt at any moment.

My Mistress pulled down my skirt to cover my indecency and left me trussed to my flogging-post, sobbing and mewling like a girl. There was a soft knock on the carriage door, and she loudly commanded entrance. The door slid open, and the lady general joined us.

'Come in, Madame General,' said my Mistress without looking up. 'You are unpunctual – rather scandalous in a German officer, don't you think?'

'Y – yes, dear Countess,' murmured the general, her voice meek yet trembling with excitement.

She bowed and put down a leather medical holdall.

'And scandalous behaviour must – be – dealt – with!' my Mistress cried, accompanying the last four words of her pronouncement with four stinging lashes of the rattan across my naked buttocks. I whinnied in anguish and looked at the general through a blur of tears.

I expected her to be arrayed in a blue and red Prussian uniform adapted for a lady, but she wore a dark blue nurse's uniform skirt – short almost to indecency! – that billowed out like a daisy and left her white-stockinged legs entirely exposed to a height of perhaps six inches above her knees. Thus, as her skirt flounced up I had fleeting glimpses of her garter straps, the belt itself, the knickerless fount, shaved bare, and the livid gash of the gleaming moist cunny I had so recently touched.

Her gait was stiff and teetering, on heels of alarming height attached to heavy medical (I supposed) boots of thick shiny rubber, laced very tightly so that her ankles and instep bulged. She removed her jacket to reveal a white, translucent blouse through which her bare breasts were clearly and sweetly visible, thrusting tightly against the sheer silk as though begging for release; beneath her breasts, a tight blue waspie, slightly narrower than my Mistress's, squeezed her muscled waist so that little pinches of flesh were extruded above and below the corse.

Her russet curls were tightly pinned in a bun. With one stroke my Mistress undid them, and the tresses cascaded over her guest's shoulders and bosom.

The general curtsied and stood at attention, adoring eyes fixed on my Mistress as her nonchalant fingers toyed with the steel spikes on the general's black leather neck-thong and began to unbutton her blouse. The general gave a little sigh as each button popped open, showing more and more of her nut-brown teats, and then I, too, gasped, for the two breasts suddenly sprang out, quite bare, quivering like jellies and holding themselves proudly at attention. Not quite bare: the general smiled happily and said she hoped she pleased the Countess by wearing her medals on parade.

She wore an array of glittering medals, whose gaudy ribbons were pinned directly into her naked breast-skin! The two largest and gaudiest, of silver clustered with painted oak leaves, were pierced directly through the stiff plums of her nipples. My Mistress struck the row of medals quite hard, making the breasts quiver and the metal jangle like gongs. The general shut her eyes and moaned softly.

'You pass muster,' said my Mistress with a lazy yawn, 'and we may proceed with parade.'

At once, the general smartly bent over and touched her toes like a schoolboy, with her legs wide apart. The Countess tipped the hem of her skirt with the rattan, then flattened it on the small of her back, baring her bottom.

'Hmm – no panties, *Fräulein Generalin?*'

'But, Countess, you have none –'

'You have peeked!' cried my Mistress in anger, real or feigned. 'An extra smarting for *that*!'

She swirled her rubber skirt over her thighs, opening it right to her fount and showing quim and mink – the general's viewpoint permitting her to spy from below the lush red gash shaven to gleaming, and with the shafts of the twin dildo clearly visible.

'And a double obispos,' she murmured. 'How powerful is your desire for pleasure, Countess. If only you could know the pleasures loving ladies can give each other. Surely whipping your slut's juicy bare bum must stir you?'

The Countess snorted that she despised the perversions of so-called nurses and sapphics and would flog such nonsense from any bum present.

'Your maid shall watch?' the general murmured timidly.

'Yes,' said my Mistress, 'I can't be bothered to cut her loose. And since you have already made her acquaintance, my dear, she will enjoy seeing how I punish a lady's wickedness – knowing her own bum will wriggle ten times as painfully as your own.'

'O!' cried the general. 'So shameful – so exciting!'

My Mistress delivered a smart thirty strokes, at intervals of five seconds, to the quivering bare flans of the general's bottom, which clenched only slightly at each savage cut, and she did not cry or squeal, her only reaction being deep and rapid sighs of pleasured excitement. I saw that my Mistress's free hand was rubbing under her furrow, to press the dildos in and out of her holes in the rhythm of her flogging. This spectacle caused me to stiffen harder, raising my skirt to embarrassment, and I squirmed painfully on the bronze cock penetrating my arse to conceal my maleness behind the statue.

When the brisk flogging was over, the lady general rose, patted her skirt down over her wealed, glowing buttocks, and sprang smartly to attention with a snapping salute.

'Thank you, Countess,' she said with a little tickle in her throat, her eyes moist in adoration.

I was sure she noticed, as I did, the trickle of shiny juice which ran down my Mistress's bare thigh and wet the tops of her stockings that peeped through the drawn rubber. The general smiled mischievously.

'I am so looking forward to my luncheon, Countess,' she said. 'O, that you would permit me to call you *Mistress*!'

'That privilege is reserved for slaves!' rapped my Mistress. 'No lesbic is my slave without *favour*.'

The general lifted her skirt and showed her wealed bare bottom, rubbing as if to beguile.

'How my bum smarts!' she said huskily. 'I bear your welts proudly – O, Galena, name your favour!'

My Mistress lashed the cane across her bare breasts, making the medals clang, and smiled thinly.

'Business over luncheon, my dear general,' she said. 'You shall dress properly – strip naked for me, my dear.'

The general saluted again and obeyed, shivering a little and smiling nervously as she unfastened her clothing. Soon she stood nude before her hostess and tormentor, the ripe muscled orbs of her croup glowing like the red ribbons of her teat-medals.

Again the Countess struck the nude lady on her teats, this time the cane tip flicking hard and expertly on the very points of the generously stiffened nipples. She ordered her to bend halfway over and clutch her buttocks to spread them fully. The general obeyed, and calmly my Mistress raised her left leg to her waist, affording us both a sight of her juice-wet thighs and the moist clump of her mink forest, then plucked from her holes the twin prongs of the dildo. The general's eyes widened.

'So big –' she murmured.

'There are bigger,' smiled my Mistress.

The naked lady's squeals of anguish were genuine as my Mistress inserted the dildo into her spread holes, pushing very hard and quite without ceremony until the twin prongs were embedded in the general's gash and bum and fastened in place by their strap.

'O! O!' gasped the general, her face contorted in pain. 'Your flogging was nothing to *this*, dear Countess!'

My Mistress said there was more, and she ordered the

squirming lady to lie down. She opened the general's bag and withdrew rolls of bandages, gauze and sticking plaster, saying that the patient must be well bandaged for an operation to cure her insufferable lesbianism! I watched agog as the general's bare body slowly disappeared under her own cargo of fluffy bandages and lint, until all of her was swathed, except her teats, fount and buttocks, and the thick wadding right up to her chin prevented her from turning her head. The bandages were secured with slivers of sticking plaster, thus still slightly loose.

'I see your body is uniformly brown, like a peasant's,' said my Mistress with faint distaste. In truth, there could not be more contrast than between her own alabaster purity and the nut-brown calfskin of the general.

The general stammered that it was the practice in the German Nursing Corps to bathe naked in the Starnberger See and to practise naked sunbathing, with healthy games like netball or wrestling all played in the nude. The Countess lashed her bare breasts very hard with the cane.

'To be fit for the coming war, you poor boobies?' she sneered, and the general grimaced and nodded yes.

My Mistress then took the roll of sticking plaster and wound it round the general's whole bandaged body save for fount and arse, tightening the wrapping until she groaned in discomfort. My Mistress came to her bandaged throat, wrapped it tight, and without comment proceeded to stick the plaster all the way up the chin and cheeks to her forehead. Drawing the russet curls into a wad, she plastered the whole of the lady general's head until only a hole for her mouth was left open. The general groaned louder, but her sighs, and the heaving of her trussed breast, denoted deep pleasure.

'We are nearly at the German frontier,' she moaned. 'I could have you arrested, dear sweet Countess, for disrespect to a German officer.'

My Mistress answered with another cut across the taped breasts and two harder ones on each swollen bare quim-lip. Then she opened her closet and withdrew a package of shiny wooden devices, which she said were a new and invaluable product for nursing in the field.

White shiny splints were placed on either side of the general's legs and arms and taped firmly in place, her arms being pinioned and wrapped fast against her sides, so that only her legs could shift; then slabs of the same wood were fastened to her back and belly, lacing her in a vicious corse far tighter than any cloth, and connected by thinner splints to the broader ones on arms and legs. My Mistress nudged the belly-pad and there was a sharp click. Two poles sprang from the ends of the leg splints, with large pads like feet; the same with the arm splints, from which devices like claws extended.

Suddenly my Mistress reached under the general's neck and scooped her whole body up to standing position.

'You see?' said my Mistress. 'Splints that become crutches, most useful in the exigencies of a field hospital, so that the wounded may be put to use, should you choose to give them the freedom of their arms. Males wounded are still unruly scum, so these prostheses are designed for their easy disciplining at a nurse's hands.'

She ordered the general to try to walk, and the general obeyed, furious at her impotence. She stamped and jerked like a marionette with wires frayed, while my Mistress laughed a soft, musical laugh.

Then she gave a smart twist to the belly-corset, and from the top of the leg splint sprang a compact frame like a handcuff with a disciplining arse-prong attached at the rear. My Mistress explained that this device was designed to immobilise the male by securing his private parts, with the optional anal restraint to cause further discomfort.

'And it can, of course, be adapted for female use, with an optional extra quim-prong. The cuff secures the male balls and penis shaft like a vice, and the female can be immobilised for discipline just as effectively.'

She fitted the clasp snugly around the general's swollen wet quim-lips and snapped it tight, causing her to squeal.

'Imagine the effect on a male's balls,' said my Mistress, licking her lips.

She pressed the belly-pad again, and the leg splints snapped wide, exposing the general's swollen red quim and furrow and spreading the cheeks of her arse while holding her legs stiff at attention. My Mistress selected a whippy willow cane and said that now, with new technology, the general's patients might enjoy healthful discipline.

She began to flog the protruding bare buttocks with vigorous enthusiasm, making her 'patient', or prisoner, squeal with unfeigned distress. This increased as the Countess switched her punishment to the spread naked fount-mouth, flicking the springy little tip of her cane across quim-lips and stiff extruded clitty with the precision of a harpist. The general moaned and shrieked wretchedly, her whole body shuddering beneath the tight swath of bandages, but her splint-crutches, and the pincers clutching her gash, prevented her from any movement more than violent trembling.

'Mmm! Mmm! O! Countess, please, mercy! *Ooo!*' she squealed as her hostess caned her bare bottom and quim, the gash now ripening to delicate mottled red in unison with the deep ridged weals that etched the bum-skin.

'I think,' said the Countess thoughtfully, 'that a generous order for my company's new field hospital equipment would be a suitable favour, *Fräulein Generalin*. I know you have the ear of the Kaiser's good lady – and, some say, more than the ear. She, meanwhile, has the same *ear* of the dashing young Marshal Ebert, so that I expect an order for our new Volchuk 80mm cannon.'

'O! Countess! Anything! Just do not stop your beating,' moaned the general.

My Mistress smiled. 'Both products are manufactured at my plants in northern England,' she said. 'The English are the finest craftsmen, and you will need plenty of supplies in preparation for the carnage to come. When England herself becomes involved in the war, I shall of course route further shipments through Sweden or other neutral countries.'

'The order is as good as signed,' sobbed the general.

'When it is, you may call me Mistress.'

My Mistress delivered a dozen cuts with machine-gun pace to the bare flans of the lady's croup, then an equal number to the gash, the cane-shaft taking her right on the cleft of the quim-lips and stroking the stiffened clitty-bud; then she abruptly ceased the beating.

The general was weeping softly as her bare bum squirmed livid, yet her beaten, bruised fount glistened with copious love-oil. The train seemed to be slowing, and I heard movements: we were approaching the German frontier.

The Countess Galena opened her skirt-front, took a hunting knife and deftly sliced a thick tuft of curly mink-hairs from her mons. She tripped up the general and sent her crashing loudly, with a howl of protest, to the floor, where the lady lay quietly sobbing. My Mistress raised her rubber skirt and mounted the bandaged woman, buttocks straddling the face with her whole weight.

The general groaned. My Mistress said gaily that it was time for her luncheon and began to feed the general morsels of mink-hair, which she moistened in her own sopping gash before stuffing them into her guest's opened mouth. The general moaned in delight, as though the wet mink-hairs were the most succulent oysters, and I saw her throat bob as she swallowed.

Her throat bobbed even more avidly as my Mistress shifted, to cover the lady's mouth fully with her spread gash-lips, and I saw her belly quiver a little as a ripe hissing sound rose from her gash. There was steam, and a delicious acrid fragrance, as the general gulped the nectar of my Mistress's evacuation, and my cock throbbed most painfully in my desire to taste the same honour. So copious was my Mistress's provender that rivulets of golden liquid ran down the general's bandaged face and shoulders, and I longed to lick up every drop!

The spectacle of a dominant and submissive lady made my balls long to spend, and the pain of the dildo in my anus now seemed the sweetest, most thrilling shame. Suddenly there came a knock at the door, and a gruff male voice announced German passport and customs control.

'Ah! I recognise your manly fist! Come in, Captain Schumacher,' cried my Mistress without moving.

A young officer in blue and scarlet uniform, with spiked helmet, stood to attention at the door and saluted.

'Everything in order, Madame Countess?' he said stiffly. 'I count three persons, including you.'

'Why, yes, Captain,' said the Countess. 'My luncheon guest is *Krankenschwestergeneralin* Hochhuth, of the Kaiser's Nursing Corps –' the officer saluted the writhing, bandaged body, glistening with the streams of my Mistress's liquid '– and the other is merely a new slave, in transit to Russia. I do not know its name.'

'Good! *Alles in Ordnung!*' the officer barked to an unseen junior, then entered, bowed and closed the door.

'If you will take your usual place, Captain, I shall attend to you in a moment,' said the Countess pleasantly. 'I am just finishing my service of luncheon.'

There was another vigorous hissing, and the general's throat bobbed frantically as she swallowed. With careful ceremony, the captain removed his boots, spurs and sword, and all his lower clothing and, with bum as bare and cock as hard as my own, took his place beside me, pressed to the bronze buttocks of the female statue.

6

Miss Bainbridge

Across Joan of Arc's shoulder I was presented with a view of the captain's bare bum and saw it was well wealed with the scars of whipping; not with the massed ridges and welts of a devotee of the rod, but etched in a crisp, crisscross pattern of scars as though by artist's design. My Mistress rose, leaving the general quivering in her bandages, and selected a dreadful rattan cane: a good five feet in length, even heavier and thicker than the instrument that had so painfully flogged my own bare.

She flexed it thoughtfully and tapped the captain at the cleft of his buttocks. This cane was not springy but stiff and so hard that it bent only with difficulty; I shuddered at the thought of that engine wealing my naked fesses. Yet the captain made a little purring sound, as though in pleasurable anticipation.

'Yes,' said my Mistress, 'the scars have formed well, and I think we can add significantly to your insignia before you leave the train. You bear my weal with pride?'

The captain murmured that no German officer could be prouder than to smart under his Mistress's cruel welts, and my Mistress laughed deep in her throat.

'Other officers show their duelling scars on their cheeks – how clever to wear them in a sweeter place.'

She took his ceremonial sword from the scabbard at his belt and swished it in the air, making a singing noise; then she said that his bum must be warmed for the duel, and brought the flat of the sword sharply down across the bare

73

buttocks, as hard as a cane. There was a loud smack as the heavy metal stroked the naked skin, and a livid pink blush appeared at once; the officer groaned, but his cheeks clenched only slightly.

She caned him again with the sword-flat, and then a third stroke followed, and a fourth, in quite rapid succession, blushing his fesses to rose while the bare buttocks started to squirm gently and rhythmically in pain.

'I think a good sixty will have your bum warm for her duel,' she murmured, and he grunted his agreement.

The sixty sword-strokes were duly delivered until his buttocks were puce. Then my Mistress announced 'one for luck', which was a further dozen, stroking him at machine-gun pace and making him actually squeal in pained surprise. When his caning was over he was panting hard, and his stern Prussian face was well flushed.

Without pausing, the Countess turned the sword round and rapped an order in German. Groaning, the male opened his bum-cheeks wide and shut his eyes in a grimace as she plunged the hilt of the sword deep into his anus.

My Mistress then delivered a vigorous buggery to the German officer, who squirmed at the thrusts of his own studded sword-hilt in his filled bumhole. His eyes were moist, and I heard sobs click in his throat as he writhed in unfeigned agony at the harsh impact of the studs.

She sodomised him thus with, I guessed, about a hundred thrusts into his anus, and then she panted gleefully to the sobbing male that it was time for him to fight like a man. Now she lifted her rattan cane and began to feint and parry, clicking it against his quivering sword-blade as though his bum were her opponent in fencing.

'Come on, captain, fight!' she cried, and her tormented submissive valiantly thrust his hips from side to side in a pretence of swordplay.

'Thrust! Parry! Riposte!' cried my Mistress, and suddenly the rattan blurred and stroked down with a fearsome crack on the top of the officer's left fesse, where it laid a dark purple welt, livid and cruel as a lady's gash.

She paused, panting, and examined the mark closely, where it bisected two other welts.

'Most satisfactory,' she said. 'A neat cross in the north-west sector.'

'I beg to thank you, Mistress,' sobbed the captain.

'On guard!' she rapped and began her swordplay once more, ending it abruptly with a further stroke to the north-east of his buttocks and pronouncing herself equally satisfied with the result.

There followed three or four further additions to the captain's mosaic of scars, until my Mistress said that he needed a refresher course in fencing and removed the sword-hilt from his squirming anus with a loud squirting sound.

She proceeded to cane his puce bare croup in earnest, carefully directing her strokes towards his existing welts, whether old and firm or the soft and livid scars she had newly laid. His breath came in harsh gasps, and his buttocks shuddered in real agony at each cut, for I could see that the old welts were opened raw at her fresh strokes, while the livid new gashes were cruelly deepened.

My Mistress picked up the sword, and at every six or seven strokes of the rattan to croup amused herself by swishing the sword-blade between his quivering thighs so that the tip expertly struck his balls, with undue harshness, I thought, for at these strokes the man growled deep in his throat and tears sprang from his eyes. He made no protest, but sighed in pleasure at his humiliance.

And his cock trembled huge and stiff, seeming to grow as the softness of his very balls was so cruelly caressed; to my horror, I saw that the helmet of his cock, revealed by a fully stretched prepuce, bore the same crisscross of tiny scars the width of a needle!

Just as he had been warmed with six dozen of sword-flat, so the captain took six dozen with that fearful rattan, with stinging slaps to the balls, until the welts of his pain shone in deep ridges on the flaming, squirming bum-skin. His eyes were screwed tight, his lips twisted in joy.

'A fine sword,' cried my Mistress, directing her voice at the trembling figure of the general.

Her bandaged captive still lay blindfold, but with her haunches squirming in pleasure at the pressure of her twin dildos, as she frotted herself in quim and anus with awkward fervour to the sound of the male's chastisement.

'However,' my Mistress added slyly, with a final groaning cut to the captain's glowing bare bum, 'I hold that the English craftsmanship is superior.'

She lashed the general's wrapped buttocks lazily but firmly with three or four rattan strokes, and the nurse gurgled in pain beneath her swaths of white. Then she tapped the tip of the captain's erect penis and said that she should prove it. She reached into the general's squirming wet furrow and with a loud plopping noise suddenly withdrew the twin dildo, shiny with copious fluid. She placed the larger prong, the quim-shaft, into the captain's recently emptied anus and then unfastened my own person from my bonds; I felt the hard bronze cock leave my hole with a deliciously painful tickling.

My cock was still rigid, and my Mistress tapped it quite severely with the rattan tip, so that I gasped. Smiling, she took me by the balls and led me to the prone bandaged figure, where she placed her arm under the belly and scooped the nurse-general to a crouching position, resting on her knees and elbows.

'A demonstration, General,' she cried gaily, 'of the finest hospital appliance English craftsmanship can offer! My new anal hygiene product, bigger and harder and more lifelike, as you shall see.'

She motioned me to keep utter silence; all the time she was stroking the naked glans and shaft of my cock to maintain her throbbing stiffness – as though that were necessary. The bare bum-cheeks of the lesbic nurse-general were spread before me, with the anus pucker crinkling open to receive my engine in the plainest invitation, for the sapphic lady moaned 'Yes, O yes' a number of times.

My eyes met my Mistress's, pleading, and at once I lowered my head in shame at this trespass. But she read my glance, knew that it was her arse I improperly longed to bugger – the spectacle of her bum-cheeks quivering under the virile onslaught of her slave Paul haunted me. She laughed slyly and said that German steel must also be put to the test. Roughly she grasped my buttocks, squeezing their lacerated skin very painfully, and pushed my penis against the general's open bumhole; inside, to an inch.

'O! O! So big! It hurts me so!' squealed the lesbic.

To two inches; her shrieks of protest turned to sobs. Then my Mistress exhorted the lesbic lady to relax her sphincter, pushed me again, and with a joyous rush my shaft sank to the root of the lady's tight elastic anus.

'No!' she howled. 'O no, no! Yes! Bugger me, sweet Countess, hurt me with that shaft. O, I know I'll spend, it is dreadful and sublime and so big. O! O! Yes!'

I needed no encouragement to begin a vigorous thrusting, for her bare squirming bum-cheeks greatly inflamed my cock's fervour. I felt a delicious rubbery pressure of her anus wall on my helmet, and she squeezed my cock with rapid, frantic shudders of her sphincter muscle. The cheeks of her fesses slammed hard against my balls, and she squealed that the dildo was so lifelike, as hot and strong and stinking as a filthy male.

My Mistress knelt beside her now, and murmured that such insulting talk earned her a spanking! She nodded to me; with a will, I set to belabour the squirming bum until both cheeks glowed smarting and red under the cracks of my palm, and I poked her clutching anus more vigorously. Her cries of anguish grew higher, and she sobbed that she should burst, and spend, and the big English dildo would split her inside out, and suchlike lady's fancies.

These cries redoubled my ardour, for I imagined that in punishing her bumhole I was taking revenge for all my indignities from my own Mistress. I shut my eyes, my hand rising and falling like a metronome as I spanked, and imagined it was my Mistress's own bare that I smacked, and her own sweet bumhole that I poked. I knew I must later confess these shameful fancies to her and merit the fiercest flogging for my insolence, and, knowing she would divine my longing for punishment, I opened my eyes. I gasped, for my humiliation had already begun.

The Countess Galena Volchuk knelt beside me on all fours, like a dog. Her rubber skirt was up above her waist, her porcelain bum-globes bare to the onslaught of Captain Schumacher's rigid pole as he buggered her with deliberate, hard thrusts between her spread fesses. Her bare teats quivered like jellies, topped by brick-hard nipples, as the officer grunted and sweated in his vigorous buggery, and her haunches and croup writhed to the rhythm of his thrusts. Her lips were twisted in a thin smile; her eyes were wide and fixed on mine, taunting me with her pleasure.

'Yes . . .' she moaned, 'O, yes, *Herr Hauptmann.*'

'O! O!' moaned the general. 'O, I'm spending! Yes! You are with me, Countess? You bugger your own arse with mine?'

I felt her bum clutch me in an embrace of steel, as her whole belly and thighs danced in the frenzy of her spend, and made bright shiny rivulets of her love-juice course on her pumping thighs until her bandages were quite sodden.

'Why, no,' panted the Countess, 'it is a lovely hot male cock – a virile German cock – that buggers *me.*'

These words cut me like a knife; I burnt with shame that my rival could pleasure my Mistress so. Her stab of contempt, together with the sight of the lesbic's squirming bum, reddened by my spanks, made my flood erupt. I filled the general's anus with powerful spurts to her root, my moans of ecstasy drowned by her own howling.

'O! O! Ooo!' she gasped, in the final tumult of her climax. '*Ach*, how can you lower yourself to *that*, Countess, when your English machine makes me come in such delight? The throbbing spurt of so much hot cream – so lifelike!'

The Countess tore the bandages from her guest's face and invited her to look at the new device that had caused her such pleasure. My unwilling paramour looked round and saw me crouched behind her, my cock still half-stiff and dripping the remains of my spurt over her white bandages

'O! O! A *male*!' wailed the general.

Her sobs of horror seemed music to my Mistress's ears, for at that moment she began to shiver and pant, and I knew her own spend was coming. Her buttocks expertly pumped the German until he moaned in orgasm, and then my Mistress permitted herself to spend, her breasts and thighs quivering violently in tune with her arse-flans.

The train began to slow again, and Captain Schumacher panted that it was time for him to disembark. He begged the honour of kissing his Mistress's feet, and this was granted. Soon I watched the resplendent uniformed figure of a German officer kneel, sword dangling on the floor, to take my Mistress's boots into his mouth and have her stand on him, crushing his nose and lips, then, with a final, hideous stab of her heels, right to his balls. The lesbic nurse-general watched the male's humiliance with glee from the crouched huddle in which she was trying to forget her own.

He stood shakily, bowed and saluted, thanked my Mistress for her kindness and begged for the honour of a further duel when next she graced the fatherland with her presence. My Mistress looked airily away.

'It depends on the progress of the war that will surely come – and, I fear, on this showing the fatherland will come off second best,' she said, rubbing the wet curls of her quim and stroking her swollen gash as though still unsatisfied. 'You see, *Fräulein Krankenschwestergeneralin*? I promised you that English equipment is second to none.'

The train stopped in the city of Frankfurt am Main, and I supposed Captain Schumacher disembarked. I was not in a position to observe our stop, nor to see much of Germany at all: no sooner had the general made her fawning departure, with promises of vast business for my Mistress's factories, than I found myself stripped of my frilly maid's uniform (of which I'd grown rather fond) and chained like a dog, naked, for a hosing to cleanse me of my male filthiness.

My trussing was worse than a dog's: I was obliged to

bend my ankles and wrists so that they met at the small of my back, in a kind of crab shape, and then they were cuffed together, leaving me nervous at the exposure of my manly parts. Though soft after my buggery of the lesbic lady, my cock now began to stiffen at the delicious humiliation of my trussing on the wet bathroom floor. My Mistress keenly directed the sharp jet of cold water to my balls and peehole; I began to groan softly, and my cock grew harder.

I must confess that my Mistress's parting words to the captain, after his buggery of her own bum, came back to me . . . about the superiority of the English product. I had witnessed her buggered by her slave Paul, and dared hope that this voluptuous duty lay in store for me.

The icy water did little to soften the smarting of my wealed nates, and I was glad – the warm pain of flogging soon becomes a familiar and trusted part of a submissive male, and so it was with the Countess Galena, my first real Mistress. From that day I have been unhappy if ever my bare bum goes uncleansed by a lady's rod. It is a (perhaps indelicate) truth that most ladies become moody without a male's cock to serve them. A lady's slave is just as edgy, until his fesses receive the cruel reassurance of her lash.

After my hosing, I lay shivering and goose pimpled while my Mistress fetched a long pole like a broomstick, with a metal clip on one end. This was fastened very tightly round my balls and the shaft of my cock, so that my erect penis looked like a squeezed fruit. She dried me with a coarse hempen cloth, then pulled me by the broomstick out into the salon, dragging me by the balls so that my eyes moistened, more in fear of discomfort than in discomfort itself.

This, too, thrills a helpless slave: the fear that his Mistress will finally lose patience with her impudent wretch and impose punishment beyond his endurance.

Smiling, my Mistress now donned the frilly maid's outfit, still warm from my own body, and said gaily that she would do some cleaning. I watched her tease me as she drew her stockings slowly over her naked thighs; fussed with garter straps and brassiere, smoothed her skirt tightly over the swelling peach – she was knickerless – and then donned a pair of high, spiked shoes of patent leather, in whose gleam were reflected the quivering flans of her bosom, and the hairy forest of her mink between squeezed thighs.

She chuckled as my erection strained hard. Briskly, she took a pot of smelly wax and rubbed it all over my left side until I was well caked. She took the broomstick and with a sharp jolt flipped me over to lie on my left side, leaving me breathless with the shock to my trussed balls. Then she began to push me up and down on the wooden parquet floor to wax it.

My pain and terror were unspeakable, and tears flowed from my eyes on to the floor now smudged with the wax from my body. Around and around the salon she went, sometimes pulling me, sometimes pushing, with the broomstick digging sharply between my spread thighs. She hummed merrily, until the whole space gleamed with the wax polish. Then she flipped me over again and repeated the process with my dry side, so that my skin buffed the floor to a shine. All the time I winced, not just at the tugs and jolts to my precious balls, but at the stinging of the wooden splinters that lodged in my skin.

'I suppose at your English boarding school you were used to performing such services, fagging for the older boys – but I forget! You had not the privilege of a proper education. How I wish my sister Dushanka were here! She is the expert – she was at Masterdale, in Buckinghamshire, you know, two years before me, and was head girl. She used to cane me, her own sister, on the bare! And I am none the worse for it! Proper and regular beating on the bare bum is all the learning a young person really understands.'

I moaned that my time at Shoeburyness had taught me a lot about bare-bum discipline, but my Mistress dismissed my ordeals merely as crudity among rude matelots. My floor-polishing came to an end, each side of my body shining with wax and grime. My Mistress laughed scornfully and said a filthy little boy must be taught to keep himself clean. I sobbed with joy at her injustice! The more so when she unfastened my aching balls and pulled me roughly to my feet, then to the closet, from which she took a bundle of clothing and told me to dress myself.

Trembling, I obeyed, and found myself in the mothballed uniform of an English public school: grey flannel shorts (but without knickers) and bulky wool socks with black boots; a white shirt, and striped tie and blazer, with a little round cap to match. The whole was slightly too small for my tall frame, and I felt quite ridiculous, especially as my appearance roused my Mistress to peals of laughter.

'We shall play an instructive game, slave. You refuse to tell me your name? Well, I shall thrash it from you.'

She picked up the rattan that had flogged the captain.

'O, please don't, Miss,' I burbled, playing my part, yet sincere. 'I am terrified of your cane hurting my bottom.'

'What, you are ashamed of being thrashed by a chambermaid? Then I must make myself proper for your instruction, my boy. Please assume *the position*.'

I gulped; I knew what 'the position' was and shivered as I obeyed. I bent over with my legs wide apart and touched my toes. She tut-tutted and said she was not going to cane me on trousers – did I not know that proper English schoolboys took their caning bare-bum? She undid the clasp of my belt and roughly pulled down my shorts to my knees.

'What! No knickers? You whelp!' she snarled. 'That bum shall smart doubly for her filthiness.'

I thrilled at this further injustice. I heard the closet open and the slither as she shed her maid's frillies; then the snap of garter and the swish of blouse, skirts and stockings being donned. I peeked between my legs as she stood behind me, flexing the rattan, and magnificent with the crisp beauty of an English schoolgirl!

She wore a black pleated skirt, very short indeed, that flounced over the tops of her thighs and revealed the wide lacy stocking tops of black satin anchored by thick red garter straps to the belt hidden beneath her starched white blouse. She had red knickers, peeping coyly under her black skirt, and beneath the knicker hem strands of golden mink-hair hung like creepers between the firm white thigh tops and strayed over the stockings in a languid caress.

Her blouse was starched and gleaming white, fitting snugly over breasts encased in a scalloped red brassiere that seemed quite too small for her teats, and thrust their proud melons out with almost insulting firmness against the tight white cotton. In the cleft of her breasts dangled a tie of plain red, matching her brassiere and garter straps, which I surmised to be the colour of her old school. Her hair was loose and cascaded over her shoulders and breasts in an unruly, girlish mane.

She purred that her uniform from Masterdale still fitted her like a glove. I marvelled at the female wile of transformation: from countess, to nurse, to schoolgirl, in each persona her lady's power undimmed. That power was enhanced by her black laced boots, very sharp and spiked, whose shiny embrace caressed her calves to an inch over her stockinged knee. The boots had pointed metal toecaps enamelled red in the school colour, and she clicked these smartly on the floor polished by my skin.

'Prefect's boots,' she purred with creamy satisfaction. 'We used these for corking miscreant girls before beating them. A really good corking is almost enough in itself.'

Without shifting her torso or her stance, she swung her booted foot back until heel touched her peach, then with a blurring motion swung it forward and up.

I shuddered at the jolt of her toe's impact and squealed without meaning to as I felt the metal point embedded in my naked bumhole, to a horrid depth of more than an inch. The point and sides of the toecap seemed razor-sharp, and my bum shivered in agony; she wriggled her toe inside my anus as though grubbing for worms.

She withdrew. I heard her grunt, and then another terrible kick was delivered to my helpless bumhole, already raw from her buggery by the bronze statue. I stood trembling and tried neither to shift nor resist, resolved to grin and bear my punishment like a slave, or Englishman.

My 'corking' continued, and she kicked me a good thirty times until I was sobbing helplessly, as much in shame as in agony. For a kicking is pure scorn, not allowing the victim the small dignity of a silent bum-whipping. The boot jolts and utterly humiliates; I wanted her never to stop.

But at last her foot stilled, and the rattan was lifted. She swished the air twice, the second time catching her toecap, which made a sharp clang.

'O! How it hurts!' she mocked. 'It pains me to apply Miss Rattan to your bare bum, my lad – I assure you this will hurt me far more than you. Tell me your name, do.'

I heard the steady clicking of her feet above the humming of the rails as she strode to the wall of the salon. There was an awful pause; the cane swished the air viciously. Suddenly the click of her boots became a harsh thud as she ran towards me, the cane whistled again, and she brought it down with full force across my naked flesh, searing my buttocks in a white-hot kiss. I bit my lip, and my tears sprang – the pain of previous floggings dimmed beside the hateful smart of the rattan. Miss Birch was a friend compared with Miss Rattan.

'Mistress! I – I cannot tell you my name,' I blurted.

In that moment I spoke truth, for I could not remember! I knew only my pain: *I was nothing more than that.*

I heard through my sobs her awful measured tread as she resumed her position for the run-up; then the thud of her boots; the whistle of the rod; the cut straight to her first weal. I danced in my agony, my buttocks clenching madly and my head shaking, eyes closed in a vain attempt to stem my tears. A deep stifled sob rose in my throat. To take me twice in the same welt was unspeakable cruelty! Unconsciously, I raised and spread my buttocks, my flamed skin and stiff cock pleading for worse.

The third stroke took me above, the fourth below the first ridges of pain. I did not need to touch my flesh to feel it puff and swell; my teeth chattered, my eyes were blinded by tears, but still I was able to stammer, to her fierce enquiry, that I could not remember my name.

'Then I shall punish you until it comes, boy,' she panted, laying the rattan across my fesses again.

This stroke was followed rapidly by three more. She did not take her run-up, but the cuts seemed twice as harsh.

'Ah! Ah! *Ahhh!*' I heard myself scream despite myself.

My body swayed and shuddered at the merciless thrash of her cane, and I knew that this was the worst bare-bum caning I had ever felt or dreamt. I reached the point of despair, of renouncing my foolish enslavement; yet suddenly my pain made me soar. My bottom's agony was the gift of her power and clasped me in an embrace of pure loving cruelty, until finally she ceased her strokes, panting that I had taken sixty, and *still* would not own up.

I looked up through blurred eyes and saw my Mistress's face flushed, her eyes hoods of savagery and desire, and for a moment I felt the power an abject slave may have over the harshest Mistress. I shook my head and said she must flog me to the very bone before I confessed.

She swallowed hard, threw down the cane and ordered me to rise and make myself decent. I did so, pain flooding my stiff limbs, and my cock straining against the woollen trouser cloth. Her breath was hard and her eyes ate mine, full of desire and hatred.

'Damn you,' she whispered. Then, in a broken sob: 'Damn you – I shall make you speak!'

With that, she suddenly placed her buttocks before my loins and bent over to assume the position! Her skirt rode up, showing her red knickers strained tight over the globes of her peach, and stained dark and moist between her thighs. She picked up the rattan and made me take it. I lifted the cane, awed by its weight.

'Bare bum,' she whispered. 'O, always lovely bare bum.'

My trembling fingers hooked the waistband of her red panties, and, careful not to sully her flesh with the touch of my own, I drew them down until they hung between her knees like a scented wet garland. Her love-juice stained the garment copiously, and I thrilled that my wealed fesses could so excite a lady. The naked globes of her bum shone wet, beckoning me.

'Cork me first, Miss,' she moaned, eyes tight shut. 'A Masterdale girl always takes a corking before her bum squirms and smarts under cane. Please, Miss Bainbridge.'

I drew back my boot and kicked out, my blunt steel toecap touching her gently in the furrow, brushing but not penetrating her anus. She moaned again that I should cork her properly, and I delivered a hard kick that had my toecap lodged squarely an inch inside her spread pucker.

'Mmm! Ouch! O, Miss Bainbridge!' she purred.

A third kick was harder and went deeper. I kicked her again and again, in a shameful fury that she should mock her slave so by humiliating her *own* sacred person. Each kick lodged my foot well inside her bumhole, and I felt her walls squeeze on my toe as I furiously wriggled inside her precious shaft, longing to hurt her and frightened of her desire to be hurt. Her purring turned to sharp wails.

'O! O!' she cried. 'O, cork my bum hard, if you please.'

After she had taken thirty kicks, I ceased the corking and raised the rattan. There was no run-up; in my impatience I took two paces back and caned her from standing. My first stroke was gentle; I could scarcely bring myself to redden that precious flesh, although her bum-skin sprang smartly pink. But her sneer of derision melted my reserve, and I began to cane her bare bum in deadly earnest, taking particular delight in lashing the same weal over and over, until it became a deep, livid trench.

The rattan whistled and made a dull, savage crack as it streaked her quivering peach, yet despite a furious clenching of her buttocks she made no sound but a satisfied rippling of her throat.

At the tenth stroke, she panted that I must have taken enough and should confess my name. I firmly answered no, and continued the caning until she had taken thirty on bare. She repeated her question: was I ready to confess and let my punishment stop? *My* punishment! Yet I understood – for a slave to conspire in his own Mistress's humiliance is punishment worse than any lash on his own croup.

Her stocking tops were beginning to shred where the

rattan's tip caught them on a stroke to the lower fleshy part of her fesses; a garter belt frayed under the same impact, then snapped sharply in two; the stockings sagged on her thighs, and I laid a mischievous stroke right on the tender bare thigh top, jolting her with a mewl of real pain.

'Ahh! Mmm!'

'Well, *Miss*!' I gasped. 'Won't you answer? You know my name. Cease your teasing! You bad, wilful girl! Miss – *Bainbridge* is very cross!'

Whoever Miss Bainbridge was! I lashed her thigh again, then her livid peach, with three hard, rapid strokes.

'Ah! Ah! Ah! O, Miss!'

The croup was now a livid mass of black and purple weals, squirming and clenching, with all trace of a Mistress's cool authority dissipated by the force of the cane on her bare schoolgirl's bottom.

My cock strained, my balls were full and longing to spend. The lesbic nurse's elastic anus, writhing to squeeze my spurt from me, was tender in my memory. Dimly I knew I should rue my insolence, but I could not resist; I lowered my shorts and plunged my naked cock full into the squirming anus pucker, then drove hard until my shaft touched her root. Now she screamed aloud.

I threw aside the cane – she had taken nearly fifty strokes – and grasped the cheeks of her purpled croup, drawing them roughly apart until the skin was stretched to a drumskin. Then I began to bugger her hard with merciless cock-strokes, my helmet hitting her root at every thrust, as though to embed myself in her squirming belly. At each stroke her body stiffened, her legs shot rigid beneath me, and she emitted a terrified squeal of distress. Her cries would not deter me. I fucked her in that tight squirming bumhole with all my might, willing myself not to spurt until she had admitted defeat.

'What *is* my name, Mistress?' I panted, taunting her.

'No – no – you'll split me with that cock!' she moaned.

Her bum flailed furiously at the savage thrusts of my cock to anus, yet implacably I would not cease buggering her until she submitted. I thought of Paul's buggering her

– *he* had a name. Any name for me would do, just to have her acknowledge the triumph of my enslavement.

She knew I would not spurt my cream in her bumshaft until I had her submission. Determined to refuse me, she began to close her arse-muscle on my cock, and thrust her own root against my helmet in time with my fucking, as she squeezed me to milk the spunk from my aching balls. I knew I could not resist. With a cry of despair and ecstasy I spurted my cream in fierce jets right to her belly's root, and her squeals of pleasured pain joined my own.

'O! You whelp! O! O! I'm coming! O, spurt your cream in my bum, you bastard. O, Philip, Philip!'

I fucked harder and harder as I came, and as I panted with the last gush of my sperm to her anus, she hissed that my name was Philip Demesne.

I paused and drooped over her buttocks, which still trembled in the throes of her own spend.

'How – how do you know?' I sobbed.

'Paul!' she cried with lilting scorn. 'Show Philip.'

The door of the salon opened, to admit the nude figure of her slave Paul, glowering and with penis fully erect. His wrists were manacled and his ankles shackled with heavy copper chains. I withdrew my softened cock from my Mistress's bumhole and sank sobbing to my knees, stammering for forgiveness. She rose and rubbed her purpled bum-flesh, wincing, and whistled softly as she inspected her ridged peach in the glass.

'My arse is raw! My, what a strong young bugger you are, Philip. But I knew that when you shouldered that heavy trunk for me. Heavy as a man's weight, wasn't it? I see by his stiff cock that Paul has enjoyed the spectacle of your discipline.'

Scornfully she kicked my arse, her boot catching my anus, and held her toe there wriggling as she corked me.

'An Englishman abroad must be wary of pickpockets, Philip,' she said, laughing.

With the hint of a grin, his eyes wide and mocking on me, Paul lifted the bundle of my wallet and travel papers.

7

Robotnik

'How dare you!' snapped my Mistress as I unthinkingly reached out my hand. 'These documents remain in my safekeeping – a slave has no property, not even his own body.'

Humbly recognising her wisdom, I covered her sharp toecaps with kisses and babbled my apology. I was silenced with a flurry of crisp canestrokes to my welts that had me bouncing in agony. My Mistress took my documents and banged them shut in a drawer, which she locked, looping the key-chain round her neck. I looked through my tears at the sombre bulk of the slave Paul, who seemed to tower over me like a dreadful behemoth – at least, his risen member did.

An erect penis is an ungainly monster. Ladies find the spectacle full of thrilling menace; to another male it causes disquiet. The stiff cock is both eye and mouth, both observed and observer. It is raw power – yet shows the fragility of power, for a stiff cock can be unmanned by the simplest, most ignoble attack to the manly orbs.

I saw my Mistress gloating at my disquiet, and she made a sneering reference to the unspeakable Tarker, causing me further unease.

'Dear Paul follows my every order,' she added, yawning, 'however distasteful he may find it. You impudently observed me at sport with him aboard ship. I may inform you that to the Tatars any bumhole is a bumhole.'

At a nod, the shackled Paul promptly assisted our

Mistress in binding me. I was bum-plugged; she wound a tight cord with unnecessary harshness around my balls and then wrapped the whole of my shamefully erect cock in the coarse chafing twine. My arms were pinned to my side with the bandages of General Hochhuth, still soiled and stinking from her body, and my legs fastened together likewise. Only my buttocks and nipples remained bare.

A pulley was lowered from the ceiling, and the Countess pierced my nipples with two sharp nails, banging them through my stiff little acorns with a practised thrust that caused a moment's agony but thereafter little discomfort – until I was hoisted by the wires from the pulley, attached to my nipple-pins, and raised with a shuddering wail to my tiptoes. I was left suspended by my stretched nipples, to contemplate my fate over the next few days of our journey to Moscow – the few days seemed eternity.

It was time for my Mistress's luncheon. Smiling, she lit a cigarette, and sauntered round me, stroking gently on my wealed bum-flesh with her cane. She was careful not to hurt: her ominous tickling presaged floggings to come. From time to time she rubbed her cigarette casually against my nipples, making my eyes moisten with the pain, though I forced myself to take it without protest.

Paul shuffled from the galley bearing a bowl of a jellied substance that I have since come to know and relish as borscht, the classic dinner of the Russians. It can be made of almost anything, as long as the basic ingredient is beetroot, and this one shivered like rich jelly, as purple as a bum-welt. My Mistress's table was Paul himself! He placed the bowl on his belly, just at the tip of his engorged cock, and in a deft movement arched his back so that he was bent in a half-circle, supported by his wrists and ankles. My Mistress sniffed the jellied borscht and calmly grasped the shaft of his penis, bending it harshly so that the helmet dipped into the jelly.

Then, with slow relish, she began to scoop quivering portions of the jelly into her mouth, using the male's contorted stiff penis as a spoon, and licking his helmet dry before dipping for her next mouthful. My fellow slave breathed hard, for the twisting of his cock must have hurt awfully; occasionally, my Mistress wiped her sticky fingers quite vigorously on his ball-sac.

She looked at me suddenly and smiled.

'Jealous, Philip?' she murmured.

I blushed furiously, for I *was* jealous. I envied Paul his humiliance in straining submission and resented my own bondage, which seemed almost demeaning in its comfort.

'My foolish slave has forgotten to add cream to my borscht,' she purred, not taking her eyes off me.

Suddenly, she began to stroke the naked helmet of Paul's cock, allowing her fingers to stray expertly over his peehole and under the arrow of his glans. Then she paused and began to rub vigorously on his shaft, pressing tight and making the helmet pop like a squeezed fruit. Her other hand pinched and tickled his balls, and I saw that Paul was tense and groaning under this artful masturbation.

'Cream for me, *robotnik*,' my Mistress hissed.

At once the slave's body jerked – he panted harshly – and obeyed. He spurted powerfully, splattering the dish with his creamy fluid, and when his convulsions ebbed she took his flaccid but still half-stiffened cock and began to stir her bowl thoughtfully. Then, with relish, she recommenced her meal, devouring the borscht until she wiped the dish clean with the cock's helmet, then swept the dish to the parquet, where it shattered.

I was livid with pain and jealousy. *I* wanted to be the slave so mockingly humiliated, and I saw a glint of triumph in Paul's eye. This episode presaged the next three days on the route to Moscow, during which we two slaves strove to outdo each other in humiliance to our common Mistress, whose scornful cruelty was fed by our shame.

The three days passed in a sort of daze – an enchanted one, to be sure, as my body and spirit survived the most extreme wretchedness a male can suffer at a dominant lady's hand. And, always, Paul and I were rivals, or wary allies, in our just humiliance. How I adored her!

After her luncheon, my Mistress yawned and stretched and said I should be punished for my hint of jealousy. She ordered Paul to rise and pick up the shards of her bowl with his lips. This done, she casually tossed him the rattan – not the harshest, but the same that had flogged me for breakfast. I hung helpless in my bandaged state, my heart chill with dread. Paul lifted the rattan with a clanking of his chains, and without preamble began to cane my bare buttocks, the chains adding weight to his strokes so that my body jerked like a marionette's.

'A good thirty should teach him his lesson,' she said.

To take cane from a male! It brought back bitter memories of Shoeburyness, even though I knew it to be a wondrous humiliation on my Mistress's orders. My cock hung limp, and my Mistress taunted me that Paul was fully erect, like a good slave. This did nothing to allay my dread.

'I shall never be a good slave, Mistress,' I panted as the cane seared my welts for the twelfth or thirteenth stroke. 'I – I deserve every punishment you grace me with.'

She laughed delightedly and told Paul to cane me harder and to take me to a good fifty. The slave's chains whirred and clanked in unison with the brutal swish of the rattan and the crack on my squirming bare bum. Tears filled my eyes; I whirled helplessly in my bonds, the nipple-pincers adding to my croup's agony.

I moaned, and I am not sure I did not lose consciousness; the caning seemed to stop, although I could scarcely tell, so furious was the smarting of my seared arse. And then I felt her cool hands stroking my welts, and she murmured that I had a bum like leather, and she was not displeased. At these sweet words, my cock leapt stiff, and she laughed at me again.

Now I was permitted my own luncheon: a bowl of watery gruel, thinly flavoured with beetroot, which she unceremoniously poured into my mouth, and of course half of it was spilt. Paul resumed a crouching dog's position on all fours, his own arse presented as though in anticipation of flogging, which I was pleased to witness. My Mistress, who had spilt my soup over me, chided Paul for the clumsiness – and I thrilled to see his bare arse writhe under three dozen hard strokes from the heavy rattan, with a few vicious swipes to his shoulders and the sides of his thighs, which I knew must hurt abominably.

Our torments were not over, for my Mistress decreed that it was time for both of us to make commode. She fetched a large chamber pot and placed it under me before giving the ordained penalty: six strokes in rapid fire from the heaviest rattan. The beating took a mere three seconds and had me squirming and smarting as a scream of useless outrage bubbled in my throat. I did my business, blushing in shame, and then it was Paul's turn; he received his six and made likewise. Then my Mistress removed the receptacle and attached his chains to my own pulley. She left us in bondage while she took her afternoon sleep.

I was pleased to see that Paul's strong face was as tear-moist as my own. We glanced at each other with nervous disdain; since neither of us spoke the other's language, this could be our only communication, save for one word.

'*Robotnik*,' Paul growled, either in dislike for me or pity for himself.

'*Robotnik*,' I gasped in proud reply, my cock stiff!

Paul was kept nude throughout the journey; my Mistress punished him with lashes if his cock wilted, and punished him harder if it was stiff. His trussing was with chain and leather thong, my own with whatever took her fancy: bandaged or roped, sometimes chained, always contorted in agony. She enjoyed twisting my legs so that my own foot was crammed in my mouth, or binding us both with our cocks only an inch apart: Paul's stiff, mine terrified and soft. There was a cruel glint in my fellow *robotnik*'s eye.

The hours passed in an unbroken routine of degrading tasks and canings for their invariably unsatisfactory completion. During these arduous punishments, or afterwards, as she contemplated her slaves in glowering bondage, my Mistress liked to masturbate quite openly and proudly, revealing her knickerless quim and plunging her fingers inside her slit while caressing her stiff little boatman. She would taunt us as she frigged herself:

'Wouldn't you like to fuck me here, in my lady's place? Just think, a juicy wet gash, all soft and velvet for your cocks. But bumhole is all a slave is fit for – hard, dirty bumhole, so painful on your tender little pricks – while I keep my cunt for my own fingers and my own pleasure.'

Her sneers cut deep, for as always she spoke truth. I did shamefully yearn to fuck her cunt.

I was pleased when, after one particularly brutal flogging, nicknamed 'forty and forty' (forty cuts each with rattan and cat), with my bumhole impaled on the statue's bronze cock, my Mistress said my own cock should be moulded. A pot of candle-wax was melted, Paul held me down and my stiff cock and balls plunged into the scalding fluid.

I cried out with the pain, and my cock wilted, but the impression of her stiffness was safe. When the wax hardened and cooled, my Mistress poured into the hole a mixture of wood shavings and glue, which set and hardened in a couple of hours, leaving a wooden replica of my stiff member. I was put to varnishing and polishing this, with my tongue, and at last my Mistress possessed a shiny new obispos, which she placed beside Paul's own moulding. I permitted myself a sly smile, for my English cock was the larger! I did not mind the punishment that followed my insolent pride: a further 'forty and forty' from her own divine arm, observed sullenly by my fellow slave in full bondage, with both feet sandwiched in his mouth and the new 'English' dildo strapped to the hilt in his anus.

On that occasion my Mistress wore her brief and tantalising school uniform, but without knickers. As she flogged me, she lifted her short skirt and openly frigged herself, accompanying her joyful masturbation with words that sneered but somehow haunted me: 'Power is beauty, and it has many guises: power is money, power is hard cock or wet cunt – but true power is the lash on squirming red flesh. Miss Bainbridge, my housemistress at Masterdale, knew it – and she betrayed me! O, how bitter my tears when Miss Bainbridge accepted the cock's dominance – married ! and abandoned the power of her lady's whip to my girlish bottom! The smell of her shoes, her stockings and petticoats flouncing in her cruel passion as she whippd my bare – how power can thrill and betray!'

Once, she demonstrated her power in a new and thoughtful way. The train stopped for an hour – I think we were near the city of Magdeburg – and she opened the rear door of her carriage to show the earth blanketed in snow, and an ice-covered lake. Paul and I were both made naked and placed in especially heavy shackles. My Countess, wrapped in thick sable over her body, nude but for stockings and garter belt, whipped us both over the ice, on harnesses attached to painful cock restraints.

Whipping us on our bare skin pimpled with cold, she made us break a hole in the ice, then dive into the freezing water. Weighed by our chains, we sank like stones. I held my breath until it seemed I should burst, and I saw Paul writhing beside me, his face swollen in the same agony. After an age, I felt a horrid tug on my ball-chain, and slowly she retrieved us from the lake's bottom, hauling us up by our balls. She laughed and whipped us at a trot back to the train, which was getting up steam.

We were both blue with cold, and she gave us each 'forty and forty' to warm us. It might have been four hundred – my numbed skin barely felt her cane's lashes. Afterwards, she pressed my buttocks to the hot stove until I was seared and could feel my welts, then did the same to Paul. I wept at her cruelty; it was the only time I saw the Tatar's cock soft. Her bootcaps were sodden from the snow, and she made us squat on them with our flaming bums, then poked her sharp toepoints deep into our bumholes to thaw the leather.

I imagined my fear of Paul's vengeful dominance to be finally allayed on the occasion when he had licked Galena's chamber pot insufficiently clean, and *I* was ordered to flog his arse with the cat. I knew we were nearing Moscow, although the Russian frontier police had not dared even knock on my Mistress's door – and I dreaded the harsher ordeal of being Countess Galena's prisoner in Moscow, where her power would be truly untouchable.

Paul was hoisted on the pulley by his own pierced nipples, but he remained naked save for a leather sheath with two cinched gauntlets for his arms and two for his legs below the knee, the two parts connected by a heavy chain. I knew this device, a Tatar glove as my Mistress called it: it was both immobilising and painfully tight.

I lashed Paul's bare buttocks, and shoulders too, with every ounce of my strength, in a vengeful fury – not least because I myself wore the frilly maid's uniform, with full wig and maquillage, and wished to avenge my own humiliation on another male body. His cock stood obstinately stiff. As hard as I striped him, she would not wilt, and my Mistress taunted my weakness.

After thirty or so she decreed a 'Graeco-Roman' wrestling match, which meant, effectively, that no holds were barred except for blows to the manly parts. She smiled in vicious delight, as though she had planned this for some time, knowing our simmering mutual resentment. Paul was unbound. He stood and flexed his muscles, which frightened me: my skills in boxing might only just be a match for his heavier build. My Mistress took a gold chain and fastened our balls, a mere two feet apart. Paul's cock was rigid, mine feeble in terror, which leapt as she announced the victor's prize.

She wore a stern costume of black rubber, like a bathing-suit, all of a piece and clinging to her torso like paint, leaving arms, legs and shoulders bare. The fabric just covered her teats, allowing the upper portion of each nipple to show, and her mound was hidden by only the thinnest thong, so that her mink bunched full and golden on either side of the narrow rubber strip. She pushed this thong aside, revealing her swollen red gash, and she began a luxurious masturbation as she smiled and stared at me.

'I command the victor,' she said, 'to bugger his foe hard in bumhole, with full cock-thrust and to full spurt.'

My cock wilted utterly at this dread command; Paul's seemed to grow huge. The shuddering of the train seemed to taunt me, just like my Mistress's scornful frigging. My very distress seemed to wet the swollen lips of her cunt.

We began to wrestle, Paul getting me in a headlock and I releasing myself with a flurry of kicks close to the balls. My boxing prowess asserted itself with blows as vicious as I could make them to face, kidney and belly, while the Tatar's agility in slippery wrestling holds matched my sturdy English mauling.

Yet I had not the stomach to win! Bound by the taut gold chain, our bellies, balls and cocks (his rigid, mine flapping soft) slammed against each other, and I knew I could not bring myself, as victor, to commit a crime against nature: better to submit to his loathsome buggery, for my Mistress's joy, than to feign pleasure in the unspeakable act myself! All the while, Galena's nimble fingers slid in and out of her cunt, and she paused to lick her juices, her eyes sparkling as they mocked me.

It was too much. I gave up the fight and resigned myself to my fate, allowing the Tatar, stinking with brutal sweat, to pinion me, his knee hard in my groin. I cried submission just as the train ground to a halt.

My Mistress unfastened the chain and ordered me to crouch like a dog and spread my bum-cheeks for this ultimate humiliance. Weeping openly, I did so and begged for mercy – not expecting it, but only to increase my Mistress's delight. She fastened Paul in a harness of chain, something like a horse's reins, and flicked it, saying that she would be the driver for his bucking.

The Tatar positioned himself over me. She flicked his reins, as she vigorously caned his buttocks with her whippy little ashplant. I felt the stiff cock brush against my buttocks as he inched the helmet towards my spread bumhole. I swallowed and looked in mute anguish at my Mistress, seeing her fingers a blur on her glistening cunt, and her belly writhing as she approached her spend.

Suddenly there was a rap at the door. Without ceasing her masturbation, or her caning of Paul's fesses, my Mistress bade enter. The door opened. She pushed the thong of her rubber costume aside a notch, baring her cunt completely, and pulled down the corselage so that her teats sprang out quite nude and with ringed nipples erect. With

97

a smile, she pulled Paul away from me and fastened his harness to the table leg, while ordering me to remain crouching and with buttocks spread.

'Now you will witness power,' she whispered.

A burly, fur-coated police officer entered, followed by three armed troopers – of the Moscow District Police, as I discovered later. The officer surveyed us and smiled, then barked something in Russian. Without ceasing to pleasure herself, my Mistress cooed back and spread her thighs wide to show her swollen wet cunt. Wordlessly, the officer led his men in, stripping off his uniform. Soon all four muscled youths were lined naked and with stiff cocks before the gently writhing loins of Countess Galena Volchuk.

She spoke to Paul in Russian, and he grunted, his face suddenly livid with anger, and strained against his bonds. Then she addressed me in English, smiling sweetly.

'You will watch the exercise of my power, Philip. This is just what I willed to happen. I feel so *fruity*! I shall take each of these brutes in bumhole, in mouth . . . O, wherever I please. *And in cunt. And you will watch, helpless!* Paul is bound – but your suffering will be the greater, for you are *not* powerless to intervene in my defilement. Crouch, slave, and weep like the abject worm you are, as I swoon to cock after cock in the cunt *you* will never taste!'

I obeyed my Mistress.

Trembling with shame, rage and hopeless desire, I watched from my crouching position as the soldiers mounted my Mistress and each huge cock penetrated the sacred pink depths of her gash. The officer fucked her first, followed in turn by each of his men, and when all had spermed in her quim, leaving heavy rivulets of cream streaking her thighs and quim-lips, the officer was erect for her again. Now she turned and crouched beside me and took his cock in her anus, while she sucked each of the others to stiffness with deep slurping sounds and bobbing of her throat.

All the soldiers took her in anus, while she continued her lustful frigging and masturbated herself to gasping climax each time a male spurted in her hole. Even then, she was

not sated, for she sucked and hand-rubbed the men to
hardness once more, making them fuck her between her
quivering bare teats, under her armpits, even rubbing their
cocks between nimble toes . . . until she insisted on taking
each of them in her throat and swallowing all their
remaining cream. All the time she smiled cruelly at me,
winking as she licked sperm from her lips.

'Power, Philip,' she whispered with a hoarse, throaty
voice. '*My* power.'

I burst into unmanly tears at my wretchedness.
Unbound, I could attempt – if only that – to stop this
turpitude. But I did not. I crouched like an abject cur,
trying to conceal my cock throbbing stiff with shameful
excitement at my Mistress's degradation – even as she
made water in full sucking of the officer's cock, and lay in
a golden steaming pool that hissed from her gaping slit.

At length the soldiers were sated, and helped themselves
to vodka and laughed with rough soldiers' jokes. All the
while my Mistress lay dishevelled and whining on the floor,
still writhing and masturbating as though she herself had
not been properly pleasured! She seemed not to notice that
she had fouled herself, as she squirmed wetly in its
glistening pool. Laughing, and with mocking motions to
their sore cocks, the soldiers bowed in mock solemnity and
withdrew.

My Mistress sighed in pleasure, then gave a whoop of
delight, and I saw her fingers flick deftly at her swollen,
throbbing clitty until after only seconds her back arched
and she howled in a spend so vigorous that her previous
whimpering climaxes seemed meekness itself.

'*Power*, Philip,' she gasped, almost sobbing.

It was too much for me to bear. I leapt to my feet and,
before she could move, had her pinioned by the teats. My
feet slipped in the warm golden pool of her fluid, and I
landed heavily on top of her, squashing her nipples,
slippery with sperm, and making her gasp. The tip of my
throbbing helmet touched warm, wet slit-flesh. Grunting, I
thrust into her until my cock penetrated her cunt to my
hilt, and I began a frenzied bucking, my balls slapping

against her thighs as she writhed and squealed, sobbing under my cock's brutal and merciless onslaught.

'No! No! O! No! You'll split me! O, stop!'

I reached between our bellies and found the stiff clitty, and I began to pummel her quite harshly, which turned her sobs into screams, and her body bucked now against mine in a slippery fervour that made my cock slam into her again and again. I really did want to split the bitch open. Her hand groped to the side and she snapped open the clasp that held Paul captive.

'Help me, Paul, help me!' she screamed.

I was near my own spend and scarcely heard the lumbering of the naked male behind me. He pinioned her ankles – she squealed again in long, indignant dismay – and lifted both our bodies up to make a space for his own! Sliding beneath us on the golden pool of my Mistress's pee, Paul forced his massive cock between her buttocks and sank it into her anus, beginning to fuck her bumhole as furiously as I fucked her in cunt.

Our three bodies squeezed and writhed, until my drubbing of her clit brought her to a convulsive spasm, and only then did I permit my balls to release their sperm to the clutching neck of her womb. She howled and shuddered and begged me not to stop coming, to drench her in spunk. Paul grunted afterwards as he discharged in her anal cavity and smoothly slid from beneath her, leaving her sobbing in the golden pool streaked with white, her body lathered with glistening fluids.

Paul and I panted harshly. Without a word, he fetched the materials of bondage for our Mistress and soon she was encased in filthy bandages, trussed in leather and rubber thongs; masked and hooded, her limbs and whole proud body immobile as a rock. Her eyes, mouth, quim, buttocks and tightly pincered nipples were left bare.

I plucked the key from around her neck, then opened the drawer and retrieved my precious documents, while Paul fetched from her closet a whip so dreadful I thought a titan must have fashioned it: four five-foot thongs two inches thick, purple and red in braided heavy leather, and studded at inches alternately with sharp diamonds and clustered nails, with razor-sharp steel tips at each thong.

'*The knout* –' she whispered. '*No* –'

I looked uncertainly at my Mistress, then at Paul, grimly smiling as he swished the monstrous whip against the wet parquet. Her face clouded in anger as she stared at me.

'Well, go, damn you, go, for a disloyal whelp! You have your precious papers. Taking the key is your act of betrayal, Philip.'

I thought she was going to weep, but she cried that I must leave her for my treachery, and if I disobeyed it was *my* bum that the knout would shred.

'You think I do not know my own power?' she shrieked. 'Damn you, traitor, for doubting! We are slowing. We are nearly in Moscow! Go now, I command you! You will ache with regret as you hear my flesh scream under the knout.'

Numbly, I got my clothing and was going to kneel and beg forgiveness, but all her attention was on Paul – she disdained even to acknowledge my presence. I slipped from the train and never felt more alone in my life. As the train chugged into motion again, its clattering was nearly drowned by the hideous crack of the knout, again and again on naked skin, and repeated screams, each rising in intensity until it tailed off in a frenzy of broken sobs. It was the slave Paul who screamed. *Her* flesh . . .

8

Miss Birch

As I sat in my droshky, a sort of hansom cab, and watched the drab snowy expanse of Moscow straggle past, I reflected that the recovery of a bundle of five-pound notes does wonders for the wellbeing of the Englishman abroad. I also thought of the beauty and pain of my Mistress – and that the mysterious Miss Bainbridge had a lot to answer for.

The droshky deposited me at the correct station, where I discovered that my passage to Vladivostok was sound, and that I had only a few hours to wait until the train departed. I bought some roubles and settled down in the station restaurant for a meal of borscht and piroshky and other stuff, all seeming to consist of cabbage, for whose accompaniment I ordered a bottle of water.

This came. I took a sip and coughed, for it tasted as foul and fiery as petrol. I soon learnt that to a Russian, 'water' means the spirit vodka, and the wary traveller must specify mineral water if he is not to be poisoned. I got my fizzy water, but since I had the vodka, and everyone else seemed to be drinking it, I took a few cautious sips and found it an admirable potion for keeping out the icy cold.

As I was tucking in, I heard a nervous cough beside me and looked up to see a very tall young fellow dressed in a spanking new sailor's uniform, complete with smart peaked cap set stiffly atop an oiled and swept-back blond mane. This person had a face of extraordinary handsomeness – I would have said beauty, except that the word did not seem appropriate for a male. The bones were high and finely chiselled, the lips broad and sensuous – like my Mistress Galena's – and he stood very stiff and straight, with a powerful chest, broad shoulders, quite bulky at the croup, and a good head taller than myself. His skin was faintly golden, as though coloured by some faraway sun. The sudden thought of my Mistress made me melancholy, and I was happy to grant his request to join me.

'You don't mind, old chap?' he said in perfect but curiously singsong English. 'Only I spotted you for a seafaring man like myself, and thought we foreigners should stick together. Going on the Trans-Siberian? I'm off to Vladivostok, to join a ship there. I am Norwegian, you see,' as though this last explained everything.

It did not explain quite everything. The young fellow introduced himself as Harald, but his voice was a deep fluting contralto, and as yet unbroken! Blushing, he explained that he was not yet of manly age, and had run away to sea, unable to stand the stuffiness of his native Tromsø. He had spent some time at a school in England and was thrilled to hear that I had been a cadet at a proper naval school. Thereafter his manner grew from respect to awe. I admit that I enjoyed being his senior – remembering Galena's opinions on the delights of power, however small.

I offered him food and a glass of vodka, which I imagined to be a necessary condiment for a sea dog. He smiled quite charmingly, blushed and sent the whole glass down in one swallow, with a little cough and a smacking of the lips. Then, with sparkling eyes, he begged me for details of my cadet days – the training, the knowledge of seafaring I had gained, and especially the discipline, a subject to which he kept returning.

'They beat you a lot, I suppose, sir?' he said shyly.

I agreed that they had.

'With whip? Or cane? O! You think me bold, I'm sure!'

I thought this a strange locution for a fellow seafarer, but I laughed and said, not without bravado, that my bum was as hard as leather after all the tanning she had taken.

This made my companion gasp and swallow in nervous delight.

'And I suppose you gave as good as you got – I mean, you've tanned other fellows, too?'

'Why, yes,' I said nonchalantly, rolling my vodka around my tongue. 'I've tanned quite a few – girls too, I might add. *They* can be *very* naughty.'

This was, strictly speaking, the truth; I was pleased at the new fascination I seemed to exert over him. He looked down shyly and whispered: 'On the bare, sir? I mean, did you flog those fellows on their bare bums?'

I laughed and clapped his shoulders and told him of course, that was the way things were done in England.

'But not girls, I suppose?' he added, blushing. 'I mean, it would be indecent – you'd have to cane them on their bloomers or petticoats, for modesty.'

I assured him that English girls were as hardy as their menfolk, and knew that a flogging not on bare was scarcely a flogging at all.

He seemed tongue-tied, so I turned the conversation to our seagoing prospects. In no time I had discovered that, being tall for his age, he had tricked his way into a cadetship with the very same line as myself – and that we should be trainmates all the way to Vladivostok. I said I hoped 'hard' class would not be too uncomfortable; he was rather embarrassed to admit that he had a little money and had procured himself a berth in first or 'soft' class.

'I am a bit shy, you see,' he stammered. 'I haven't been in foreign countries before – England doesn't count as foreign, sir – and I wanted to ensure my privacy. But since we are to be shipmates, and you seem such an awfully good egg – forgive my being so forward – there are two bunks in my compartment, and I'd be honoured if you would share.'

It was dark already, and soon time for us to board the train. For one so young, Harald proved surprisingly deft at dealing with the hordes of porters, servants and officials, all wearing uniforms that vied with each other in threadbare gaudiness. The Trans-Siberian seemed like a large village on wheels, with jostling vendors, tethered pigs and sheep and even donkeys, and furiously shrieking babushkas, ladies of indeterminate age who bargained over rolls of cloth while their menfolk squatted, drinking and smoking and spitting, at their lightning-fast card games.

Harald chattered at them in a singsong language that he explained was part Norwegian, part Finnish, and part Russian, a sort of lingua franca of the Baltic Sea. We fought our way valiantly through the pandemonium and soon found ourselves cosily ensconced in a peaceful and spacious compartment of a luxury to equal my Mistress Galena's private carriage: scented with pine panelling, snugly heated by a stove, and with comfortable bunks, soft chairs and a cheerful pile carpet.

The train whistled and roared and clanked, and we set off into the Russian night. I was finally on my way to Vladivostok! A pleasurable chill made me shiver, and drove away my sadness at forsaking my first true Mistress, Galena. We were well provided with tea, and had the remains of our flagon of vodka. Both excited, we neither of us felt like sleeping and passed hours in excited chatter about Russia, our future and the world as young men dimly see it.

Harald explained that Russia was incomprehensibly vast, and that the pompous trappings of the Tsarist state were a cloak for raging poverty, violence and lawlessness; that there were huge tracts of Siberia, for example, where the Tsar's writ did not run, and bandit gangs – 'Tatars and the like' – oppressed a servile populace, raping and robbing any foreigners unlucky enough to be caught by them. We pored over his map and its magical place names: Kazan, Omsk, Khabarovsk. Russia did indeed seem frightening.

'Why, the train crosses Siberia,' I said, 'but I imagine we are safe. From raping, at any rate – sturdy fellows like us!'

Harald grinned nervously and said that he carried his gold coins – the only real currency east of Moscow – in a very safe place, which it would be indelicate to mention. I said rather cruelly that I had some acquaintance with Tatars, and that was the first place they would look.

He switched the conversation back to my cadet days and to his fascination with corporal punishment. Warmed by tea and vodka, I was happy to play the wise elder, and airily told him of the fierce beatings my naked bum had taken, and how a seaman's bum must be hardened to teak; that discipline east of Suez was as brutal as in the old days, and we young officers might expect no mercy if remiss, though of course floggings would be in private. Harald blinked nervously.

'That's just it,' he murmured, gazing at me now with wide, bright eyes that might be timid or mischievous. 'I don't know how to say it, sir, without seeming bold.'

His eyes were big and sad and lustrous, and he seemed like a lost lamb. I put my arm round his shoulders and said he could speak freely to me, as a chum.

'My bottom has never taken a *proper* beating, sir,' he whispered. 'Only spanking, you know, and I am frightened – I don't know if she can take cane or whip. I fear it will take me a while to adjust to discipline at sea, and in the meantime I shall taste plenty of that discipline. I should hate to let the side down through inexperience, sir.'

'Why, Harald,' I said, 'you don't mean –'

'Yes, sir. I'm afraid it is a favour I must beg.'

'You mean, beat you in sport, Harald? Why, there is no need to beg. I myself know –'

I stopped myself from admitting my own passion for bare caning and released him, fearful he should feel the beating of my heart. Man to man – well, it is not the same as a proper lady's caning, but still the squirming of bare red bum gives that luscious chill of power to the caner, whatever the sex of his victim, and I knew it would be all in healthy sport, between chums.

'Of course I'll beat you, Harald,' I said with surprising tenderness in my voice.

'Bare bum?'

'Why, of course.'

'But you'll let me keep my knickers on, for modesty? I wear only a little seaman's pouch. You'll get a clear swipe at my arse, sir. I mean, swipes.'

'As many as you like, dear friend, or can take. Why, we

106

have a whole week to get your bottom tanned to leather. And perhaps I might ask you to return the favour. I cane hard, and you'll feel like having your revenge, while for me a week is a long time to be – out of practice.'

'Cane you, sir? O, I could *never*.'

He blushed deeply. We laughed and shook hands, and said it was a bargain – after all, I must recompense him for sharing his carriage.

'Well, sir,' he said, his voice suddenly brisk and manly, 'there is no time like the present.'

Unbidden, Harald unbuckled his trousers and lowered them to reveal his bare arse. In truth, his silken undergarment was a mere slip, the thong buried in his furrow and supported by a waist-string, like a girl's, but with a pouch for his manhood, which I glimpsed only briefly. His arse almost took my breath away: pear-shaped and soft and sumptuous, not hard and bony like my own, but fleshy and curved like a girl's. My appreciation made me feel guilty; I told myself it was purely artistic, as one might admire a stallion's crupper.

He took off his jacket and folded it neatly, then lifted his shirt and knotted it under his ribs, showing the golden downy hairs like gossamer at the small of his back. That bum looked indeed as though she had never tasted cane, and I feared to hurt her. I suggested that a mild slippering should be enough to start his 'treatment'.

'O, no, sir,' he blurted. 'I have brought the necessary from home – if you will kindly open my portmanteau.'

I did so, and withdrew a superbly menacing birch, already fashioned, with fifteen or sixteen long, stiff twigs, bound with a brass clip for a handle. Harald said he had made it himself, from the trees in his garden, and supposed it to be the correct instrument for proper English discipline. I agreed, reluctantly, and at his insistence lifted the heavy bush of birch twigs over those soft bare nates. Gulping, I brought it down in a gentle swish, intending only to tickle him. He tut-tutted.

'Why, sir, I hardly felt that! Harder, if you please! Don't treat me like some silly girl.'

107

I was rather annoyed at his peremptory tone, and swished the birch much harder for his cheek; his bum reddened suddenly and he sighed in satisfaction.

'O! *That* was tight! More, please, I beg you.'

I lashed his bare bum quite hard, my strokes growing more rapid and harsher as I saw the naked flesh weal and darken, and now he was clenching his buttocks well before each stroke – merely at the swish in the air. By the fourteenth or fifteenth stroke he gasped that it smarted abominably.

'I never realised . . . O! O! O! Gosh, you are cruel!'

Alarmed but without abating my lust for flogging – if not to receive, then to give! – I continued to birch his squirming bare, admonishing him that he must not think me cruel, that I was merely doing my shipmate a favour.

He took a good forty with the birch, until his bum was purple and I decided it was time to retire to our bunks. His eyes moist with tears and his face glowing with the flush of pleasure I knew only too well, he grasped my hands and seemed about to plant an unseemly kiss on my lips, then checked himself and thanked me profusely.

'The same tomorrow, sir?' he pleaded.

I agreed, somewhat taken aback.

'Once in morning, and once in evening, I think,' he said brightly, then shuffled on to the top bunk and fell asleep.

Sleep was some time coming to me, partly because of Harald's deafening snores of contentment and partly because of my own itchiness to take birch myself. I did not *want* to be beaten by a male, especially one who called me 'sir', but 'any port in a storm', as we matelots say.

Harald was as modest in his toilette as he was in lowering his trousers for his twice-daily flogging, and I saw nothing of his body except his nates bared for the birch. He was, in fact, equipped with several birches, and for the next two days bore my strokes until each one was quite denuded, that is, about seventy or eighty strokes. I marvelled at the leathery resilience of his croup, which was now as livid and puffed as my own. He reassured me, as I reassured myself, that his birching was good sport, between chums.

On the third day we were somewhere near Omsk, and as usual Harald lowered his trousers for his after-breakfast birching (breakfast on the Trans-Siberian was primitive but wholesome – boiled eggs, black bread, jam and, of course, cabbage). I lifted the birch and with a now easy rhythm delivered a brisk dozen before pausing, so that his ridged fesses had time to redden for the new day's crop of welts. I looked through the window at the vast, dreary Siberian plain, its treeless waste broken only by a clump of marsh grass or an occasional stunted bush.

I myself longed more and more for a flogging, the warmth of life in the midst of this melancholy wilderness. Harald fixed me with an odd, fierce expression through his tears of pain and smiled grimly, as though reading my mind, and I wondered, not for the first time, which of us really lay in the other's power. I continued the birching, laying my strokes very hard, and clustered three or four in succession on the same welt, so that his wriggles and moans became quite frenzied, as though my harshness would subdue my own desires. Yes, I *did* want to be flogged, on the bare bum, by this – this *beautiful* young man!

'O . . . O,' came the moans, as the birching continued, as hard as I could. His squirming bare buttocks were now a mass of livid purple and black weals – and the moans were my own.

By the eightieth stroke, my birch was almost bare of twigs, and little shards of broken wood littered the carpet around Harald's body, like a sacred circle. There was a crash of splinters as I laid a last, ferocious cut that jolted the young man and made him cry out in sudden anguish. His croup was livid and puffy and streaked with black, and I resisted my urge to touch her with soothing fingers.

Harald rose, unbidden, and now had a fierce gleam behind his tears. He rubbed his flamed bottom and whistled.

'You do lay it on tight, sir,' he whispered, 'and now I think it is time you took some of your own medicine – as you requested! O, how I have longed to – I *must*!'

I gaped as he removed a fresh birch from his

portmanteau, bushier than any I had used on him, and containing a good two dozen rods. Then his strong fingers had me by the back of my neck, and he forced me down across the arm of the chair. I wriggled and protested – it was too sudden, I was not prepared – but he laughed as cruelly as my Mistress Galena, and I felt his strength as deft fingers unfastened my clothing and ripped down my trousers.

He delivered a contemptuous spank with his palm to my bared bottom, laughed and then obliged me with those steely blue eyes to make myself quite naked for my beating. Numb with dread, I wriggled out of my garments, as though seeing for the first time how tall and strong Harald really was.

My arms were pinioned behind my back, and strong cords fastened my wrists, then my face was pushed into the cushions and my legs kicked apart to put me in the correct position with my bare bum spread high and helpless across the chair. I was jelly. I could only moan feebly, sensing that this beating was *not* to be sport among chums. And to my despair I felt my manhood stir – I *wanted* the beating, wanted my bare croup to be birched raw by a strong hand!

The first lash bathed me in liquid fire. I quivered and sighed bitterly at the pain of my reacquaintance with Miss Birch. The cuts followed in quick succession, and I felt myself squirm and clench my fesses as the pain jolted the breath from me and my eyes filled with tears of humiliation. Harald was ruthless and strong.

I resolved to be brave – I had, after all, shown no mercy to his own bottom – and took a full thirty-five without squealing until he laid a particularly clinging and savage stroke whose tongues of fire seemed to lick every inch and crevice of my flaming bare bum, and I gasped: 'I say, it's a bit rough, you know. Steady on, old man!'

Harald emitted a strange cry that was almost a sob, and the birching ceased. I felt long, cool fingers stroking my bare, caressing every ridge and welt, and his soft contralto voice cooed in sympathy. Then, to my horror, I felt the cool fingers delve under my spread furrow and gently clasp my balls and the shaft of my cock! I started in anger, and Harald said I was well stiffened, and the beating must excite me as much as it excited him.

'Look, old man! I know we are chums,' I squealed, 'but –'

Harald cut me short with another jarring cut of the birch, which knocked the breath from me.

'*Old man!*' he laughed bitterly. '*Chums!* Six of the best for my chum, eh, old man?'

Before I could reply, he delivered six of the cruellest birch-strokes I had, or have, ever felt, and at intervals of only half a second. Now, the breath was crushed from me, and I howled in the agony to my raw, puffed bare. I looked round, my face contorted with rage, and saw his hand at the back of his neck; in an instant, a flowing mane of snow-blonde tresses cascaded over his shoulders, and I saw his epicene face framed by a goddess's hair. He began to unbutton his shirt, down to his breast, which I saw to be tightly swathed in hospital bandages.

He undid the bandages, impetuously ripping them. From them swelled two delicious golden breasts, topped with large strawberry nipples, their points tingling and erect. The magnificent teats stood proud, thrust out and heaving in the new joy of their freedom. Swiftly, Harald turned and fumbled with the opening of the trousers, exposing and pulling aside the pouch, to reveal a beautiful shaven hillock, a perfectly formed golden mound of Venus, and thick ruby quim-lips glistening with moisture.

'Harald –' I began, half-rising from position.

'If only you knew, sir!' he cried. 'The pain of birch is nothing to the pain of deception! From the moment I saw you – O! O! How I regretted my foolish disguise!' And *she* burst into thoroughly female tears.

Suddenly, the train lurched and whistled, the wheels screeched, and we jolted to a stop. At once there was uproar. We looked fearfully at each other. I heard horses' hooves, the bang of doors and – unmistakably – the discharge of rifles. Harald held the birch high, as though frozen in terror: we must be attacked by bandits!

There were crashes and yells in the corridor, then thuds on our locked door before it was smashed open with a rifle butt.

'My name is Haralda!' cried my companion, trying to conceal her exposed womanhood. 'Please save me, sir!'

She flung herself beneath me, and as the door splintered at the protruding impact of a rifle I dare say we made an incongruous sight: myself, a naked male with a glowing wealed bum, and a tall, stately female, a blonde goddess, her breasts and quim on immodest view, vainly trying to shelter between my thighs.

I struggled to rise, shielding Haralda as best I could, and faced the intruders, forgetting my nudity and my erect penis in the righteous fury of an Englishman disturbed by foreigners.

'What is the meaning of this!' I cried, and felt Haralda cling to my leg in recognition of my manly fortitude – absurd, since the meaning of 'this' was gloomily obvious.

I was faced with a dozen soldiery, massive in snow-crusted fur greatcoats and fur hats, their faces wrapped in woollen scarves of surprisingly gaudy colour. Their eyes were covered by dark goggles with rubber straps, like a sea-diver's. As well as rifles, they carried slingshots, or catapults, at their belts. Through the smashed window I saw the Siberian landscape now carpeted in a dazzling shroud of snow that fused seamlessly with the icy sky. I blinked and looked away, understanding the need for sun-goggles.

The goggles were torn off, revealing big sloe eyes wide with excitement, and there was a jabber of some Siberian tongue – the voices were the sweet lilt of females! The largest of them stepped forward almost shyly and grabbed my stiff cock in her big leather mitten, squeezing and whirling it round like a child's top. She giggled nervously, and then in delight, and her giggles were followed by her sisters, who crammed into the compartment and vied for a chance with this wonderful new toy. I admit that to be the centre of ladies' attention, however menacing, does urge the male to rigidity.

The leader reached down and pulled Haralda to her feet, delving roughly between her naked thighs and fingering her quim, then holding up her fingers glistening wet; this caused more giggles. The others began to maul Haralda's bare teats, squeezing the nipples and flicking them like pellets, to Haralda's nervous moans of discomfort. There was further excited jabbering when the birch was lifted, swished in the air and suddenly swished right to my bum-welts, making me squeak in surprise. Haralda was bent over, her own wealed bum inspected and stroked, with coos of appreciation, and then a mitten came off to reveal a shapely, delicate finger, the nails long and pointed and painted a delicate mauve, like any London society lady.

Haralda was held down, and without fuss or preamble was birched quite soundly, as the still-scarved leader held on to my cock as her trophy. Haralda's squeals of pain made her birching all the harder, and I admit that I was as fascinated, and lustful, at the sight of her squirming female buttocks as our captors seemed to be. She took a good thirty, the birch crackling in fierce echoes above the tumult outside. I thought back on my guilty delight at birching those naked fesses and freed myself of any shame. My pleasure at 'Harald's' submission was explained: I must have known her true sex all along – I *must* have!

My cock was stiff under a harsh lady's fingers as I scented new enslavement and new joy; also at Haralda's golden silky bum-flesh writhing and clenching and graceful even in her birched agony. How could I have been so foolish as to mistake those pear-shaped orbs for the croup of a mere male! A lady's smooth fesses are perfection on this earth . . .

Suddenly Haralda's purpled buttocks were spread, and the lady holding my cock plunged a mauve-lacquered fingernail right inside her anus, pushing hard until the finger was buried and Haralda was squealing in unfeigned distress. Her distress increased as the probing lady cried in triumph and, with burrowing movements of her sharp finger, extracted a column of gold coins, one by one. The jabbering in the Siberian language grew fervent. At that moment there was a sharp and fiendishly loud whipcrack from the corridor, followed by a scream. Another, much taller lady appeared, wielding a knout.

'Speak English, you sluts!' she cried.

The soldier-girls were suddenly mute, their eyes wide in terror.

The soldier holding my cock suddenly relinquished it and squealed aloud as the knout crashed across her buttocks, with an impact that made her shudder even through the thick fur greatcoat.

The new lady looked imperiously at me and disgustedly at the naked squirming bum of Haralda. Then she slowly unwound her own scarf to reveal a wide, red mouth curved in prim distaste. Her face was something like Haralda's, but not as soft or girlish: the high cheekbones and large dark eyes, and her air of cool superiority, reminded me of Countess Galena, although this lady was her senior by perhaps five years, with the regal poise of a lady's ripe experience. A few wisps of bright chestnut hair peeped from beneath her fur hat, and she brushed them away languidly as though they were impudent servants.

'Hmm!' she said. 'Meagre pickings on *this* train! Not a European to be seen . . . But what prize have we here? If he's suitable, I may spare you gels a flogging, for speaking your barbarous tongue. But I don't suppose he is even English – a proper Englishman would not be caught in shameful nudity with a foreign *gel*.'

She pronounced the word 'gel' in the impeccable accents of the well-born classes of England, such as I had heard on the lips of officers' wives at college.

'Begging your pardon, Miss, I *am* English,' I stammered, hoping this would help Haralda and me. 'And Haralda is Norwegian, which is almost the same thing.'

I was rewarded with a hard spank to my left fesse, which hurt abominably on skin already raw from birching.

'O! I am sorry . . . Mistress!' I cried, lowering my head, and got a harder spank to my right one, which set me tingling and, to my embarrassment, made my rigid cock twitch. She noticed this and smiled.

114

'So – a mere slap on bare excites you, filthy boy,' she said. 'Now I see why you and your hussy were trifling with the birch! Abominable behaviour! The birch is sacred here in Siberia, and only for the arses of the highest.'

Her voice sounded quite magical to me, despite my discomfort. She daintily pronounced our sturdy English word 'arses' as 'osses', with a lovely pursing of her wide lips.

'Well,' she said, 'I think we must be off, gels,' languidly pronouncing the word as 'orf'.

At once, Haralda and I were bundled quite naked over strong ladies' shoulders. I felt the fur silky on my belly as we were removed from the carriage, and our bags rummaged behind us, with any poor items of value gone to me for ever. The same process took place all along the train, and the girl soldiers – none of them could have been more than twenty years of age – obediently transported their loot to a fleet of packhorses waiting docilely at a short distance.

They were strange-looking animals, more like Shetland ponies than full horses, and were covered, all but their doleful, placid faces, in long matted hair, like ropes, that trailed in the snow. Haralda and I were roughly draped over the back of one of these beasts, and now my belly was scratched by the coarse fibres of its hair. Our wrists were knotted to our ankles, and slung thus we formed part of the plunder train. I saw there was one proper horse, a thoroughbred, and it stamped haughtily by the engine of the Trans-Siberian, its rider I assumed preventing the alarm. The 'gels' cried 'Giddy-up, hosses!' in the same fluting English as their Mistress, and we began a rapid trot across the featureless blank waste.

The train dwindled to a speck in the distance, and then I saw a flurry of snow-dust as the horse left the engine and sped towards us, now that we were at a safe distance. I strained to look to the horizon; no possible destination was in sight, and I felt the cold of that snowy emptiness begin to sear my naked body. I felt Haralda beside me, and saw her teats turning blue with the cold; both our bottoms were thrust upward, fiery glowing beacons against the blanket of white.

'I say, Amanda, don't the new scum look like lollipops, their filthy bums all red!'

'*I* think they look like clowns' noses, Ethel!'

'They won't be clowning when the Mistress shows them what scum they are.'

'The Mistress's knout, you mean, Wendy.'

'And on bare! The lovely knout on lovely bare, all black and trenched and raw, and the scum naked and squirming and screaming with no one but the snow to hear!'

A sharp impact from the senior girl's catapult, on one or other befurred bottom, stilled the schoolgirl banter, which made me giggle despite my discomfort. To come all this way and be kidnapped by bandits whose voices were the music of the English shires!

'What are you laughing at, you filthy boy?' cried a stern and familiar voice, and I was jolted by an agonising lash across my wealed bare arse.

I looked up with tears in my eyes and saw the Mistress, with a long black riding crop raised and quivering. I was convinced my awful smarting was from the knout, but her knout was coiled at her waist, along with an intriguing array of whips and flails. The Mistress rode the black, lathered stallion and had only now caught up with us.

Haralda was now shivering quite alarmingly, and I whimpered that it was cold.

'Well below zero, boy! This is Siberia! But there is only a blanket to cover one of you scum.'

Of course, I begged her to cover Haralda, and she ordered one of the girls to see to it. By now, my own teeth were chattering, and I was bold enough to ask how long we should ride. My impudence earned me a flurry of crop-welts across my bare arse, which had me squealing and writhing in my distress – the stiff upper lip of taking punishment in silence did not seem to apply in this white desolation. The Mistress laughed harsh and loud, her voice dry and dwarfed in the snowy immensity of the steppe.

'Scum, Miss?' I snivelled. 'But I am an Englishman, as you sought.'

This earned me another flurry of strokes on the raw, at least a dozen in quick-fire succession. The Mistress delivered them with her back ramrod straight, not stooping or faltering in her control of her stallion.

'All new students are scum, to begin with,' she snapped. 'Some remain scum for ever. My crop will keep you warm for the journey, scum, no fear,' she said. 'We should be at Masterdale by dusk.'

Despite my scalding agony, I pricked up my ears. 'Masterdale!' I blurted. 'I thought –'

'Scum that thinks!' she sneered. '*What* did you think, scum?'

My bum clenched to another dozen from the crop. When I could cease gasping I was about to tell what I knew, but an instinct told me to dissemble.

'O – just that I had heard the name, Miss. A famous academy for the education of young English ladies.'

'For the education and *correction* of young ladies,' she rapped, 'and here in Siberia, young gentlemen too. What do we call young gentlemen, gels?'

'*Scum!*' cried the soldier-girls in fluting unison.

'And what may scum expect to get at Masterdale?'

'*What for?*' came the eager chorus.

'Built of the finest Scottish granite, shipped from Aberdeen to Archangel, and rebuilt stone by stone in the pure, vast nothingness of the Tunguska,' said the Mistress with awed satisfaction. 'There!'

Haralda and I craned to look, and I saw a black mound at the horizon.

'Impregnable Masterdale!' crowed the Mistress.

I was at a loss to see how a place could be impregnable, as it seemed without natural defences of any kind. However, after a jolting hour, during which my tender buttocks were seldom left unlashed, the convoy paused. Clumps of reeds told me we were at the bank of a frozen river, curving a good mile wide in a loop across the plain.

Masterdale itself was beginning to take shape, and I

117

discerned towers and buttresses, like those of an English castle. I expected us to proceed across the ice directly, but we did not; we skirted the flank of the river for about three or four miles, until the soldiers as one turned their ponies (I later learnt they were called Tunguska ponies) to face the ice; in single file we proceeded across.

Then I learnt the reason of our detour: one of the ponies slipped and tumbled, and immediately cracked through the ice, falling into swift water along with its rider. All the girls laughed gaily as their willing arms helped their comrade and her steed, who were a hair's breadth from being swept to destruction.

The river looped and meandered all around Masterdale, and only in this one spot was the ice thick enough – fortified by a wall of bricks – to allow passage. Any assailant force would be destroyed instantly on trying to cross the frozen river. I later learnt that every summer the brickwork ford was demolished carefully, so that the turbid river afforded no crossing at all, save to the fleetest of messengers trained to swim their horses.

The sun was low and the land darkening when the Mistress and her troop, with two naked, well-flogged scum, passed through the granite portals of Masterdale Academy.

9

Scum

That grim trek led me to expect the utmost degradation
once immured in Masterdale Academy, and yet it was not
so. Apart from the first week, I found myself in a spartan
but prettily appointed establishment run with polite
severity, much like the English public school that
Masterdale purported to be – which Masterdale *was*.
Perhaps polite severity is not the right phrase, or at least it
is if the most decorous yet cold-blooded rigour can be
served politely.

The place functioned along an impossibly arcane and
intricate network of rules, the slightest infraction of which
led to the harshest but *fairest* punishment, so that much of
my time was spent cribbing the niceties of disciplinary
procedure – only to discover that by the time I had
mastered one rule, some shadowy Mistress had changed it
altogether. Rules, I soon learnt, were to be obeyed rather
than understood, since true discipline is its own function;
thus does an English gentleman gain backbone. But I must
not omit that first week: our painful reception, and the
deliberate squalor of a new scum's 'breaking'.

I think it was a week – it might have been more. Time
lost its meaning during the breaking of myself and
Haralda. We halted in the tidy courtyard of the academy,
with its neat lines of leafless trees like sentinels, and flanked
by bushy evergreen firs. I observed that the buildings were
all in dazzling white, rather than the normal drab brown
of the English nineteenth century Gothic revival, and that

these squat towers had the modest Romanesque style of the early Middle Ages. I had never heard of a Romanesque revival and wondered briefly if these buildings could somehow date from the original period eight hundred years before.

The girls joined together in lifting a heavy iron manhole, and Haralda and I were bundled naked down a flight of steps, lit by only two or three guttering candles. Fearfully, I plunged down into the darkness, sensing no alternative, turned a corner, and found myself in the light. I turned to clasp Haralda, who was crying and shivering, but was slapped on the arse by a prefect's whip. (Almost my first instruction was to distinguish between 'fillies' – prefects – and monitors and, of course, the teachers who ruled overall, subject only to the Mistress herself.)

The light came from above: Haralda and I were in an open cage, with mud and straw on the floor, and heated to surprising warmth by a wood stove, whose fuel was a pile of frozen sticks in the corner, which we duly had to break off with ragged fingernails to keep us from freezing. Above us, mischievous smiles mocked us as the 'fillies' peered down from the courtyard. Our cage was right underneath the central pathway, and almost at once a barrage of rotten apple cores and the like pelted down on us, until the prefect barked that we had not yet been yoked. This was not long in coming; another prefect arrived through the narrow aperture of the cage, which opened out into a dank corridor and was adjoined by similar, empty cages. She carried the trunk of a sapling birch, about ten feet long, with iron hooks at each end.

Haralda and I were whipped apart with a needless flurry of rapid strokes on the buttocks, to the length of the birch trunk, and our necks clipped in the hooks, which, though thankfully loose, gave us hardly any freedom of movement, and that little severely limited by our fastening. The length of the sapling prevented us touching in any way, a punishment as cruel as it was intended.

The presence of the stove was a comfort; the outer ring of the cage was icy cold, well below freezing, I guessed, while the hearth was scalding hot. In the corner stood a wretched slop-pail, our only consolation that its surface was frozen over. Our yoke meant that only one of us could approach the stove, or the slop-pail, at any one time; I naturally placed myself at the rim of the cage to let Haralda sink to the filthy straw, sobbing, and my heart ached that I was unable to shield her from her portion of the muck that rained down on us both.

The prefects locked the door on us without a word of explanation and left two miserable naked scum there, alternately toasting and freezing. I could not but emulate Haralda, and I sank to the floor, my body spattered with rotten eggs and tomatoes, with the worrying thought that these slops might be intended as our only sustenance. There was a water barrel, fed by melted snow and thinly crusted with ice, from which we could drink after laboriously making arrangements to shift our yoke.

At first we were too exhausted and bewildered to sleep, sullenly I realised that I had what I secretly craved: I was a cowering slave of unknown and powerful women. I pitied poor Haralda even as I longed to worship her, lusted for the touch of that glorious golden body, the dugs standing proud, and the buttocks tensed and firm, even under their sorry carpet of weals. Her gash, wetly naked amid filth, still shone to me as a radiant fold of glory. After a while, I dared to speak.

'It could be worse, Haralda,' I whispered. 'If only I'd known you were a girl – and so lovely! I'd – I'd have – O, I think I shouldn't have birched you half so hard.'

'You would have, sweet sir,' she said coyly, with a blush to her cheeks, 'because I should have made you.'

I was about to reply with some morsel of tenderness when without warning two prefects returned and entered our cage. Our yoke was seized and we were dragged to our feet, then the yoke was hooked high up on the cage bars, making each of us stand straining on tiptoe, struggling and gasping for mercy.

'Scum may not talk,' snarled the first prefect, a tall, rather thin but muscular girl of my own age, with raven hair cropped short, and thick pointed thigh-boots of shining black leather. She kicked me three or four times in the cleft of my buttocks, the sharp toe of her boot piercing my anus, which made me squeal in shame, and I saw that Haralda received the same from the second prefect, though she suppressed her cry of pain with a bitter grunt.

Squeal! We were both howling before our inevitable beating was half over. I took a vicious rattan cane, well over four feet long and an inch thick, while Haralda was flogged with a short quirt, like a cat only with a dozen or more braided thongs. The lashes, and our piteous cries, rang out through the academy, accompanied by roars of laughter from the schoolgirls above who redoubled their pelting with rotten fruit as our bodies shook below them.

The prefects said nothing more, not even when they released us and stamped from our cage, leaving Haralda and me sobbing in our filth. I had taken thirty strokes on the bare buttocks with that fearful rattan, and my flesh was wealed raw. Haralda, I guessed, had taken the same with the quirt, and her bare bum was a mosaic of black and purple. I wanted to tell her that she took her punishment like a man.

Neither of us could sit; we lay on our bellies, sobbing bitter tears, as our raw, bare buttocks were spattered with ordures from the mischievous schoolgirls above. I shamefully wanted nothing more than to stripe every girl's naked bum in the darkest of welts with the hardest knout!

The day passed in sorrow and lonely, silent pain, each of us longing to speak, but ashamed at not daring to. Darkness fell early, and we huddled as best we could by the comforting glow of the stove, while all around us icicles crackled and snowflakes cascaded to the ground, melting and hissing as they struck our steaming urn.

Sometime in the night we were aroused by shuffles and jangling noises, and I opened my eyes to see the cages on either side being opened to admit their occupants: naked and yoked just like Haralda and myself. I shuddered at the sight of bare wealed bodies burdened by their birch neck-thongs, yet the sight gave me hope: we were not the only scum! Somewhere, in the cruel councils of Masterdale Academy, there was a plan for us; however cruel and hideous, a plan seemed better than neglect.

I do not know if our fellow scum were schooled to be part of our own degradation; all I know is that they achieved it. All day I had lain looking at Haralda's wealed nude body, every scar and bruise making her more precious to me, making me long to throw myself at her feet and kiss her filthy toes, begging her to lash me a thousandfold as vengeance on the world's brute use of her!

I knew her to be submissive, and some remnant of male arrogance in me willed that she should submit to my own longings for slavery. If she whipped me with trembling and unwilling hand, all the greater would be her submissive joy, and all the lovelier my shame as I writhed in guilty passion under her lash.

The new arrivals were also yoked in pairs. On my side of the cage were two nude females, in a state of fearful squalor, both full-breasted and ripe-arsed, but with all those sacred hillocks well striped by canes, and their tangled pubic bushes matted and filthy. They leered at me and wiped their slavering lips, patting their bellies with lewd motions; it seemed that they had just been fed.

On Haralda's side were yoked two males, tall but scrawny fellows who seemed to feel no shame at the exposure of their long fat cocks, bare to a lady's eyes. On the contrary, they made their own lascivious gestures, which modesty forbids me to describe. To my horror, Haralda did not turn her eyes away but gazed in lustful fascination; then I saw that the males each carried hunks of sausage and scraps of chicken bones squeezed between their buttocks and thighs. One, the stronger, was pressed against the cage bars, while the smaller waited his turn, coming as close as the yoke would allow. The same applied to my two sirens.

I turned and saw the two females delve into their quims and extract for my own teasing hunks of sausage dripping from their cunts. They waved the sausage at me, making the motions of eating, and pointed to their open gashes.

The implication was clear: I should enjoy the succulent meat if I offered my own in lustful bargain.

I looked horrified at Haralda, but her eyes were on the proffered food and the swelling cocks of the two filthy males. And when my eyes turned again to the vixens, of whom the more massive was scarcely two feet from me, I smelt their food and the juices from their open cunnies.

Both females were openly and lustfully rubbing their quims, showing me glistening pink flesh as fragrant as the meat that dangled alongside. Their lips pursed, they made sucking, teasing noises, batting their crusted eyelashes in a hideous parody of flirtation.

I looked at those pink gashes as their owners shamelessly masturbated to my gaze, and my cock began to stiffen and rise. This made them redouble their onanistic contortions, and in no time my cock was pressed hard and throbbing in supplication against the bars of my cage.

Only a tug on my neck birch made me remember Haralda. Bound to me, she was kept at a foot's distance from her own two tormentors, both of whom had erect cocks pushed through the cage grille inviting her to pleasure them for food. And I saw that Haralda herself was masturbating for their eyes. She gestured at me to hurry with my business, so that she could be about her own.

I reached out and grasped the proffered cunt, soaking wet under the matted dirty mink; found the stiff clitty and began to rub vigorously. I was rewarded with sighs and grunts from its owner, who rubbed her huge stiff nipples up and down against the cage as she writhed at my touch. This gratified me; a glimmer of warmth in that frigid desolation! My cock begged to enter her warm place; she spread the fat swollen lips of her cunt in urgent invitation, and I felt her moist and velvet on my glans as I plunged the shaft of my arrow right to my balls inside her slopping tight quiver.

Then the cage bars began to rattle as I began a vigorous – nay, furious – fucking of that soft wet cunt, poking her brutally and masturbating her clitty very hard to make her climax before my own spurt came. In this way, I reasoned, I should have power enough to pleasure both the vixens and be released, so that my yoked Haralda might be soiled by the cocks of her meat-bearing males.

As I fucked, the delicious humiliance of my role added power to my hard penis. I was a slave pleasuring a voracious female, in order to enjoy the shame at my beloved fucked by two brute rivals, my own charms as nothing compared with theirs.

My vigorous masturbation of the clit paid handsomely, and the female cried out very loudly as I brought her an orgasm, with her cunt-juices cascading very freely down my hand, and making little rivulets on her thighs. I saw from the corner of my eye that the cunt-juice slowed in its flow as it passed her knees, then fell to the ground with little tinkling crashes, having crusted into icicles. I was sure the prefects should come, but I was past caring; the fragrant sausage meat filled my eyes and nostrils.

Her spasm over, the woman moaned and slavered, seeming reluctant to release my throbbing cock. Yet her comrade began to mewl and shake the yoke, demanding her turn. A reluctant reversal of roles was made, and now I was presented with a taut white bum, superbly ripe and muscled, bent over with the cheeks spread to reveal a crinkly little bum-bud, open for my entry. This second vixen was busy masturbating her own clitty and delving into her quim, and it was clear that my role was to bugger her in bumhole.

Without a pause, I plunged my cock into the brown anus, surprisingly loose and comfortable like a glove, and I surmised that many cocks had entered this passage before mine. This, too, gave me a shameful thrill (what male has not dreamt of many powerful cocks spurting in his lady's cunt before his own, whether the lady be honest wife or *demi-mondaine*?); so did Haralda's glance of disgust as she turned her head from the spectacle of buggery. My heart beat with hope: if I could make Haralda thoroughly despise me, then perhaps I could induce her to whip me with true and undisguised contempt.

The vixen's long legs trembled and banged against the cage as I buggered her with sincere frenzy. I wanted to shame her lewdness, and shame myself for my joyful acceptance of it. Her arsehole closed and squeezed on my cockshaft, and now it was as tight as a vice, with evident practice in the art of buggery. The tip of my helmet slammed at her root, and she writhed and moaned with familiar enjoyment, squeezing my cock with her elastic anus as though to milk my spunk from me.

I saw that her comrade at the other end of her yoke was waving the shiny sausage at me, tantalising me; then she bent and presented me with her own anus, into which she pushed the thick sausage until only an inch of meat protruded from her bumshaft. She pointed at it as though I must reclaim my dinner from that unseemly place. This extra shame quickened my fucking in the white-bummed vixen's arsehole, and I felt the spunk well honeyed in my balls and cried out as I spurted my hot cream long and hard right at the root of that squirming deep bum-slit.

My cock slipped with a raw plop from the tight little arse-bud, and I sank to my knees, sobbing and gasping, and looked round to see Haralda masturbating herself most vigorously. Her lips were still twisted in contempt for me, but an avid clit-mashing betrayed her real excitement. The males had stiff cocks now, and Haralda stretched out one bare gazelle's leg to tickle each of them on the balls with outstretched toes, and I saw she could dextrously twine her big toe around their cock-tips for a lascivious frotting.

Now the larger vixen, whom I had cunt-fucked, approached me again, arse first and wriggling so that the tip of the sausage danced before my eyes. My chin was moist with drool. I pressed my hungry mouth to the cage, willing to accept the worst degradation. But she sneered and motioned that I was to present my own bum. I feared a flogging, even though it was obvious the bars would not permit it.

Much worse was in store: the slut held a rough chunk of wood, about the size of her muscled forearm. She lifted her hand and stuck two fingers against my arse-bud, then at once sank them right into my unprepared shaft. I squealed at the pain, as the fingers burrowed deep inside my bumhole, without waiting for my sphincter to relax and permit that soft swooning passage which is I understand so delicious to devotees of buggery.

I writhed and moaned, in full view of Haralda, whose toes were busy frotting the stiff cocks presented to her through the cage, and the spectacle of my wretched pain-wracked face seemed to increase the fervour of her clit-frotting. I could see her boatman standing stiff and wet as her thumb and forefinger pummelled the throbbing organ; she gasped hard at the pleasure of her fierce diddling.

Meanwhile I was forced to accept a third, then a fourth finger right inside my anus. I thought I should faint from the agony. The vixen began to move her hand back and forward in a vigorous poking as though it were the harshest dildo, and to my horror I felt my buttocks begin to squirm in time with her poking and my sphincter to loosen to willingly accommodate this torment.

My flaccid cock began to stiffen again, provoking a cry of triumph from my tormentress! At this, her four fingers were joined in that congested passage by her very thumb, and, squealing, I felt her hand ball into the hardest yet daintiest of practised fists. Now a true fist-fucking began in earnest, and I felt my sphincter pummelled by her vigorous blows, the knuckles punching my root as though in a prize fight, then withdrawing to the wrist before plunging inside me again. My cock was ramrod stiff!

I felt the most curious tickling amid my agony, and suddenly there were jeers from my two vixens and loud gasps from Haralda as she masturbated herself to climax. I looked between my legs and saw my shaft jerking and bucking all on her own, the drops of spurt jetting from my peehole to fall crusted into icicles on the floor. That fist-fucking had brought me to spend, and in my agony I had scarcely noticed.

The vixens were not quite satisfied. To get my reward I had to accept the piece of frozen wood as a dildo instead of that cruel fist. Its gnarled length sank to the root of my mauled bumhole, and I was instructed by gestures to hold it inside me if I wished to feed. Then I was allowed to shift position, and with a good eight inches of that cruel wooden shaft embedded in my anus I was obliged to squat and present my nose and lips to the parted cheeks of the vixen's naked arse. Greedily my teeth seized on the tip of the sausage and began to suck it from her anus.

She resisted, squeezing her bumhole so that I had to fight for each morsel that passed my lips, glistening with the juices of her belly. I did not care, and felt only the glorious warmth of nourishment in my stomach. At last, every inch of that sausage had been sucked from her hole and swallowed, and I began to release the burning shaft that I had fought to keep embedded in my own anus.

As I chewed the very last morsel of food, suddenly she whipped her hips around and again I was faced with the hairy swelling of her mound, placed atop my face. I gasped as the wooden dildo plopped from my bum, and then felt a hot surge of golden smoky fluid bathe my face with a hiss. Through blurred, moist eyes I could see her gash spurting golden liquid over me, to her peals of laughter.

Then there was a furious jerk on my neck-yoke, and I was dragged away from the cage bars. The droplets of golden woman-piss fell from me, turning to icicles as they spattered the floor. Haralda had lost patience; she knelt by the cage and was avidly sucking the cock of the stronger, hairier male, taking the shaft right into her throat and making furious bobbing motions like a pigeon, at the same time allowing the male's bare toes to frot her gash-lips. I thrilled in degradation: that my pure Haralda should abandon herself so lustfully to another male.

The male began to groan as his cock bucked, gleaming with her spittle as she sucked; then, deliberately, she rose, to bend over and present her buttocks. But cunt was not on the brute's mind. I watched as Haralda took his massive ten inches of flesh inside her anus and began to masturbate her clit anew, slamming her bum on his cock and squirming with every sign of pleasure.

It was not long before her squeezing anus made the male cry out in spurt, and, directly, Haralda playfully squeezed the stiff nipples of her breasts and gestured that she was not yet sated. His companion therefore shifted, to present his own member and recommence the buggery in her bumhole still dripping with the first cock's spend. This fellow was not treated to the same writhings as the other, and I sensed that Haralda wanted to keep his cock stiff for greater pleasure. She looked at me and winked, then wiped her hand over her bedrooled lips.

Suddenly she jerked forward, leaving the stiff cock standing and flapping between the bars, and gleaming from her bumhole's secretion. She wiped it with straw, then pressed her hips to the male, spread her muscled thighs, and engulfed the cock in her cunt, to its full length.

She began to slam vigorously against the bars, and I saw that her bucking was so hard that the male's balls were smacked at each of her thrusts. He began to moan and then gasped long and loud as I saw a stream of golden fluid spurt from Haralda's cunt, over his thighs and balls, while her nimble fingers dancing between their bellies did not cease from frotting her ramrod pink nubbin.

She spasmed at the same time as he did, his creamy spurt mingling with her golden rain to crust into a cascade of tiny little icicles by their ankles. Then Haralda sank to her knees and was rewarded by a scornful hail of chicken bones that spattered her breasts, cunt and piss-wet thighs. She greedily picked up every morsel and crunched it – meat, grease, bone and all – and when she had finished she rolled on the filthy straw with another wink at me, as of a lady thoroughly satisfied.

Our tormentors melted away into their own darkness, their whip-scarred bare bodies glowing in the eerie stove-light as they fell asleep. Haralda pointed at my own cock, which was hard again at the spectacle of her lustful degradation, and spread her bum to show that when possible I was to bugger her too. I shook my head, outraged that my delicate and mysterious lady had turned so suddenly into an animal willing to sacrifice all modesty for a scrap of food. Of course I know that there is no mystery to ladies, only the lust for power, the dripping cunt hungry for cock, and the vengeful song of the whip on bare skin. Perhaps that is precisely their mystery.

Suddenly there was a chorus of catcalls and jeers and ironic applause from above: our spectacle had been watched the whole time! I saw fur-clad schoolgirls pelting us with ordure and offal, and Haralda and I at once scrabbled for rotten muck to eat. Then I understood that we were no different: we were both scum.

For two days we lived thus, enduring the taunts of the females above us – themselves, as I was to learn, the subject of frequent and odious persecutions by their caning prefects. The most hideous part of our silent ordeal was our uncertainty: no one came to see us, no one even bothered to lash our bodies into submission, since our submission was assured by our first awful whipping.

The same ritual of debased lust was repeated on the second night, when our neighbours returned naked and whipped but bearing the prizes of their own punishment. I surmised that they were privileged to receive these scraps after a whipping-feast, and remembered it was the custom of Russian nobles to amuse themselves over their borscht with the screams of naked slaves under the knout. My truest and deepest wish was to be ennobled by a whipping-feast!

I was almost grateful when on the third morning our cage door burst open and the two prefects entered, accompanied by the distinguished lady who had been in charge of our prison cortege. She wore a glorious sable coat, with a collar of gleaming silver spikes, like a wolfhound's, and high gleaming leather boots, which kicked me to the ground, while Haralda was toppled by a flurry of canestrokes to her bare breasts.

Helpless and subdued, I jerked under at least a dozen bumstrokes from a rattan until I was trembling and quiet to her satisfaction. Then she put her foot on my buttocks, grinding my wealed flesh most painfully, and let the sable coat fall open. I saw the glorious sheen of a frilly basque corset, with a brassiere that scarcely contained the superb pale melons of her teats, topped by the swollen and brick-hard wide nipples, and with garter straps attached to sheer silk stockings, the whole in the most girlish and adorable pale pink.

There were no panties to cover the succulent hairy fount, whose hillock swelled as proud as Haralda's pert bare breasts. Beneath this fount peeped a pair of swollen fleshy quim-lips from which suddenly emerged a stream of gold. The hot smoky liquid splashed my face and belly, as her boot held me still with the point wedged firmly in my arse-bud. The magnificent dominatrix coolly allowed one of her prefects to light a cigarette in an ivory holder, and she smoked contentedly as she pissed on my bare body.

I twisted my head and caught some of her precious golden fluid between my lips! My tongue lapped, and I moaned in submission to Woman! Her own lips curled in a lovely sneer.

'It seems you are ready to be shown to the academy, scum,' she drawled, flicking ash from her cigarette on my face. 'And you might be graciously whipped and fed.'

Her accent was the same poetry of the English shires.

'O, thank you, thank you, Mistress!' I babbled, licking the last droplets of the piss that cascaded from her gleaming pink cunt-lips.

I was rewarded with a further six or seven strokes of the rattan, which seared my wet bottom horribly. If I mention these beatings so casually, without describing the agony of each stroke, it is because they were inflicted so casually, the pain of strokes no more than the pain of my degradation. A beating inflicted with due ceremony and anticipation hurts more than one given to scum, who accept their welts as a dog accepts fleas. The lady inflicted my strokes nonchalantly, then frowned and brushed a stray lock from her forehead. She dislodged the glowing butt of her cigarette, threw it on my bare bum and lifted her boot to grind the ember into my flesh. But after a moment's searing pain it rolled on to the ground and she contented herself with four sharp kicks to my tender anus bud.

'You do not address me as Mistress, scum,' she said evenly and with some amusement. 'That is for the Lady Dushanka herself. You address *me* as Miss Bainbridge.'

10

Harnessed in Rubber

All my memories of the Countess Galena came back to me as Haralda and I were unyoked and thrust outside into the narrow wire corridor. Our neighbours, too, emerged into the cold pale daylight, blinking and rubbing their eyes. We were unshackled; I reached out an arm to comfort Haralda and got five painful strokes on the bare bum for my trouble before Miss Bainbridge lifted a restraining finger. The noise of my caning resounded above the birdsong of laughing schoolgirls in the distance.

I knew I would be caned for impudence, but I wanted Haralda to see I cared for her. Sadly, she seemed to think nothing of my gesture, but gazed with mischievous coyness towards the two brutes who had pleasured her so abominably for the last two nights. I admit my eyes turned to the females who had misused my own person and was ashamed that I found them both attractive in daylight, though dirty and covered in a scum's horrid welts and whipmarks.

They were not the misshapen sluts of my imaginings, but tall and well-formed young ladies of my own age, proud of breast and bum, and deliciously large in both. Simpering and fluttering their eyelashes, they gazed unabashed at my exposed balls and penis, which could not help stiffening. Haralda observed my modest excitement and was not pleased; she redoubled her own coy glances at the naked brutes.

One girl was ash blonde, not as light as Haralda, the

other, smaller, a cherry brunette, and I saw that both the quims I had pleasured were hidden by swelling hillocks whose big straggly minks were in need of combing. The thought flashed that I should like to kneel and groom these ladies' founts! But I sighed inwardly: I had not heard them speak, and imagined some unmusical foreign tongue.

Miss Bainbridge was attended by the two prefects we had seen previously, the senior and crueller of the two with the bony face, a rangy, mannish body and the cropped raven hair that gave her a certain cruel charm in my submissive eyes. It was she who had lashed my bottom, and the welts stung; like a booby, I treasured them.

The other prefect was softer and more ladylike, voluptuous of bosom and with a large pear-shaped croup scarcely disguised by the tight leather greatcoat, shiny and black, which both prefects wore. In addition to their hand-held canes, each had at her belt a coiled stockwhip and a dangling cat-o'-nine-tails. Both ladies wore chokers of plain steel, but without the spikes of Miss Bainbridge's, and their necks were bare; the greatcoats were buttoned up tightly, and I suspected that like Miss Bainbridge they wore only skimpy underthings beneath.

I later learnt that the practice of Masterdale was for easy access to bare flesh; that even a prefect's exalted status did not protect her from whipping by a senior, and that the greatcoat, a badge of power, could easily be stripped from her to reveal the flimsy corselage inside, which left the buttocks almost entirely bare for whipping by such as Miss Bainbridge. I also learnt that Milady Dushanka, the Mistress of Masterdale, liked to be attended by girls and boys ready to be pretty for her.

Now, the prefects separated us into lines of males and females, side by side, so that I was sandwiched between my two brute rivals for Haralda, and stood opposite the blonde girl, authoress of my two nights' abasement. To my surprise, she gave me a little simpering smile that was not in the least sluttish – she was of my height, her firm young breasts stood proud only inches from my hands, from my very lips – I resisted the impulse to bend and kiss those cherry nipples, standing brick-stiff in the cold, though I longed to kneel and kiss her dirty feet, whose ripe smell assailed my nostrils. All of us shivered, while Miss Bainbridge smoked, a sardonic smile on her lips as she inspected our goose flesh.

'Rowena Tushingham!' she barked suddenly, and my ash-blonde companion made an automatic curtsy.

'Everything all right?'

'Top hole, Miss Bainbridge,' said Rowena.

'You have performed your duties with the new scum?'

Rowena nodded.

'Any complaints?'

'Useless to complain of smelly males, Miss. But I did my duty and made him suffer. He took it hard in the bum.'

To my astonishment, her English accent was as crisp and faultless as Miss Bainbridge's own. Miss Bainbridge smiled and blew a plume of smoke in my blushing face.

'True, Philip Demesne?' she said softly.

I bowed my head and said in mortification that it was quite true, not forgetting to use her proper title. It was clear that only my indignities counted; Rowena's lustful submission to my cock was the privilege of a lady. I wondered what had brought Miss Bainbridge, legendary betrayer of my beloved Countess Galena, to this outpost.

'And have you any complaints?' she asked me. I shook my head and replied that my treatment had been quite fair.

This extravagance of speech got me a further three strokes of the cane on my bare bum at a nod from Miss Bainbridge to the raven-haired prefect. The prefect seemed avid to continue beating me, but Miss Bainbridge drawled:

'Enough, Fitzhurst, save the choice meat for later.'

She addressed the larger male as Denning and asked him the same as Rowena. He smirked a little and said he hoped he had done his duty with the dirty foreign filly. I was pleased that this extravagance in turn got him strokes of the cane on his bare from the second prefect, who flogged him very fast, with an angry gleam in her eye, getting in five stingers before her ardour was stilled by Miss Bainbridge, who addressed her as 'Marpole'.

'You are still scum, even out of your cage, Denning,' said Miss Bainbridge, flexing her own cane. 'Scum speak only when spoken to, and then sparingly. The same applies to slaves, if you are privileged to become one.'

The prefect Marpole was named 'ganger' of the three females, and Fitzhurst of the males. We were shackled by waist and ankles, with our wrists cuffed behind us and a chain from the cuff leading to our balls, which were bound tightly. The girls had corresponding clamps applied to their quim-lips roughly spread. As though there were anywhere to escape to in this wilderness! But our bonds were a symbol of our status as scum.

I was apprehensive that Fitzhurst was our ganger, for I suspected – accurately – that once out of Miss Bainbridge's sight her cane would lash unsparingly.

I have omitted to describe our casual beatings in detail. I must advise that a ceremonial beating from a lady's hand is unbearably thrilling: the tension, the scowl of displeasure or scorn, the first cleansing cut of whip or cane on bare bottom, and the music of a lady's dainty voice counting her cruel strokes. Yet short beatings at whim soon fade, if there are pauses between them, and the flogged croup learns to absorb frequent short pain.

There is a slave's pleasure, too, in casual cruelty: the cuts carelessly given to bare hide, as though their number, or the anguish of the receiver, were of scant concern. It was the same with Miss Bainbridge's action in wishing to stub her cigarette on my bare bum. She was unable to do so but did not mind, and her very indifference thrilled me. To be punished by a lady who does not care if you smart is great joy to a slave.

Miss Bainbridge dismissed us, and we were marched off at a brisk hobble, the male cortege following the female. I saw that Denning's demeanour was not at all as sullen as his fellow's; rather he shuffled quite jauntily even under the menacing swishes of Fitzhurst's cane.

'Come on, Fitz,' said Denning, 'don't be a rotter. You know I can be good for you, ever since we –'

Fitzhurst's bony visage coloured in a blush, and she cracked the cane hard across the top of Denning's arse.

'Silence, scum!' she hissed.

'My hide's like walnut, Fitzy,' said the cheeky young man. 'Cane me as you please, I can take it. I've done my duty – *la* Bainbridge approves of me – and I'll be a proper slave soon, out of your jailhouse.'

'I've done my duty too,' announced his comrade, who was rewarded with two strokes on his croup, which made him yelp.

'You too, Crocker,' hissed Fitzhurst. 'You are scum until I say otherwise.'

'Until *Miss Bainbridge* says otherwise,' sneered Crocker, and this time it was *I* who received the cuts on bare croup – five hard ones, and with a gleam in Fitzhurst's eye, as though my caning pleased her more than the others', for her eyes were on my hard cock.

'At least *you'll* be scum for a long time, you whelp,' she spat at me, then added, with a sly look at Denning: 'A true submissive's cock needs real taming.'

This remark excited me! Denning glanced at my cane-stiffened penis and swallowed nervously, looking jealous. Haralda, too, looked at me with darting, amused eyes that did not displease me. I said nothing but concentrated on keeping in step; we were headed for a low building whence scurried a gaggle of laughing book-laden schoolgirls wearing thick woollen coats and stockings, with heavy boots. They jeered at us and bent down to make snowballs, until warned off by Fitzhurst's cane lashing the snow.

Our column of three females and three males entered a vaulted corridor, redolent of the sweet smells of girls' bodies, perfumed with youth, sweat and eagerness. We shuffled into a large changing-room, with lockers, sporting apparatus and a bathroom gurgling sullenly at one end. Without being loosed from our shackles, we were herded into the bathroom, all of us jammed in stinking proximity, and the two prefects at once turned violent hosepipes on us, drenching us with icy water and making the girls shriek.

Fitzhurst in particular got great pleasure from this, and turned her nozzle directly to the male organs which we tried in vain to shield from the spray's pummelling; Marpole amused herself by swishing the girls' bare titties until their nipples stood stiff. At length we were cleansed and led shivering into the changing-room, where the hot stove soon dried our steaming bare bodies.

Now the prefects unshackled us, and, as though it were the most natural thing in the world, Fitzhurst ordered us to bend over and touch our toes for a caning. All of us obeyed smartly and without question. I stole a glance and saw the wealed orbs of five nude bottoms perched high for the cane – one of nature's sweetest sights! Fitzhurst inspected the line of croups, swishing her cane, and with one hand rubbing inside her coat at her fount.

She dealt each bare bum a resounding six stingers that had the girls sobbing and hiccuping, and even Denning was moved to whistle 'I say!' as the cane caught him the third time on a particularly livid welt. Excited by the beating of bottoms other than mine, I peeked – interested in the customs of each sex under cane. We all squirm, of course, but the male clenches and shudders with great drama, as though to show off his manly fortitude; the female buttocks wobble and shiver most delicately, like lively striped jellies, as ladies are concerned not to appear vulgar even in the extreme agony of a bare-bottom caning.

This capricious beating had the desired effect of quelling any rebellious instinct, so that our 'robing' could proceed apace. I saw that eyes were on my person, and realised why: mine was the only cock excited to stiffness.

'You, Crocker and Denning, and Misses Arkright and Tushingham –' it was the first time I had heard the brunette girl's name '– shall now be privileged with robe. Before, as new scum, you were obliged to make ordeal naked and filthy. Your robes will keep you warm and dry.'

'The new scum too?' whined Denning. 'That's not fair.'

'Fair?' screamed Fitzhurst, her bony face flushed with rage, and lashed him hard on the wet buttocks. 'Was *that* fair? Did you come here for fairness? Is *that* fair?'

At her last remark she grasped the shaft of my stiffened cock and squeezed it, then pulled it very hard as though she wanted to wrench it from its root. Her pert breasts and arse strained against her coat leather.

'Oo,' she moaned, half in anger and half in suppressed desire – and looked me briefly straight in the eyes with an expression of such luscious loathing that my cock stiffened fully under her touch. She squeezed my balls so hard that my eyes moistened, then let go.

'No,' she muttered, 'not *fair*.'

Marpole opened a large locker to produce a pile of neatly folded black garments, which we were ordered to don. I looked at mine: a skimpy thing of fragrant black rubber with curious attachments. The girls dressed faster than the males; I saw Rowena Tushingham cased in a rubber corselet which pinched her waist very tightly, like a waspie. The huge teats were left bare, although the upper hem of the corset pressed them up and out very firmly, tightening the titties so that the pale flesh gleamed like moons. There were no panties, and no crotch piece or even a thong; instead the vulva, mink and fesses were left entirely nude.

Four straps hung from the hem of the corselet, attached to thin rubber stockings, the garment being all of a piece. Rowena fitted her long shapely feet into the toepiece and swiftly pulled the stockings up over her quivering bare thighs, tightening the straps for a snug fit. Haralda was not far behind her, while I dawdled, my balls tingling at the sight of two blonde girls with bare flesh melting into a soft black carapace.

The other girls caught up, and soon each wore a rubber costume of corset, stockings and gauntlets up over the elbows; to our dismay, we males realised that our costumes were exactly the same as the girls'. Denning opened his mouth, but his protest was stilled by three fierce canestrokes from Marpole which flamed his welts nicely; I was secretly thrilled to be dressed with the same beauteous indignity as the ladies, and hurried to robe myself. Surely I could not be the *only* willing slave of females!

'Feel like a cissy!' hissed Denning under his breath.

All of us were tightly and very warmly encased in the

black latex, but all our genital parts were exposed, including bare buttocks for all and bare titties for the girls. The strangest was to come: our remaining garment was a hood that snugly cased the entire head, with holes for eyes and nose, and a mouthpiece that snapped shut by a little metal clip, so that eventually we six stood as black ogres, our sex identifiable only by our naked pricks, teats and gashes. I envied Haralda and Rowena their proud, firm titties with the nipples standing so stiff!

Fitzhurst smirked and said that now we were decent for exposure to the classroom and also waterproofed for the muddy tasks and 'gauntlets' that awaited us. She seemed to ignore the exposure of our most sensitive parts.

We were pronounced ready to proceed to our tasks, but before leaving the changing-room we were harnessed. Our shackles were replaced by a single silver chain binding males and females together. For the females, heavy pincers were clamped very tightly to their nipples, and the chain looped across their bellies to be attached with two further clamps, one on each quim-lip, before snaking through the cleft of the buttocks to the next girl in line.

Males were treated differently. Our part of the chain contained a small apparatus for confining the balls and penis: the chain looped around the base of the scrotum and was fastened with a padlock, then Fitzhurst fully drew back our foreskins to reveal our naked bulbs. The chain was looped very tightly right under the ridge of the helmet and clipped shut. It was obvious that any stirring of the penis should cause extreme discomfort.

Mine was the only stiffened penis! My fellow males looked with a mixture of envy and distaste as my cock and balls were subjected to a further icy shower to make me subside. I did not; if anything, my excitement was greater at this public humiliation. Fitzhurst leered at me.

'We cannot show you to innocent schoolgirls in such a state, scum,' she said, then turned to Haralda.

The pale face stiffened under her rubber mask as Fitzhurst coolly told her to open her mouthpiece, then suck my cock and swallow the spunk, to get me soft for

140

binding. Haralda blinked – I hoped against hope that she would demur – but swiftly she slid open her mouth fastener and her pink tongue stuck out and waggled teasingly at me.

Her eyes were wide and guileless but did not look at my face. Without more ado she squatted before me and I felt my stiff cock engulfed in her hot velvet mouth, right to the back of the throat, with her tongue and larynx pressing eagerly and hungrily on my naked helmet. My joy at this voluptuous tonguing was made bitter in the knowledge that Denning had enjoyed the same only hours ago; Rowena looked jealously on, as though she had missed something in concentrating her humiliant efforts on my bumhole.

Ordered to hold my hands behind my back, I watched Haralda's bobbing rubber head, the teats mashed together and the nips rock-hard as she squatted, as though making an evacuation. This thought excited me despite my shame; that she should think so meanly of me as to make commode while tonguing me so intimately. I felt the wet pressure of that throat again and again, tickling my glans and peehole while her lips were busy under the ridge of my bulb; I could not withhold a yelp of ecstasy as I felt my balls surge and my cock buck in her mouth, and I spurted long and hard in that slithery pink throat-cunt, which writhed as she swallowed every drop of my spunk.

It happened so fast, so briskly! I sobbed a little, partly in shame and partly in satisfaction. The act of oral pleasure is normally seen as a female's obeisance to the power of the cock, yet Haralda had managed to service me with such cool and effortless skill that she made me feel I was in her power – as I longed to be! Her sly and lascivious grin as she licked her lips glistening with my spunk taught that my enslaved cock was one among many.

Fitzhurst at last pronounced my penis soft enough for harnessing, and I was duly fastened to the rest of the gang. Linked by our vicious, dainty silver chain, we were led out again into the thronged school yard. This time Fitzhurst did not dissuade the schoolgirls from pelting us with hard snowballs and sneered as we struggled to fend off the missiles. Waterproof our costumes might be, but the snowballs struck our uncovered parts with deadly aim.

Wincing, we entered the larger classroom building. The obedient queues of smirking schoolgirls parted to let us pass – not in respect, but in distaste. I recognised some of the warriors who had kidnapped Haralda and me; now they were demure and rosy as any English maiden, with short pleated skirts, dark blue stockings and tight cotton blouses that clung to their braless bosoms with tantalising transparency. They wore striped neckties of different colours showing the house they belonged to.

At length we were led into a deserted classroom and ordered to stand at the rear. Marpole and Fitzhurst took each end of our chain and hooked it to the wall, high enough that we were obliged to stand on tiptoe, with our hands behind our backs. Flexing her cane, Fitzhurst passed along the ample runnel behind us. I jerked at a sharp stroke to my tensed buttocks, then felt the chain jerk again as each of us received the same.

Assured of our attention, Fitzhurst told us that we were to be privileged to witness a class of fillies. This was the state to which Rowena, Arkwright and Haralda might aspire to join, and the state that Crocker, Denning and myself might aspire to serve and worship as slaves; for in the hierarchy of Masterdale any male was a mere *robotnik*, subservient to even the meanest female. As for the girls, lest they fall into smugness, a girl who neglected her books, was impudent or failed to take ordained punishments with a stiff upper lip would soon find herself reduced to scum once more, for new breaking.

'The purpose of Masterdale,' she sneered, 'is to train the race of females, whatever their origin, as English ladies – skilled in all the arts, and especially that of total submission. This art leads to equal knowledge of dominance, and, thus schooled, our girls advance the cause of women's supremacy over the male. Males are here to learn submission and nothing else – to the same end.'

The class duly filed in, their giggles turning to silent

smirks as they saw us, with little surprise. Their flushed faces were enveloped in scarves and their bodies in woollen greatcoats; each girl at her desk stripped off her outer garments and hung them neatly on the appointed pegs. The mistress entered the classroom, brandishing a pile of books and a long sheaf of birch rods gleaming darkly at her dainty waist, which she carefully leant against a squat flogging block beside her lectern. All the girls were neat and pretty in their uniforms as they rose and bowed to the mistress, chorusing, 'Good Morning, Miss Grant.' She ordered them to be seated and to open their books. The lesson, I gathered, was Latin.

Miss Grant herself wore a uniform scarcely different from those of her charges, except that beneath her white blouse a black brassiere was clearly visible over her deliciously full breasts – some of her charges were equally endowed, but their rank forbade them the dignity of cover, and they were obliged to show the entirety of their titties and nipples through the thin school blouse. Miss Grant's pleated skirt was heavier and longer, just covering her knees, and she wore black stockings in a fishnet pattern, with vivid seams over her calves, with shoes of gleaming patent leather that perched on elegantly high heels that ended in sharp points.

Across her shoulders was draped a miniature scholar's gown, which brushed the points of her breasts. Her auburn hair was swept over her head and pinned in a lush, towering bun, and she stared sternly through tortoiseshell glasses, glancing at the chained scum as though we were specks of dust on her blackboard. She spoke in a gentle Scottish burr and told one or other of the girls to begin translating a passage from Caesar's *Gallic Wars*.

A tug on our chain made us stand up straight and still. The chosen girl began to translate her passage in a trembling voice; she was pronounced adequate, and another girl was chosen to continue. Three or four girls gave of their best, until Miss Grant decreed that one Emma Porritt should continue the translation. Emma was a tall, superbly fit girl with an hourglass figure, a lush and unruly blonde mane and breasts that swelled in open competition to the harnessed teats of the mistress. I sensed a little gloating in Miss Grant's selection of her, and indeed poor Emma fumbled and stammered, mixing up the gerund with the past participle with the ablative absolute to such an extent that I feared for the legionaries' safety. Miss Grant smiled thinly and swept off her spectacles, brushing a stray hair from her forehead and sighing quite deeply.

'It is obvious you have not done your prep, Emma. And in front of new scum, here to observe how a lady is made! Will it do, filly? *Will* it? You will stand, please.'

'No, Miss,' said Emma meekly, as she stood. I saw her hands clasped behind her, nervously rubbing the ripe peach of her bottom in its tight blue skirt.

'Well, what are we to do, Emma?'

She lifted the birch from its place at the block and swished it in the air with a menacing crackle, then stroked the tips on her palm. I saw her glance more than briefly at our row of trussed bare bodies, in particular at the male cocks – and I blushed as she lingered on my own. But any stiffening was discouraged by the painful *corniche* – the ring that bound us by the ridge of our helmets.

Emma sighed and murmured: 'I must take punishment, Miss.'

'Yes,' said Miss Grant, rolling the words around her tongue, 'you must take punishment, Emma. Perhaps you will kindly be more specific.'

She stroked the birch rods as if they were kittens.

'I must take birch, Miss.'

'And?'

Emma gulped, and her voice was almost a sob. 'I – I must be birched on the bare cheeks, Miss – kneeling at the block with my bottom raised.'

There was a shiver of delicious apprehension from the class, and I, too, felt a vindictive glee at the prospect of this ripe filly stripped of her neatness, with bum bare and raised for the crackling birch rods.

'I cannot hear you!' Miss Grant rapped.

'O, Miss,' Emma sobbed. 'I must be birched, please, on bare bottom, and kneeling at the block, if you please!'

144

'That's better, Emma,' said Miss Grant, breathing heavily and licking her lips. 'Now advance and present yourself for punishment.'

Emma rose and marched unsteadily to the lectern, where she knelt over the flogging block, with her belly on the saddle and her calves, knees and thighs fitted into the concave rests, with straps on either side. Miss Grant ordered Emma to raise her skirts right over her back, and the filly lifted first her navy-blue skirt then a pale blue petticoat, draping them snugly on the small of her back. Thus was revealed a pair of matching baby-blue knickers, cut quite high and allowing a generous expanse of firm white buttock-flesh to be seen.

This was not enough. Miss Grant bent down and herself lowered the knickers to the offender's knees, leaving her bum bare and trembling, framed by the baby-blue garter belt and suspenders which held up the darker stockings. The orbs of her fesses were a true peach, ripe and succulent, and Miss Grant licked her lips again. I felt a trembling in my cock. I looked at my fellow males and knew they felt the same, but a twinge from my *corniche* dampened my ardour.

Her white bum-globes were already sullied with livid purple marks, and I gasped in dismay at the cruel beatings she must have recently taken. Then I peered closer and saw that they were signatures, in some kind of tattooist's ink. Miss Grant scrutinised these marks and pursed her lips.

'Let's see. Six with yew cane from Miss Wickham; six with rattan from Miss Bainbridge; a further six from the prefect Sturges. My, you *have* been naughty, Emma.'

'Miss, if you look at the dates you'll see I've been a good girl for a week now.'

'Why, so you have. The welts have faded to almost nothing. Let us see if you may blossom again from my birch, Emma – for your own good.'

'Yes, Miss,' said Emma miserably.

'How many, then? On bare bum, with full birch, mind.'

'O, six, I suppose, for my horrid naughtiness, Miss.'

Miss Grant clucked. Briskly, she buckled Emma's thighs

and calves in the restraining straps, drawing them as tight as they would go.

'Six! But I counted at least ten errors in your work, filly, so I think you have earned ten. Shall we say a dozen for round figures?'

'Y–yes, Miss, if you please,' Emma sobbed. Miss Grant lifted the birch to her shoulder.

Is not the birch the most sublime instrument of human correction? The crackling, hissing twigs seem the most soothing whispers of a lady's voice as they redden a naked bottom; each smarting caress is a joyous reward. Small wonder that the entire class observed the flogging with bated breath, and that we scum joined in their delight.

The first crack of the birch jolted Emma's whole body, and she wailed aloud. Her firm bare arse-globes glowed instantly with a pink flush.

'One!' cried Miss Grant.

The second stroke took her in the same place, and her furrow clenched and she gasped hard, three times.

'Two!'

Miss Grant dealt each stroke hard and accurately, aiming her birch so that every inch of Emma's buttocks was covered, from the sensitive upper fesses to the soft thigh tops. She brought the birch down straight from above, then gave swingeing thrashes from each side, or full under the flogged bottom. As her beating progressed, and her bare bum gleamed mottled and puffy, Emma's gasps and panting grew more piteous. Each stroke slammed her bare thighs against the restraining straps, which cut into her flesh. Her bottom turned rapidly to dark red, and at the softer edges it was purpling cruelly by the eighth stroke. Four more awful cuts completed her punishment; the girl's puffy, wealed bum-globes and her whole body were shaking horribly.

Miss Grant sighed in satisfaction, her own breath no less rapid than her victim's, and produced a pen. With shaking hand she wrote on the lower portion of Emma's buttocks, as a painter would sign his work. She read out the day, date, number of strokes and offence, signed with a flourish, and stepped back satisfied. Then she looked round, her flushed face signalling a desire for approval.

Her eyes fixed on my cock, and my cock alone! Forgetful of the painful *corniche*, my organ had been so enthralled by the beauty of that birching that she had strained and risen almost fully. Miss Grant gasped and pointed.

'An – an outrage!' she stuttered. 'Who is in charge – responsible for this scum?'

There was a deathly hush; not one girl dared to turn and peek, cowed as they were by that sensuous artful birch.

Fitzhurst swallowed nervously.

'It is I, Miss Grant.'

'Fitzhurst, eh?' sneered the mistress. 'Do you find your duty irksome? You have left your scum undisciplined.'

'O! I beg you! No, Miss.'

Miss Grant's sneer turned to a smug smile of triumph.

'You may deal with the scum at your discretion – but now it is *you* who must be disciplined, as a warning to my fillies, here, should they attain your rank. Lay down your rod of authority, Fitzhurst, remove your boots and coat, and present your body for punishment.'

Glowering bitterly, Fitzhurst gave her cane to Marpole and unbuttoned her leather greatcoat. It peeled from her body to reveal a basque corselet like Miss Bainbridge's, but lime green in colour. The frilly garment clung to her pert, conical titties and flat belly, and the superb muscles of her back, the frothy girlish confection at odds with that hard body but thus showing its full feminine power.

The trim, hard buttocks, swelling like apples, were almost entirely bared by the thin thong of the corselet. Beneath, the stockings revealed four inches of taut thigh muscle, and the swelling of a mink whose lustrous raven curls spilt over the edge of the green silk and dangled far down between her thighs. I clearly saw the forest extending over the slab of her belly, up to the deep whorled navel. She patted her hair and smoothed the basque over her thighs and buttocks, then stepped forward on stockinged feet, long and lithe as a panther's. She looked back at me and hissed: 'I'll have you for this, Philip Demesne.'

11

Product

The unfortunate Emma Porritt was permitted to replace her knickers, and after bowing to her punisher she shuffled painfully back to her seat, where she winced audibly on sitting down. Then Miss Grant nodded to Fitzhurst, who began her sullen progress up the aisle to the lectern and flogging block. Her words stung with their raw, powerful lust. To *have me*. I imagined a million delicious cruelties, and my cock throbbed, the *corniche* lacerating my glans as though Fitzhurst had already begun her vengeance.

Miss Grant observed me, and I saw her swallow; her eyelids fluttered and she pursed her lips, taking a deep breath as Fitzhurst presented herself and curtsied, her garter straps tightening to take the strain of her green stockings that swelled with thigh muscle. Miss Grant held up the remnants of her birch; a mere dozen to Emma's bum had quite denuded the ragged thing.

'This won't do,' she said, a malicious gleam in her eye. 'Fitzhurst, you will fetch another for your own bottom. Go to Miss Bainbridge's office and explain your mission. Beg her for the loan of her stoutest birch.'

'Coatless, Miss?' asked Fitzhurst bitterly.

'Quite so,' said the Scottish lady, her breasts swelling in satisfaction. 'You will go as you are – that will be part of your punishment, *filly*.'

I could see that this insult stung Fitzhurst more than any birch could. When she was gone, Emma Porritt put up her hand. She was shifting in obvious discomfort on her hard seat, and when allowed to speak she asked Miss Grant's permission to stand. The mistress glowered at her and barked that she was a cissy indeed.

'A mere dozen! Very well, filly. But you must lower your knickers again, hands clasped behind your back, and stand in the corner – on tiptoe – like a dunce.'

We were treated to the sight of the sobbing girl quivering tiptoed in the corner, with knickers down and skirts up, showing the welts of glowing bare arse-globes.

Fitzhurst returned shortly, bearing not a birch but the fearful rattan that had flogged me on my arrival in scum's cage. She curtsied to Miss Grant and said that Miss Bainbridge sent her best wishes, but had only one birch of sufficient strength to tan a prefect's bare bottom, and feared that Miss Grant's prowess at chastisement would render the instrument useless. She hoped that the rattan would suffice for the delicate task. Miss Grant took the thick rattan reverentially and stroked it like a pet. However she feigned displeasure.

'Will this do?' she cried, as though asking the class. '*Will* it? A birch is the finest tool for the flogging of a lady's bare – the rattan a poor thing, fit for brute scum and *robotniks*. However, we must make the best of things, eh, Fitzhurst? You may proceed to take position.'

Fitzhurst approached the block, pulling the corselet string tightly up into her furrow. Miss Grant frowned.

'That is not quite enough, I'm afraid. There is too much bottom flesh still covered, and I would not wish to damage that pretty green frilly with an errant stroke of my rattan. Take it off, if you please.'

'You wish to flog me naked, Miss?' gasped Fitzhurst.

'Quite naked.'

With a shrug, Fitzhurst doffed her frilly green slip, folded it neatly and placed it on Miss Grant's lectern. Then she knelt with studied nonchalance on the flogging block. Her body was a joy; unlike, say, Emma's, or Rowena's, her femininity expressed itself in the compact neatness of her form: every muscle and curve was sinewy and sculpted, like the body of a thoroughbred racehorse. Her pert breasts were hard as muscle, and her arse swelled quite massively under a pencil-thin waist. Most impressive was her pubic bush – I had never seen a mink so thick and lush, the hairs straggling far up her belly and dangling tousled in a clump beneath her gleaming moist gash-lips, which themselves were very thick and extruded.

Her lips twisted in a sneer, Fitzhurst fastened the leg straps herself, well tightened, then bent over and raised the huge globes of her bottom high in the air, spreading her thighs so that the clump of tousled mink-hair protruded like a woolly mitten. To my astonishment, her bum was not pale white but bore the flush of a recent flogging, and there was a scrawled signature on the lower left fesse. Miss Grant at once noticed this and bent to inspect, lifting her tortoiseshell glasses over her brow.

'Well! So you have been beaten recently, Fitzhurst? A naughty prefect indeed! And who did this to you? I cannot make out the signature, a very sloppy piece of work. The first letter seems to be "D" but the rest is a disgraceful scrawl – why, I'd like to cane whoever did this!'

Fitzhurst looked alarmed, then suddenly smiled slyly.

'Why, Miss Grant,' she said in feigned modesty, 'it was Milady Dushanka herself who caned me – a mere six, for her pleasure, not for any peccadillo I committed.'

Miss Grant hurriedly replaced her spectacles and paled. 'O!' she said. 'O – well, that will do. Milady Dushanka herself! My words were only in jest, of course.'

She composed herself, and there was a deathly hush in the classroom as she lifted the rattan over Fitzhurst's helpless naked buttocks. After her unwise outburst, Miss Grant now assumed her former icy fury, and her caning arm was stretched straight above her head.

'Dear me!' she said with malicious humour. 'I forget myself. There is the small matter of the number of strokes. Milady herself awarded six for no crime at all, so we had better warm your bottom with that, Fitzhurst.'

Suddenly the rattan flashed and whistled in the air and landed squarely in the centre of the girl's bare bum, at once streaking it a livid pink. Fitzhurst was taken unawares and cried 'Ahhh!', her arse shaking in pain. Miss Grant smiled thinly and followed the first stroke with a second on the very same place, and now the prefect's buttocks clenched tight and she wriggled against her straps, but she did not yelp, merely gasped deeply.

'Yes – I cane tightly, Fitzhurst. Feel free to moan or blub, if you like,' said Miss Grant in false pleasantry.

The third stroke took the naked girl slightly higher, on the tender skin at the tops of her nates, and the fourth likewise. Now Fitzhurst was gasping rhythmically and her eyes and lips were tightly shut. The last two of this 'warming' landed on the soft underside of the buttocks, nearly at her thighs, and I saw the clump of protruding mink-hair stir as the tip of the rattan caught it.

Fitzhurst's buttocks continued to writhe and clench even after this segment of the beating was complete, as though her deep weals had given the powerful bare fesses a life of their own. Breathing hard, Miss Grant paused. I could see large dark sweat patches under her arms, and the front of her blouse clung wetly to her black brassiere, which was an artful and frilly creation like Fitzhurst's corselet.

'Had enough, girl?' said Miss Grant hoarsely.

'N – no, Miss,' spat Fitzhurst through chattering teeth. 'I *beg* you, please give me a proper punishment.'

'And how many strokes would you, a prefect, award for such vileness?' asked Miss Grant, her voice calmer.

I, the cause of this vileness, seemed forgotten, even though my stiff cock must still have given offence.

'Why, I don't know, Miss,' said Fitzhurst drily.

'You don't know? A prefect who doesn't know? Will that do? I had better tell you, Miss. You shall take three dozen with the cane you have so kindly brought from Miss Bainbridge; when your punishment is finished, you shall return it to her after passing through school on your hands and knees, with your bare fesses raised, and the cane between your teeth. Do you agree to your punishment?'

Fitzhurst slapped her own bare bum as though impatient! Now her flogging began in earnest. She took another six heavy stingers quite rapidly, and thereafter

Miss Grant's pace slowed, though not the force of her cuts to the naked flesh. She took off her scholar's gown and delivered six more, raising her arm right above her head for every stroke and lashing the bare croup with a genuine fury. After this twelve, Miss Grant asked Fitzhurst if she felt comfortable.

'Quite comfortable, Miss,' sobbed the prefect, every muscle of her arched body tensed and straining.

'You do not cry out – that, fillies, is what makes a prefect – but I intend to cane you with my utmost force, Fitzhurst, so I won't take it amiss if you do.'

Fitzhurst's naked bum was puffy and livid after the eighteenth stroke, and her cheeks clenched in a frenzied rhythm of shuddering. The clenching of her bare wealed arse seemed a wave that sent ripples of agony shivering up her whole body. She rested her entire weight on the flogging block, her arms and head drooping like a broken doll and her proud back and buttocks quivering convulsively. Still there were eighteen stingers to come, and she refused to cry out. Miss Grant's face was red, her blouse soaked in sweat.

'You will excuse me, class,' she said faintly, and rapidly unbuttoned her blouse, shedding it and throwing it carelessly on top of her victim's neat frilly slip.

Now I saw her armpits tufted with thick glistening hair, her belly taut and heaving with the effort of the lash, and truly massive breasts artfully – perhaps painfully – restrained by the tightest of frilly black brassieres, exerting the pressure of a corset and making the succulent teat-flesh spill out over the straining cups.

Six more strokes followed. Miss Grant's skin sparkled with sweat, and she paused frequently to wipe her brow and under her tufted armpits. Still Fitzhurst's squirming bare body uttered no sound except for panting gasps of agony, and in the awed stillness of that classroom I sensed that a duel was taking place; the world seemed far away. Miss Grant wiped her body with her blouse, itself sopping, and said faintly that we were all ladies together, and a lady knew the value of comfort; she proceeded to unbutton the back of her skirt and shed it as rapidly as her blouse.

Smirking faintly, she stood before us wearing only her high shoes and fishnet stockings, the straining bra, frilly garter belt in the same design and panties that were the merest of thongs, showing her ripe, firm buttocks almost to the full, with the cheeks seeming to close like a robe over her tiny furrow-string. She had a small diamond-shaped tattoo right at the base of her spine, atop those swelling arse-globes, and it seemed to be in the shape of a diamond, though modestly obscured by the string; peering, I saw that it was a female vulva, depicted with painstaking clarity, with gash-lips parted, tunnel open and clitoris erect.

The cup of her panties was in the shape of a butterfly and clung sweat-drenched to her mound, showing almost all of her bare and shaven hillock, a cake of sweet white sugar that gleamed with her sweat-drops. Her shaven pubis was in impish denial of the unkempt tufts under her arms, or perhaps it was the other way round. Her stockings glistened with juices flowing from that little cunt-patch.

'Twelve more to go,' she gasped, and ran her palm over Fitzhurst's puffy bare bum. 'My, you are obstinate! This rattan should make the boldest filly whimper.'

For the last twelve, Miss Grant took the rattan with both hands, and made the dozen into one full set, delivered very rapidly with scarcely a pause between cuts. Fitzhurst's wealed buttocks clenched madly in and out like some tortured bellows; her thighs and the slabs of her back muscles tightened and shivered in the same rhythm. Still she would not please her chastiser with a squeal, though her breath came harshly in choking sobs. Both females seemed oblivious of their audience as these final slashing strokes cracked on the prefect's purpled bare.

Miss Grant's agitation grew feverish; she could not make her victim scream even under that pitiless thrashing. Yet as the flogging mistress gasped 'Thirty-six', Fitzhurst's body shook convulsively, and now she did cry out, long and high in staccato moans, and between her yelps she gasped: 'More, Miss – that won't do!'

'O! You hound!' cried Miss Grant, and recommenced caning the girl's frantically squirming bare bum.

She was oblivious to our gaze; without shame, her free hand touched the butterfly at her crotch, pushing it aside and openly rubbing the alabaster hillock of her shaven fount. Then her fingers delved to swollen red cunt-lips, and pushed inside the wet gash, while an artful thumb diddled the clitty that trembled atop her cunt-folds.

'O! O! Will this do? There!' she cried, and her bare belly shuddered, and a hissing golden stream suddenly cascaded down her stockinged thighs and calves, wetting her shiny shoes before forming a yellow puddle on the floor.

Then she, too, cried 'O! O!' in loud yelps, and her caning arm faltered. The fingers at her fount, and inside her gash itself, grew to a blur, and she trembled, knees buckling as she dropped the cane. In the distance a bell clanged, signalling the end of the lesson. Emma Porritt, who had peeked all the time at the beating, was herself quite red in the face, and as she drew on her knickers they immediately stained dark wet at her crotch.

Both flagellant and offender returned almost at once to scholarly decorum. Still in underthings, Miss Grant signed Fitzhurst's still-quivering bottom with a flourish of her pen. Then she told us we could go, my offensive cock seeming quite forgotten. Fitzhurst, face as flushed as her welted bottom, unfastened her bound legs, revealing deep strap-weals, then rose groaning to her feet, and gravely curtsied to her chastiser.

'I expect you wish to go to the infirmary, Fitzhurst. You took extra strokes, so I shall excuse you from returning the cane to Miss Bainbridge, and you may leave your scum in the charge of Marpole.'

'Thank you, Miss, but that won't be necessary,' said Fitzhurst, her eye fixing its menacing gleam on my person. 'First, I have to teach the scum some manners.'

As she donned her basque, she slapped her raw buttocks through the green cloth as though careless of her welts. Then she stepped close to her tormentor, who was still cased in tight underthings and trembling at Fitzhurst's intimate gaze. Coolly, the prefect reached behind Miss Grant's back, tweaked the string of her panties, and drew it back to reveal her vivid cunt-tattoo in its entirety, and with a loud 'ping' let the rubber smack on the mistress's bared buttocks. Smirking, Fitzhurst swaggered back to us with a sensuous roll of her flogged bum.

The girls filed dutifully out, as though from a perfectly normal Latin lesson, but Emma Porritt was told to stay behind. Fitzhurst belted herself in her leather coat, patting it snugly over her rump, and marshalled us with sharp canestrokes out of the classroom and towards the outside door of the building. From Miss Grant's room I heard a commotion and glanced back, ignoring Fitzhurst's bark of 'eyes front'.

Through the misted glass panel, I saw Miss Grant. She was still in her underthings, except that her massive breasts had escaped from their restraining cups and poked over the flogging block like ice-creams, topped with the huge, stiff cherries of her nipples. Her bum was bare and her thong panties strung between her thighs, and baby-blue knickers were wadded in her gaping mouth. Her naked fesses already quivered pink and puffy under the rattan wielded by Emma Porritt.

'Will this do, Miss?' trilled Porritt, lashing her on the bare arse, then smartly across the nipples.

Miss Grant raised her head from her squashed teats and nodded quickly, raising her buttocks to greet the cane.

'Mmm!' cried the flogged mistress through her gag.

On leaving Miss Grant's classroom, we scum were paraded around the academy, as much to shame us before the giggling schoolgirls as to show us the workings of the establishment. Our 'training' was subtle, in the guise of humiliation. We went outside, into grounds as spacious as the vast Siberian plain allowed, and I glimpsed the reason for the bizarre isolation of this English college so far from home. Masterdale *was* home, the harsh comfort of her discipline a protection from the loneliness of the snowy wastes. Exile from the academy was terror.

The academy itself proved a veritable warren of alleyways and passages, more like a town than an educational establishment, and with intimate knots of uniformed females busy in their nests, as though the whole place huddled in on itself for comfort against the desolation outside.

But these obedient schoolgirls, pretty in their neat uniforms, were also hardy warriors, accustomed to long treks through the freezing wilderness in search of booty and 'recruits' – human prey like myself, for enslavement and training in female virtue. This was not the soppy 'virtue' of our European civilisation but the ancient Roman 'virtus' – meaning prowess, merciless strength and unquestioning obedience.

We saw the life that awaited us on our acceptance as slaves, or fillies, and always we were whipped through the scenes of education, unable to ask questions or do anything except smart under the prefects' lashes and the schoolgirls' jeers. Yet the lot of these carefree fillies – who had all been new scum once – was scarcely less onerous than ours, as the harsh discipline meted to Emma Porritt had proved.

There were male slaves, or *robotniks*, and, to my surprise, among the twisting lanes and turrets of the village that seemed to grow around the towers of Masterdale, there was a race of female slaves too, called serfs, and lower than the fillies they served, though still higher than any male. There were intriguing skeins of servile relationship: a filly might 'have' a slave or a serf, and the serf in her turn 'have' a pet *robotnik*.

Later I learnt how rewards and loyalties were distributed. Prefects ruled with cane and whip over these lower classes, and the monitors – mistresses were monitors who chose to give lessons – ruled over all. Except for the curious interlude between Fitzhurst and Miss Grant, which made me suspect that bonds of rank might be loosened by strange affections; I was reminded of my parting from my adored Countess Galena and her willing screams under her slave Paul's whipping.

The cottages that nestled in the twisting lanes all seemed to be workplaces. There was a forge, ringing with the sound of hammers, and white fires glowing as smudged fillies clad in heavy leather jerkins and trousers made tools and shoes for ponies, and worked on intricate iron devices of loops and clamps and brackets, whose purpose I could only guess with a shudder. Here, the male slaves served only to carry the heavy metal and hot coals, while the females were in charge of the craftwork.

One male dropped his load, hurting a female's bare foot. His punishment was severe: he knelt before the furnace and presented his naked bum high, with thighs spread, and his bare nates were flogged with a length of iron, like a crowbar, which had only minutes before been glowing red hot. His squirming and gasps of anguish made me shudder. He took thirty strokes before the iron was plunged hissing into cold water, and his bum was livid with welts. Yet he kissed his chastiser's feet and proudly returned to his duties.

It was the same in the adjoining cottage, served by the same furnace, where the goldsmiths did their work. Gold, annexed no doubt from the unwilling travellers on the Trans-Siberian, was melted down and fashioned into new jewellery, or else clumped into glowing ingots for storage in unseen vaults. Haralda's gold, so innocently concealed in her (not so innocent!) anus, was among those pieces. The craftsfillies here wore supple suits of heavy rubber, permitting more intricate work than the blacksmiths, and their heads were shielded from hot spurts by masks of glass and rubber, giving them the aspect of deep-sea divers.

Yet the sensuous moulding of their breasts and bottoms made them more like mermaids, and the obscuring of their faces behind the misty glass of their helmets gave them an other-worldly and spiritual beauty, as though the mask hid the individual face and only the ripeness of the body suggested the female beneath the rubber coating.

One or two of the goldsmiths worked completely nude, like the *robotniks*, apart from face masks – in punishment for slacking – and shuddered whenever a hot droplet of molten gold spattered on to their naked breast or belly. But they did not yelp. Sometimes they winced as the gold hardened, adorning nipple or even bellybutton with bright fire before they were obliged to give up the fragment.

There were greenhouses, where *robotniks* laboured naked in the heat, tending plantations of tomatoes, lettuce and other healthful produce. Their faces were red and sweating, and they scratched their bare bodies under the raids of numerous insects; their female supervisors wore cool protective robes of tight satin and were not slow to add whipmarks to the insect bites on the males' bare bums.

In the slaughterhouse, carcasses of elk, reindeer and other tundra beasts were chopped and filleted by females this time, the males again being used to haul the heavy cadavers. Here, both males and females were naked, despite the cold of the naturally refrigerated chamber, for their work made them sweat, the females grinning as they slashed and chopped and sliced with flourishes of gleaming steel.

Fitzhurst spoke to the monitor in charge, who wore a costume of wine-coloured rubber, and the monitor nodded. Our prefect then told us that since we had not eaten we might take our luncheon from the floor. All of us scum, males and females, were permitted to kneel, hands behind our backs, and forage with our lips for scraps of meat and offal which had fallen carelessly to the icy floor. My few mouthfuls of liver and heart consisted mostly of frozen greasy sawdust, and I could not chew in comfort under the insistent lash of the prefects' canes on my bare croup – I thought they singled me out in particular, though Denning's and Rowena's yelps made me not so sure. To finish, we were permitted a few mouthfuls of water from a trough.

'Thank you, Fitzhurst,' we chorused as she lashed us to our feet.

In the distance, naked slaves had broken the ice of a small lake and were diving in to return with fish between their chattering teeth. I saw that most of the slaves were male, but there were some naked female serfs among them, their mixed nudity strangely chaste in the democracy of blue chilled flesh and the whip that warmed the buttocks of a serf or *robotnik* who emerged gasping but fishless.

Beyond the lake was an oval of ground cut into lanes, which Fitzhurst said tersely was the racetrack and sports ground. Beside it, we saw the marshalling yard, at the academy's perimeter, where ponies stamped and steamed, departing on expeditions with a few fur-clad fillies under the control of a monitor, or else arriving exhausted with their cargo of meat or booty. I did not see any human captive among the foraging expeditions, as Fitzhurst quaintly called them, and realised that to be taken prisoner by the academy was a great privilege, for male or female.

'I have served in all these places, as a mere filly,' Fitzhurst intoned proudly. 'You see, scum? All of us serve the greater purpose. The product is all.'

She nodded towards two squat adjoining buildings standing isolated just beyond the marshalling yard.

'The infirmary and the punishment block,' she said softly, licking her lips. 'Necessary parts of the whole.'

Then she gestured towards the great central hall, or kremlin as she called it, whither the prepared viands and foods and metal goods were dutifully transported on wealed male backs. The gateway to the central courtyard was open, and the centrepiece of the yard was a massive flogging frame built round a central post, like a pillory. I could see that a whipping was in progress.

A filly, naked but for a thin waspie around her pinched waist, was suspended between the outer posts of the flogging frame, which were rather like football goalposts, and her arms and legs were weighed down with heavy shackles, so were stretched to their fullest and most painful extent in an X-shape. Her fount and belly were pressed hard against the central pillory and strapped tightly; unseen, but as I learnt later, twin massive dildos of gnarled wood, protruding from the pillory shaft, would have been embedded in her cunt and bumhole.

Two monitors, clad in corselets of shiny black rubber and wearing executioners' hoods of the same, flogged her bare body, one attending to the buttocks, the other to the shoulders. Even from this distance I could see every ripple of her flogged muscle, every twitch of her creamy white skin and every line traced by the whips on her body, delicate as some antique etching.

The girl was well striped and her flesh wealed; she wriggled like a fish, and against the background of stillness and vast snow her squirmings seemed of no more importance than a fish's. The thin and useless modesty of her pinching corset gave an unbearable poignancy to the scene. A flock of scavenging birds hovered high overhead in the grey sky, placidly flapping their wings. Her pain amid such desolate beauty was beautiful in itself, and as I stared at the naked woman under the whips of two cruel dark mistresses my penis stirred in lustful sympathy, or envy.

'The final *product*,' emphasised Fitzhurst. 'Milady Dushanka says that Masterdale is communism in action – isn't that a lark? After her final chastisement and adornment, the filly will leave Masterdale proud and serene, that most superb of all creatures – an English lady!'

Then she turned and saw the stiff trembling of my cock. My *corniche* began to pain me, but I was powerless to stop my excitement at the flogging. Fitzhurst's nostrils flared, her eyes widened and her face paled in fury, as though she chided herself for having neglected my correction.

'You filth,' she hissed. 'Not content with your vileness in Miss Grant's class, you dare to insult me here in public view! Belly on the ground, worm, to hide that shame.'

Her cane prodded my balls very sharply, dragging on my bonds I lay belly down on the frozen rutted earth. She ordered Denning and Crocker to hold me down by my wrists and ankles, and, enthusiastically, they splayed me hard. I heard the slither of her cat-o'-nine tails being unclasped from her belt and tensed myself for the lash.

There was a hiss of leather, a hard whistling, and I jumped as my bare buttocks were seared with a dozen tongues of fire. How abject the receiver of a just flogging! Every lashing feels the worst ever – under cane, he longs for the female embrace of birch, under birch, for the manly force of the cat, under cat, for the brisk simplicity of cane. In truth, the cane, though vicious, enables one to localise the pain of each stroke. If it takes the lower end of the buttocks, one tries to feel from the upper; if the cut lands square in the fleshy arse centre, one tries to feel from the extremities. With the cat there is no escape.

Every inch of bum-skin is flayed at once, and all I could do on that freezing earth was wriggle and jerk and slam my shameful cock against the frozen splinters of rock that lacerated my belly as cruelly as Fitzhurst's cat seared my fesses. I took twenty strokes in rapid and furious succession; it was agony, and I thought I could not bear it. Yet I was bound by the shackles to my fellow scum and held by strong arms. The scavenger birds had drifted towards us, circling my body convulsed in pain.

After twenty, there was a pause – I thought my wealing complete and looked up, tears streaming on my face. Fitzhurst leered savagely at me.

'It is time for the ladies to take comfort,' she snarled, nodding to Rowena Tushingham, Arkwright and Haralda – who grinned at me with an impish glint in her eye, and a face flushed with glee at the sight of my bare welted bottom. The males held me tighter than ever; the three females squatted over me, crooking their thighs, and three golden jets of steaming fluid arched across my back and buttocks. I sobbed in my disgrace, as I felt the hot stream of Haralda's piss soak my face and neck! The girls giggled as they made water, increasing the beauty of my shame, and vied with each other to direct their fierce hot jets into my bum's welts and ridges from the cat.

'Scum! Scum! Pee on the scum!' they trilled.

At length the girls' piss was exhausted, and I heard Fitzhurst lift her whip again. Maddened with pain and shame, I scarcely cared as the thongs bit once more into my bum-welts soaking in cooling piss, the strokes of the cat all the more painful on bare wet skin. The girls continued to giggle, and I heard chuckles from the two louts against whose grip my wrists and ankles jolted in vain.

'Pee on the scum! Whip his bum!' cried the girls, giggling, and Haralda's voice the loudest.

My belly writhed, scratching my cock and balls on the jagged icy ground, and locked in this shame – aware of the eyes of the whole community and of the music of

161

schoolgirls' laughter – I took twenty more from Fitzhurst's skilful cat.

At length the beating stopped. I was scalded by my agony and scarcely felt the prefect's cool fingers begin to stroke my bare buttocks flogged raw.

'You poor scum,' soothed Fitzhurst. 'You can't take it, can you, silly boy? I'll take you to the infirmary and make sure the nurses take care of you properly.'

She ordered Marpole to take charge of the other scum; I was released and helped to unsteady feet. Fitzhurst's eyes gleamed, her lithe panther's body tense with excitement.

'It's all right, Miss Fitzhurst,' I sobbed. 'Begging your pardon, but I've taken worse. I'll manage.'

Fitzhurst's eyes widened and she smiled happily.

'The infirmary, Philip,' she said. 'I insist.'

12

Smoking Zone

I found myself in a cheerful antechamber decked with flowers, whose perfume did not quite conceal the antiseptic infirmary scent. All that distinguished it from an ordinary reception room were the walls: they were of sheet rubber, cream in colour, and so was the door.

'My, you *are* a sight,' exclaimed its occupant, a spectacularly tall lady dressed in a spotless white matron's smock, with a pretty bobbed cap and very handsome, if discordant, fishnet stockings peeping below her starched pinafore. She wore a pretty bundle of birch twigs suspended from a tight white belt that girdled her hourglass waist and had high spiked heels on black boots.

I estimated her age at twenty-five or twenty-six. Her face was as handsome as her stockinged legs, broad-lipped and dominated by piercing blue eyes and high, strong cheekbones, and framed by a lush mane of corn-blonde hair quaintly arrayed as two large pigtails with pink ribbons.

I say she was tall – I could not remember seeing a lady so tall. She must have stood over six feet. Her body was trim and lithe in proportion to her height, so that her figure swelling beneath the decorous matron's robe comprised a bottom and breasts that were beyond ample: in perfect harmony with her strong frame and muscled legs, so long and powerful they seemed like pistons stretching almost to her teats. I have learnt that ladies buy their underthings and measure their bosoms in inches – her breasts must, I reckoned, have extended to forty-six or even forty-eight. And the panties to girdle the massive globes of her peach must have raised many an envious salesgirl's eyebrow.

Fitzhurst curtsied. The lady put down the document she was studying and rose from her position sitting sideways on her desktop, smoothing down her skirt and thick layered flounces of a black petticoat as she did so.

'Another new scum you've had at, eh, Fitzhurst?' she said brightly. 'My, you do thrash 'em tight.'

'It is all they deserve, Matron,' pouted Fitzhurst.

'That's the ticket! Philip Demesne, eh?' said Matron, glancing again at her document.

She cast a practised eye over my wounded bottom, and I felt her cool fingers appraising my weals.

'Not beyond redemption, I warrant,' she said, her accent similar to Miss Bainbridge's but betraying a foreign lilt in the vowels, and otherwise perfect, as only a foreigner's studied English can be. 'But then, no male is. Horrid tough buggers the lot, and this one an Englishman to boot. You can flog an English boy until his bum's a pineapple, and he won't squeak. Will he, Philip?'

With that, she playfully goosed me! She poked a forefinger right into my furrow and flicked it against my bumhole. I was too astounded to reply, and allowed myself to be led through the swing doors into an examination room.

This small chamber was more surgical in nature, with an array of jars, tubes and syringes, and with cream rubber walls. The floor, too, was of cream rubber. There was an operating-table in the centre, a hot stove, and a large pumping-machine of some sort. I was ordered to stand still; Matron knelt and, humming a tune, stripped off my rubber costume and unfastened my *corniche* and chain. She took the helmet of my cock between thumb and forefinger and squeezed it hard on the weal left by the *corniche*, at the same time rubbing my peehole and the top of my glans.

'My, what a big one!' she trilled. 'It's quite the biggest pudding I've ever seen! And the glans quite untried! I dare say there will be some filly-fights over *this robotnik*. Does she harden well and often?'

This last remark was addressed to Fitzhurst, who said that my vileness was the cause of my thrashing, and Matron replied merrily that her nurses would soon teach the young lady to behave – meaning my cock, referred to with playful scorn as female. I feared knowing what a virgin glans was.

Stark-naked I was ordered to hop on to the operating-table and to lie face down with my bum 'on parade'. I protested feebly that I was all right and fit to return to my duties, then yelped as Matron's little birch suddenly flicked from her waist and lashed me hard on the bare.

'One extra, you silly boy!' she laughed. 'And plenty more if you are cheeky again. Now be still while I get you cleaned up, and then we can park you in the chamber of horrors for an hour or two.'

She laughed again, gesturing to the swing doors marked WARD 2, from which muted murmurs filtered. I felt swabs and cloths rinsing me and applying soothing ointments to my inflamed buttocks, and gradually my pain ebbed. I saw Fitzhurst idly inspecting the procedure, and to my surprise she withdrew a packet of cigarettes from her greatcoat pocket, lit two, and passed one to Matron, who took it between her lips and sucked heartily. Then Matron began to busy herself with the pumping-machine, which emitted gurgling noises. During this, Fitzhurst nonchalantly spread my buttocks and placed the tip of her cigarette in my anus! Shocked, I quivered as Matron, now with rubber gloves, wheeled her machine towards me and laughed.

'*Ach! Prima!*' she cried, and slapped her thigh with a shiny rubber-gloved hand.

I trembled, feeling the hot tip of the fumable approaching my tender bumhole, my confidence in Matron's medical robe suddenly dissolving as I was reminded of my lowly status as scum and of powerful ladies' infinite love of mockery. The burning began to be painful, when suddenly Fitzhurst retrieved her cigarette, tapping a finger of ash on my back. Matron's rubbered fingers began to grease my bumhole with oil, kneading my

165

buttocks and furrow very hard so that I was obliged to spread and relax the orifice. I felt cool rubber as one finger delved inside, and then another; with two fingers in my bumhole, she plunged steadily towards my root, until I groaned and squirmed at the pressure of this harsh greasing. Matron sniffed.

'He's been golden-showered, I take it?' she said.

'Of course, Ma'am,' said Fitzhurst. 'During punishment, by the female scum.'

'Capital,' cried Matron. 'Teach 'em manners, eh?'

She withdrew her fingers abruptly, causing a discomfort that was sweet and shamefully pleasurable. Grimacing, I looked round and saw Matron unbutton her starched tunic.

'Have to dress for the fray, eh, Fitzhurst?' she said. 'Plenty of splishes and sploshes in hospital work. Better stand back if you want to keep your coat on.'

'Mayn't *I* disrobe, Miss Hochhuth?' pouted Fitzhurst.

'Thought you'd never ask!' said Matron gaily.

Fitzhurst sloughed off her greatcoat and stood once more in her green basque, bare bum glowing proudly with the marks of her recent flogging. Matron paused in her own disrobing and whistled. 'Who ever gave you that whopping?' she asked.

'Why, Miss Grant, Matron,' said Fitzhurst smugly.

Matron nodded and smiled impishly. 'I had Miss Grant in here only the other day,' she mused, then coyly told Fitzhurst that her welts became her, and that she was awfully pretty of bum.

Then the white medical robe fell from her body. Her petticoat was frills of black rubber, layered with thin petals like a mille-feuille pastry; above it her arms were bare, and her torso totally encased in a tight black-rubber singlet tightly stretched over her teats, and revealing a cluster of rings fastened to each huge and clearly outlined nipple. The proud, massive titties seemed to jut unsupported by anything except the tight latex, and the magnificent V of her back and shoulders rippled like a leopard's down to her narrow waist, her body pausing there as though with a wink before the sudden swell of the peach.

With a flourish, she unfastened her petticoats and stood in studded calf-boots and fishnet stockings; the rubber garment was a basque-like corselet, covering her pubis but cut very high, and had garter straps to which the stockings were affixed. I saw that the intricate fishnet, too, was made of strands of latex rubber. And at the massive hillock of her fount – the smoothness of the rubber coating indicating complete depilation – I saw a cluster of rings at her cunt-lips to match those at her nipples. Her thighs rippled against the stockings like a stallion's eager for the race, and her breasts perked and thrust at each breath.

Without pause, she picked up a long brown-rubber tube and stuck it deep into my bumhole, making me writhe in pain. She pushed and pushed until the cold rubber nuzzled my root, and then I shuddered and suppressed a squeal as I felt the cramp of icy fluid bloating my anal passage. I clung to the sides of the table trying not to wriggle.

'Will you take it like an Englishman?' said Matron.

'Or must we strap you?' added Fitzhurst.

'It is no more than being buggered,' Matron cooed. 'All English boys are buggered, not true?'

I was not out of Fitzhurst's clutches in this infirmary. And I gasped, for it *was* like being buggered, like the powerful dildos I had felt cleave my anus at cruel ladies' direction. Much as I feared that terrible filling, yet I craved it too. Feebly, I blurted out that I should take it like an Englishman. The pressure mounted in my bumhole, and I filled with the horrid smelly liquid until I sobbed with fear I should split – and that I *wanted* a lady to split my bum. At last the hideous pumping stopped, and I felt Matron withdraw the tube and cap my anus with a large painful plug to prevent the fluid from escaping.

'You'll hold it for one minute before evacuating,' she said nonchalantly, and for a whole minute I counted the seconds until she removed the plug.

My bumhole ached, worse, I thought, than under any caning. Yet as the seconds progressed, and my body warmed the invading douche, I began to relish my fullness, as though I were indeed buggered by Matron's cruel tube.

At last she ordered me to the open commode, and I lurched to my feet and squatted to make my evacuation in full view of the two ladies, who were smiling at me and holding hands as though at a fête or circus. I gasped with blissful relief as I felt the fluid hiss into the can and gasped once more as I was ordered back on to the table for the process of 'lavage' to be repeated, this time with hot fluid and with a holding time of two minutes.

Matron nonchalantly lifted her birch, saying nothing. I took another dozen on bare, very tight. The ladies giggled.

My third lavage was almost scalding, and I was obliged to 'hold for three'. I took another round dozen with Matron's birch, the strokes irregular and teasing. I squirmed, my clenching bum as uncontrollable as my sobs. Fitzhurst placed herself mockingly by my face so that I had a close view of her scarred fesses. She mocked, but her scorn excited me, as did her weals and soft, puffed flesh. I discerned Miss Grant's neat signature, and the other, messy one, which her pen had not quite obliterated. I looked up and smiled at Fitzhurst, but she was smoking another cigarette and waggled her buttocks in scorn, her hand stroking Matron's rubber crotch as she beat my buttocks.

Suddenly she accused me, quite justly, of peeking.

'The wicked scum!' she cried in mock outrage. 'May *I*, Miss Hochhuth?'

Matron had her birch ready, and with a broad grin handed it to the prefect, who under laughing medical eyes proceeded to lash my wealed buttocks with a further dozen stingers from that tight snaky birch. The effort of keeping the fluid inside my anus while the birch twigs danced on my fesses was almost too much for me, and as I writhed and sobbed a squeal escaped my lips. Matron clapped her hands.

'O, the rotter!' she cried, and suddenly hoisted herself on to the table to sit on my face.

My head was turned sideways, and I felt myself pinioned in darkness by rubber-clad thighs that clamped me and almost stopped me breathing with their muscled power.

She put her whole massive weight on me; I smelt the ripe aroma of her womanhood mingling with the scent of rubber and felt my face wet as a tiny trickle of warm oily fluid seeped from the thin rubber cunt-string. Her thighs clamping me, Matron writhed enthusiastically on my face as though I were a Tunguska pony for the taming. Through the rubber, I felt the stiff nubbin of her clitty rubbing rhythmically on my scalp; her cunt-juices flowed faster.

'O, the naughty boy!' she murmured. '*Der Hund!*'

At long last I evacuated, now enjoying the slithery spurt as the fluid rinsed and cleansed my aching bumhole. I foolishly stole a glance at Fitzhurst's blossomed bum and the signatures adorning her. She saw me and understood. *I knew her secret.* Her face paled, and she hissed to Matron that this scum deserved special treatment.

'Let's have some fun before we bandage him,' she cried. 'Teach him to *keep his mouth shut.*'

'Super idea,' gasped Matron, rubbing her wet crotch.

'His back is bare of flogging,' said Fitzhurst.

'And his glans,' said Matron. 'I cannot stand a male with an untried helmet.'

'Splints. I have some my sister sent from Germany.'

'Then put him in the tank with the flogged bitch – the one to be bangled.'

They both laughed lustfully, then stopped, gazed into each other's eyes, and embraced. They kissed full on the lips, and their hands stole across their bellies to each other's crotch, where each lady frotted gently.

'You're wet, Fitzhurst.'

'And you –'

'Naughty prefect.'

I thought and hoped they had forgotten me, but Fitzhurst said she had to pee and spat at me 'just wait for it', as though my presence on commode was a further crime. She stood above me and pushed the thong of her corselet aside, revealing her cunt-mound contemptuous in its nudity. A thick golden stream of piss emerged from her swollen red cunt-lips and spattered my face and breast.

Matron clapped her hands and laughed, saying '*Ach! Ja!*'
And when Fitzhurst had finished my humiliation, Matron
suddenly knelt and licked her dripping fount dry. She
clutched Fitzhurst's bared buttocks, kneading them as she
had kneaded my own, and her mouth chewing the naked
gash-lips like the sweetest food.

I was pulled to my feet, and they saw my own cock
trembling to stiffness at this lustful exhibition. Both ladies
agreed I should receive the most careful restraint.

'He is clearly dangerous,' said Matron with relish,
licking her lips, at the same time casually frotting her own
rubber-clad vulva and making little mewling noises.

'First, we must plug and clamp him,' said Fitzhurst.

I was ordered back on the operating-table, and, sniffling
abjectly, I obeyed. I lay on my back, my cock awkwardly
splayed across my belly, and Matron flicked my balls hard
with her birch. Fitzhurst, who seemed as familiar with the
surgery as Matron herself, fetched a metal appliance rather
like a scold's bridle; it had a huge shining dildo with a
circle of steel, and a round clamp at the end, evidently
designed to tighten round the balls of the male miscreant.

I braced myself, but my readiness did not lessen the pain
as the huge shaft of metal was plunged without ceremony
or lubrication into my arsehole still tender from her lavage.
While Matron did that, Fitzhurst had the ceinture around
my waist and the clamp firmly squeezed and fastened on
my scrotum. Both ladies pretended to be shocked by my
penis rigid under this shameful constraint.

Then, slowly and with relish of my fear, they tightly
wrapped a thick roll of gauze around my whole body from
neck down, and fastened it with pins that stung me,
omitting my genitals and buttocks which were left bare. The
gauze itched my weals abominably, but worse was to come:
another roll was produced, this one of thick rubber, and the
wrapping was repeated, adding inches to my girth and
making me sweat in the hot chamber. Again, my cock and
buttocks were left bare, but now the wrapping enveloped
my whole head, leaving only slits for eyes and mouth. I was
cased like an Egyptian mummy in stern black rubber.

The two women paused to kiss and frot each other in my full view, and despite my discomfort my cock rose at the sight. Fitzhurst removed her fingers from Matron's wet cunt and put them in her mouth, licking the fluid, then scornfully wiping the residue on my balls; Matron did the same to the giggling Fitzhurst, until my balls were sticky and oily, as uncomfortable as my trussed skin.

Matron said that my glans was untried and must bear duelling scars like a proper slave's. I shuddered, recalling the German officer in Countess Galena's carriage, and longed for the Countess herself to be present, to witness my humiliance with her cruel, sweet laughter.

Fitzhurst said the worm must be properly strapped, for he would whine and blub and couldn't take it like a man. I did not protest as my wrists and ankles were locked in metal cuffs – emblazoned with an eagle – at the sides of the operating-table, and also a steel cincher was compressed painfully around my waist. I could not move.

Matron fetched another metal device, an open cylinder with pins at its side, which she slid over my throbbing cock and rested on the platform of my constrained tight balls. Fitzhurst took hold of my prepuce and pulled it harshly all the way back, exposing my naked helmet. Those readers whose prepuce has been removed at birth may not know that the male foreskin has a tendency, if pulled back, to creep back to his rightful place.

It was to prevent this that Matron now fastened the edges of my prepuce with little clips, tightened on wires to my ball-clamp. This hurt me and I bit my lip, but my eyes widened as I saw Matron remove from her belt-pouch a little whip – a miniature flail of shiny piano wire, about seven or eight inches long. The wires were studded along their length with tiny weights that gleamed dully like heavy lead, and larger ones at the tips. She lifted this little quirt over my erect penis and stroked my naked bulb. I shuddered, for the quirt was heavy. Then she lifted her arm to her shoulder and smiled at me.

'A dozen each, Fitzhurst. Turn about!' she said. 'First one to make him squeal is the winner.'

She lashed my naked glans hard, and my rubber-trapped body jerked in the utter misery of my pain. The glans, tender to the caress of soft cunt, can, like buttock-flesh, taste pleasure curdled to harshest agony. I gasped at each stroke of that wicked flail, looking down to see the pink of my glans turn dark red, then puffy puce, under those agonising whipstrokes. After a dozen the quirt was passed to Fitzhurst, whose stroke was even harder, and, as she watched, Matron masturbated openly at my agony.

They lashed me in turns until I was delirious with pain, and through glazed eyes I saw each lady frot her clitty and cunt-lips quite openly, with thighs churning and thrust lasciviously forward, as the other flogged me. It was Matron who dealt the final blow: complaining that my gasps and squirms did not constitute a cry, she brought the quirt down squarely on my peehole itself.

I screamed. Matron dropped her quirt, and the two ladies embraced again, gurgling with cheerful pleasure and masturbating each other's wet slit the few strokes to moaning orgasm as I lay writhing in my rubber bondage and straining hopelessly against my thongs. My penis bulb was puffy with tiny welts and mottled dark purple.

Yet still I stood throbbing and erect, with honey longing to spurt from my trussed balls, at the splendour of my wretched humiliance and the ladies' superb cruelty. That a nurse, tender and caring, should show such cruelty towards the male was a delight undreamt of.

'I win!' cried Matron happily. 'The brute squealed!'

At once, she began to strip herself of her rubber corselet. First the garter straps were unfastened, so that the fishnet stockings flopped on her thighs but stayed sluttishly in place. Then she peeled the garment away from her teats. The naked breasts stood proud and trembling like giant flans; pierced right through the wide pink cupolas of her erect nipples were three jangling silver rings for each breast. The rings were soldered in place and could not be removed, and the holes in her nipples gaped large, leaving room for more rings. The rubber stroked her belly and her thighs, and was kicked to the floor to show a shaven mound big as a ripe fruit, with three identical rings pierced through the cunt-flaps. They, too, were welded in place, and the holes in the lips left room for more rings.

Matron sank to her knees with her face on the rubber floor, while Fitzhurst assumed a massive strap-on triple dildo. She pushed aside the thong of her corselet and inserted one prong into her wet cunt, then strapped on the waistband and manoeuvred the two other prongs against Matron's spread pink furrow, where her crinkly arse-bud shone wet from her juices.

First, she lit two cigarettes and poked them into both Matron's holes, ordering her to smoke! Matron sucked and puffed smoke with cunt and anus, down to the embers, which the laughing Fitzhurst knocked aside; the two prongs penetrated her holes at the same time and sank deep into the sopping slits, provoking a moan of satisfaction and a vigorous clenching of the bum. Her arse-globes began to buck even before Fitzhurst's haunches thrust, and both ladies had streams of cunt-juice visibly flowing on bare skin and rumpled slut's stockings.

Groaning and sweating, Fitzhurst composed herslf enough to grasp Matron's birch and vigorously apply it, first to the flanks of her heaving bare fesses and then, after striping her deeply to a couple of dozen, she transferred the flogging to Matron's rippling shoulder muscles, which seemed to stiffen and bristle under the birch's caress.

The birch is normally for bare bottom, and I found this a novel and exquisite approach, for the lash on bare back made a harsher crackle than on fesse-meat. Matron's shoulders wealed very quickly with livid pink stripes, and I saw why her rubber costume covered her back.

Matron lifted one arm from the floor and began to masturbate, frigging her clitty as the dildos punctured her arse and slit, and sending lovely shiny rivulets of juice from her swollen cunt. She groaned and sighed, and suddenly could not contain herself; alongside the pool of quim-oil on the rubber floor appeared a golden lake of steaming piss.

'You *would*, would you?' cried Fitzhurst. 'Lucky you haven't a male to flog you!'

'Don't be dirty!' gasped Matron.

Fitzhurst flogged her back all the harder, and her own replenished vessel emptied anew, as she showered heartily over the deep weals of Matron's bare buttocks. Her hot piss sank into the furrowed birch-welts, trickling over the bum's flesh like streams down a hillside and into the recesses of the sloppy fishnet stockings, which were by now well soaked with piss and love-oil. Fitzhurst, too, was frotting her swollen clitty quite methodically, taking the stiff pink organ between thumb and forefinger and tweaking it like the ear of a miscreant schoolboy.

I was hypnotised in submission. My cock stood throbbing and my balls ached to spurt, but my constraint forbade me. My bondage now seemed a caress, and the embrace of these vicious females before my eyes a delicious insult.

'Miss Grant, eh?' gasped Matron, shrill as though her spend was coming. 'O! I'll have words with that patient. O! O! I'll stripe her arse well for her cheek.'

'You don't own me, Miss Hochhuth,' spat Fitzhurst, swivelling her hips to spray the last drops of piss over the small of Matron's squirming back. 'And what about *la* Bainbridge? *She* feigns abstinence from cane's pleasures.'

'Every wench is my patient: serf, filly, monitor or praetorian guard. O – you've no more gold for me?' wailed Matron. 'O, Fitzhurst, flog me harder, I command you. O! I shall come, I shall spend, my cunt is so wet under your cruel lash! O! O! Please, do my bum again – she's nice and wet from your piss – the birch will hurt horribly. Ahh!'

Fitzhurst obliged by renewing her assault on Matron's wealed, wriggling bum, and Matron cried out in the first throes of her spend.

'*Ach* – I'm coming! Faster! Harder! O, flog me raw, you sweet bitch! Flog my bare, whip me to bone! O! *Ja! Ja!*'

I saw that her words excited Fitzhurst, for she, too, increased the pace of her masturbation. Her belly quaked and heaved under its tousled green corselet, and she cried out in a spend, the lashing of the birch twigs slowing to a faltering crackle until I saw that the instrument was almost denuded.

Their lusts were not sated – dominant ladies' lusts rarely are. No sooner had each convulsed in her spend than both eyed my stiff cock. Matron leapt to her feet and tightened the clamp on my cock and balls, saying this would stop me spurting before my service was complete. No sooner was I clamped, my cock smarting and raw, than Matron clambered on top of me and nuzzled my flogged glans against her spread arse-pucker. She clutched her own flogged buttocks and sank down on me, crushing me with her weight, and I felt my cock sink into the tight channel of her bumhole right to her root, which seemed to clutch and squeeze my peehole with artful muscles.

The thrilling weight of a woman, her anus tight on cock, is sublime submission. Matron pirouetted on my penis, showing me her wealed peach, and I wondered if many females had flogged her: yes, but surely no males – quite unspeakable – and certainly not one who signed with 'D'.

13

Punishment Ward

As Matron's buttocks squirmed on my cock, squeezing and rubbing the stiff member with the elastic walls of her bum-tube, Fitzhurst climbed on to my sheathed head and lowered her bottom firmly on top of me, emulating Matron's dominance – called 'queening' – of minutes before. Fitzhurst's arse was firmer and bonier, but the weight of her intimate places squelching wet and agile on my face seemed just as heavy.

Droplets of her piss and flowing love-oil entered my mouth, and I swallowed the acrid mixture as I struggled to bear the weight of two writhing female bodies intent on my humiliance. Fitzhurst jackknifed forward and pushed her mouth to Matron's vulva, where I heard her greedily drink the cunt-juice from the gash with slurping gasps of pleasure as great as my own in drinking *her* secret fluids.

'O, Fitzhurst,' moaned Matron, the prefect's tonguing increasing her anal squeezes on my cock. 'O! You are the stronger! O, diddle me, sweet slut!'

Any submissive male, which is more of us than care to admit, will see that I was in a kind of paradise: my flogged bum raw with whip-welts, my whole body tightly and cruelly encased in rubber and bandages, strapped down and ravished by two heavy, strong females at once. Yet a small part of my mind discriminated. My introduction to slavery was at the hands of ripe women with lush manes: the Countess Galena, Haralda, Rowena Tushingham and now Matron herself, a more powerful and vivacious

176

version of my longed-for Haralda. I thought of my sweet Becky herself in faraway Essex.

Fitzhurst was bony, strong and mannish, her hair brutally cropped, her teats perky but small, like crab apples, and the massive buttocks – bigger than Matron's, and harder, like two lions' skulls under whipcord flesh – and long colt's legs seemed to be an afterthought, as though her body wished suddenly to remind her of her femininity. She was puzzling and ambiguous: I wondered if I should ever have a permanent mistress, and if she would be on the model of Matron, who was essentially soft and, I sensed, submissive to the harder female; or the hard female herself, like Fitzhurst. Yet here again was her puzzling side, that I knew she had taken cane from a male, an unthinkable impropriety in the female world of Masterdale.

And if she had taken cane, then I guessed buggery and gash-fuck as well – for where does one exist without the others? – from a male scum, from the brute Denning. I thought suddenly of Denning's cock inside her, buggering her anus and fucking her in cunt; his spunk washing her root as mine longed to do. I hated Denning all the more. Her juices cascaded over my lips as though she guessed my fury, and she tasted as sweet as the ocean.

Fitzhurst's voice growled, muffled by cunt-lips, that she must have her turn at the cock. Matron moaned again, and the ladies swapped places, my mouth and face now engulfed again by the massive quim-scented weight of Miss Hochhuth, my tongue lodged in her gash-rings. Now my cock entered a soft, wet velvet place, right to the sucking womb's neck, and I knew I was in the cunt of Fitzhurst.

Her thighs and buttocks pounded heavily on my loins, slamming and thrusting as her slit milked my cock – yet I could not spurt due to the cruel pressure of my cock-clamp. She swivelled round, and I felt the metal of my clamp rubbing her stiffened extruded clitty, diddling her as she fucked me. As she presented her spread bum-cheeks to Matron, I felt the blonde lean forward, her rigid nipples and teat-rings squashing against my belly.

177

Again, I sensed the difference between my two dominas. Matron was eager to please, both herself and her companion, while Fitzhurst wanted only to take and subdue: her pleasure a mere by-product of her delight in power.

'O yes, Matron! Your tongue in my bumhole! Lick me until I come!' Fitzhurst cried fiercely, knocking her stiff clit back and forth against my cock-ring as her gash drenched my cock in slimy love-oil.

The walls of her cunt squeezed my penis quite mercilessly, raw and brutal despite her copious lubrication, as though she wanted to punish rather than pleasure the organ of a male. I was dazed and insensate; many times these partners in lust swapped and came to orgasm as they used me in quim and anus. But sometime later my pounding stopped, with my cock raw and seeming to burst with the cream roused in my imprisoned balls.

I felt their eager hands bind me further, this time in wooden splints that were fastened to my arms and legs, and recalled those I had seen in Countess Galena's railway carriage, binding General Hochhuth. It could not be a coincidence; Miss Hochhuth, with her exclamations in German and her penchant for corporal chastisement, must be a scion of the German nursing clan.

I was hoisted to my feet and encouraged to walk, which I did with stiff, awkward clumping movements like a broken rubber puppet. Both ladies made lengthy commode, then made me lick them dry, and finally used my hands to wipe their bums and cunts. They made themselves decent once more, and with a flounce of her rubber mille-feuille petticoat Matron placed a crutch under my armpit. Like this I was able to hobble through the rubber swing doors into Ward 2.

The ward was much larger than the outside of the infirmary suggested. It was bright and airy and prettily adorned with flowers. There were a dozen or so cots in which fillies were strapped in various contrivances of straps, pulleys and plaster casts, and, sympathetic though I felt, it did not look like a chamber of horrors. Busy

178

nurses all in white, with starched cotton aprons over tight rubber skirts, with rubber boots and shiny rubber stockings, bustled brightly along the ranks, dispensing drinks or adjusting legs precariously raised in thick plaster casings.

Since the ward was so hot from the central stove, most of the patients were at their ease and lay with bosoms bared, or else completely nude except for their splints and plaster casts. A few unfortunates were bandaged and splinted over their whole body, like me, and their eyes met mine in brief sympathy. Above every bed was hung a neatly pressed schoolgirl's uniform of skirt, blouse, petticoat, panties and stockings, like docile pets awaiting their mistress's return. All the fillies had shaven legs, arms and founts, for hygienic medical reasons, I supposed, and in every case, whatever the bandaging, the crotch and buttocks were left bare, so that I saw many bums heavily bruised (the fillies lay on their bellies) yet not from whiplashes. I recognised a few of the ladies who had kidnapped me from the train and suppressed a vengeful smile.

There seemed to be no place for me. Besides, the ward was all female, and my captors led me towards its far end where another rubber door announced WARD 1. Matron said that *this* ward contained victims of sporting accidents: the sports ground I had glimpsed was used for races of various kinds and also for wrestling tournaments, which were held sometimes outdoors and sometimes indoors, at Mistress Dushanka's 'whipping feasts'. This was the second time I had heard this awesome phrase.

The most popular races were pony races, where a filly was harnessed and shod just like a pony and was obliged, solo or in pairs, to pull a jaunting cart around the track under the lash of a horsewhip wielded by their 'driver', who might be a prefect, another filly or even a monitor. The crowds for these contests got very excited and sometimes a small riot ensued between rival supporters, so that the praetorian guard intervened to restore order, with frequent injury. Fitzhurst explained rather sullenly that the guard was an elite group, selected by Mistress Dushanka herself, and very much a law unto themselves; even monitors curtsied to them, although not strictly obliged to.

A praetorian guard could administer corporal punishment to any resident of Masterdale save the Mistress herself, and on any pretext or even without one. It was well to keep on the right side of a guardsgirl. Their full dress uniform was a bloodcurdling suit of domina's armour, with leather jerkin, spikes and chains and steel caps for teats, knees and shoulders, and with spiked helmets and visors. However, the guards did not always choose to wear their uniform, and sometimes went nude with a whip worn in ceinture.

'In fact,' trilled Matron artlessly, 'sometimes we are not even sure who they are! But in Russia, you know, we are one big family.'

Fitzhurst was of more contented tone in informing me that the worst rioting and the worst injuries came from the wrestling tournaments, or the pony races of male *robotniks*, where there was no time limit, only the limit of endurance, and no limit to the whipping of the harnessed naked males. We reached the rubber doors of Ward 1 and passed through. I gasped: this was the chamber of horrors.

Along the walls at intervals were gaunt whipping-posts. I saw a rack, a pillory and hooks and pincers hanging by chains from the ceiling. And in the centre of the chamber was a huge fish-tank or aquarium, with steps leading up to its lidded top. The room smelt sweet from the crowded banks of flowers which festooned it, and each frame of discipline had its own fragrant flowerbed nestling at its base. Amid honeysuckle and roses hung whips, chains and canes, with heavy metal irons, pincers, branks, restraining corsets and hoods.

Several fillies, completely nude save for heavy plaster casts or splints, lay on their bellies, with wrists and ankles shackled and chained to bed corners, and their naked bums livid with severe whipmarks. Their heads were either encased in rubber hoods or else branked – gagged by a metal scold's bridle so that their tongue was depressed to stop them squealing. Matron said gaily that they were there to recover from floggings – but that treatment continued their punishment.

'As soon as one welt fades, another is applied,' she said in her lovely girlish lilt. 'Our infirmary is for the relief of pain, of course, but it is also for its celebration. Infirmity itself can be turned to discipline. There are no male slaves here. Bed space is too precious to waste! If they come whining, they are given fifty lashes with the rattan and thrown out naked into the snow, to fend for their snivelling selves. However, Nurses Cadogan and Goode and their staff –' I counted four other nurses '– will see to your special needs most effectively.'

Foolishly, I blurted out: 'Special – why, Miss?' I scarcely felt the cuts of the cane on my naked fesses that followed. Matron tapped my erect penis, on which the two nurses' eyes seemed fixed.

'Big pudding, black heart,' she said, licking her lips.

Inside the tank, the trussed and rubber-clad figure of a young girl was suspended by her bound wrists from a harness at the rim of the tank. Like me, she was immobilised by splints and bandages, wrapped in thick rubber; her ankles were bound, too, so that she dangled like a black fish in the water, and her head was hooded with slits for eyes and mouth. A single rubber tube led from her mouth, allowing her to breathe. Her breasts, buttocks and fount were unbound, and her bare croup was livid with whip-welts, as were her teats. The big purpled plums of her nipples bore the marks of severe flogging.

Only her hair was allowed to peep under her hood and float across her shoulders. Her eyes gazed at me piteously. Suddenly I knew that hair . . .

The water-bound girl was the same maiden I had seen flogged in the kremlin courtyard. And her eyes – they, too, spoke to me, from far away. My mouth hung foolishly open. I felt a tube thrust against my tongue. Nurses Cadogan and Goode pinioned me and bound my ankles with heavy chain, lifted me up the steps to the rim of the tank and gently lowered me in until the water enclosed me up to my ears. Then my wrists were cuffed and forced above my head.

'The nurses will take good care of you, Philip,' said Matron, giving the taller nurse a light cut on the buttocks with her cane! 'They are vicious serfs – yes, serfs! – and have nothing to lose. By the way, Philip, if you think that one day, when you become a *robotnik*, there will be an end to your supplice – be assured there is no end to it.'

With that I was lowered into the icy water and felt myself drowned in a silent world, facing my fellow prisoner and unable to touch or comfort her.

Nurses Cadogan and Goode were handsome in the English county way, raw-boned lasses and full in croup and breast; tall and rangy, with long legs like Fitzhurst's, yet their bony power slightly softer and swathed in a more obvious femininity. Their eyes glittered with delight in power. I wondered why they were serfs, or if they chose to be.

Both ladies had long hair of brownish hue tied back in ponytails. They wore traditional nurses' costumes, like those in Ward 2, all in white rubber, but had whips and handcuffs at their ceintures, and wore high boots in a curiously girlish pink, offsetting their blouses and skirts. These skirts were slit to the waist, allowing an occasional glimpse of stockinged thigh and fesse in high tight G-string, and covered in the delicate rubber filigree of their fishnet stockings under tight white suspender belts of the same latex. Each had buttocks well emblazoned with cane-stripes. The fishnet stockings were woven, too, in white filaments, and beneath the stockings, on her inside thigh, each nurse bore a tattoo of a serpent, the head hidden by the short slit skirt and seeming to crawl up into her fount.

Goode, who had taken Matron's playful canestroke, did not flinch at the cut or even seem to notice it; perhaps the tight rubber skirt that sheathed her bottom protected her from sensation. Both nurses grinned at me through the water then padded off separately to their duties.

The four other nurses bustled silently in the ward, like

grim wraiths. Their heads were hooded in black latex, their hair not visible at all, their legs, arms and titties bare, with heavy pincers like workshop tools clamped to each nipple as though for their own punishment. Their only clothing was a waspie or ceinture which brutally squeezed their bellies and from which looped a thin thong very tightly between extruded naked fesses.

Their bums were all marked by livid blue tattoos that depicted a mosaic of whipstrokes! Apart from that, the naked fesses were well striped with recent raw pink, even though these nurses themselves carried instruments of discipline: one a short metal quirt of five or six vicious shiny thongs that jangled as she walked; one a curled stockwhip; one a long rattan, about four and a half feet, which she carried in both hands, idly flexing it and making it twang; one a simple wooden paddle, with three holes, about three feet long by six inches wide.

These under-serfs were all long of leg and wide of croup and thigh, with heavily muscled arms, and all completely shaven, thus scarcely distinguishable except by the disciplinary instrument they carried. Some of the splinted and plaster-cased female patients had completely shaven heads, their scalps shining in the smoky light, and I wondered if the nurses' hooded scalps were shaven too. Somehow the thought of a lady's head and body completely naked and denuded of all hair was exciting to me, and I felt my cock stir and stiffen. The trussed girl beside me in the water noticed my erection, and her eyes widened; her lips moved on their rubber lifeline to crease in a smile.

At the far end of the ward, a handsome filly lay face down, her legs in plaster casts and her bare bottom high in the air, suspended by a pulley. Her arms were rigid in splints and her ankles weighed down by manacles, and her face pressed to her pillow in a pretty corona of hair. Her naked bottom was covered in bruises, but they did not seem to be whipmarks: rather the result of some fall or contusion. I saw that her bare shoulders were marked as though by a harness and that her hair bore the imprint of a pony's bridle, and I surmised that she had been a victim of some racing accident – or its cause.

Goode consulted a chart and barked orders. The four hooded nurses glided to her bedside, and I saw Goode bend over and wave her finger, as though admonishing her for some error. The girl shook and seemed to sob, then turned her face on her pillow, and I recognised the sweet angel's face of Emma Porritt. My heart beat in sympathy; was there no end to the humiliance of this poor maiden? But I was aghast when Goode seemed to pose a question and receive an enthusiastic nodding of Emma's head in reply, with a broad smile.

At a signal from the senior nurse, the hooded wraith lifted her paddle and proceeded to spank Emma's bare bottom, not very hard at first, but after a few dozen, enough to make her bum blush a lovely pink and have her clenching by the end of the tanning. Emma smiled again, grimacing a little and with moist cheeks, and nodded.

The second serf-nurse then lifted her rattan and dealt full two dozen strokes to the naked fesses. I had nothing to do but count and watch as Emma's bare bum reddened and squirmed, her splints and plaster casts shaking as her helpless body writhed.

There was a short pause while Emma's quivering croup gradually stilled, and then the steel-thonged quirt was lifted. The thongs flashed like knives as they stroked her bare bum very rapidly, spreading artfully to embrace the whole expanse of the buttocks at each stroke, so that not an inch of Emma's soft bum was left unmottled, her deep puffy weals darkening to purple. Yet the clenching of those bare fesses was sweet, the squirming and clenching of the croup making the line of her peach-cleft wriggle and dance like a serpent. Her bare bum raised at each stroke and jerked sharply as it took her, as if in surprise or welcome.

This flogging was speedy: four dozen severe lashes were administered, and Emma was sobbing and squirming in visible agony. Goode bent over and spoke to her again, and Emma vigorously shook her head.

After a respite of three or four minutes, the stockwhip

was uncoiled, and the hooded tormentress took position a good six feet from Emma's bed. The stockwhip snaked high in the air, flashing its cold leather thong, and caught Emma with lightning accuracy in the centre of her wealed bare peach. Her whole body jerked and her face contorted in pain, flushed and streaming with tears.

The stroke was followed almost at once by a second, the long stockwhip not seeming to pause, but rather to curl and loop in a sensuous ballet. The second stroke took her with deadly accuracy right at the soft underflesh of the buttocks, close to her quim and bumhole, and stroked the tops of her thighs, leaving a livid welt.

Emma's body began to shudder and her face banged in frantic rhythm against her pillow as though she was trying to hide from her pain, but the merciless stockwhip cracked on her bare bottom without respite. I could not hear anything in my silent confinement, but I fancied I could feel the air shudder at each blow.

The force slammed her shivering body tight against her bonds, but she had no escape. The whole ward craned to look; Emma took six dozen, slow and lingering, with the stockwhip, and her bare buttocks were black and purple as she shuddered to the beating's end.

Cadogan now advanced and applied ointment to the inflamed fesses, while Goode opened the far door of the ward to admit a shackled line of male *robotniks*, led by a girl whom I recognised as one of the fabled praetorian guard. Goode and Cadogan, and the four hooded nurses, curtsied deep to the girl, whose body presented frightening power.

Six feet tall in high heels, the lithe and muscled guard was, with the insolence of brutal authority, almost nude. She had a loincloth or string of tight black rubber, cut very high over her haunches and topped by a thick rubber belt from which dangled whips and canes right around her waist, like a skirt of correction.

Her ripe pubic mound was hairless and almost entirely exposed by the waist-garment, which was not pouched but was thin leather cord, all of a piece, and snaked tightly through her furrow and the very lips of her cunt, exposing their swollen fleshiness to gaze; the lips were pierced with no fewer than six clustered rings on each side of the thong.

Her nipples were pierced in a similar manner, with big silver rings that should have weighed down the bare breasts; yet these stood proud and pert, despite the weight of the rings and their own flesh, like hard, trembling gourds. The very tip of each nipple was covered in a conical, pointed silver thimble, but I could not see if this, too, was pierced or merely clamped to the wide nipple-peak.

The neck was encased in a cluster of spiked metal collars about six inches in depth, and her arms were covered by leather gauntlets that came up almost to her shoulders and were also studded in spikes right down to the backs of her hands. Her black-leather boots, too, came almost to her cunt-rings and were spurred and spiked, with heels and toecaps that were daggers of pure steel.

Her helmet was of shiny steel, sculpted and close-fitting to her skull, with not a hair peeping out, and spiked like a German officer's with a pink plume of feathers; a steel tongue protected her nose, with a corresponding chin-piece, and a band enclosed her eyes, leaving thin slits for her vision.

I say she was almost nude, but she seemed otherwise, for her entire skin, including her face and lips, was adorned with vivid and chilling tattoos. They depicted many-headed goddesses, swords and whips, stars and moons, toothed fish and flames; her buttocks were a tableau of a naked maid strapped, hooded and flogged raw by a dominatrix, naked also but for her own hood. The two figures seemed beautiful, like two petals of the same flower.

The praetorian guard received the curtsies with icy indifference and cracked her long rattan cane smartly across the buttocks of the first male in the shackled line. There were six males in all, each of them dirty, hulking brutes, naked but for a woman's frilly pink shift, like a nightdress, but too short to cover their naked balls and pricks, which were locked in brass restrainers.

186

The praetorian handed a bunch of keys to Cadogan, who curtsied again and unlocked each of the males from his restrainer. I permitted myself to smirk: none of the cocks was as big as my own implement. Then the guard cracked her cane in the air, and the males, staring sheepishly at Emma Porritt's flogged bare fesses, at once bent over and touched their toes.

The guard replaced her cane at her belt and drew out a gleaming stockwhip, which she uncoiled and lashed in the air; it was feet longer than the nurse's whip that had punished poor Emma. The guard stood back to six or seven feet and cracked the whip hard across the row of bare male bottoms, touching and wealing every one with a smart pink stripe. She lashed again and again, some forty times, until the bare bums of the boys were quivering and reddened and their faces glistened with tears. But every one of them was erect under his whipping.

Their chastiser spat on her whip and rubbed it, then coiled it and replaced it at her belt, drawing her rattan once more. Now Goode stepped forward and spoke to Emma a final time, to receive the same nodded agreement. The praetorian nodded too, and smacked one raw croup with the spiked back of her glove, leaving a raw gash.

The brute clambered on to Emma's bed, his cock fiercely stiff, and lifted his shaming girl's nightie to his neck. Now, under a warning stroke from the guard's rattan, he positioned his swollen hard cock at Emma's furrow, drove until his helmet pierced her arse-bud, then, as his bare wealed arse was lashed again, plunged the erect cock right to the balls inside Emma's gaping bumhole.

Her body shuddered, her head jerked up from her pillow, her mouth widened in a ghastly rictus of pain, and then sank back like a broken doll's as the boy began a vigorous bum-fucking, spurred by occasional, languid strokes from the guard's rattan. His haunches and balls slammed against Emma's splints and plaster casts in his furious buggery.

It was not long before he, too, shuddered, as his spurt came. He drove frantically into the squirming girl's anus as though to split her with the force of his sperm-jet; immediately afterwards, he was lashed off the helpless body of the buggered girl, her bumhole wet and thighs dripping with his shiny cream, and his place was taken by the next erect slave. Emma gave a broad smile of contentment!

Emma Porritt was buggered six times, until her thighs were a glistening sea of spend and her open bumhole shone like a pink raw gash. Wordlessly, the guard nodded to the nurses, who curtsied again, very fearfully, and refastened the males in their heavy brass cock-harnesses. Then, with a series of cane-cracks across bare croups, she drove the shivering naked males out again into the snow.

Almost at once I felt hands seize me and saw that my companion, the flogged girl, was taken too. We were hoisted from our tank, the rubber breathing tubes removed, and frogmarched towards the end of the ward, very awkwardly in our bondage. Numb, I scarcely noticed the lashes from Goode's and Cadogan's whips as the hooded serf-nurses marched us; my companion's eyes were joyous, and she smiled!

Our paths diverged; she was strapped to a sort of operating-table while I was marched to Emma Porritt's pillow. I was permitted to survey her wealed bare bottom for moments, and could not help becoming fully and shamefully erect. The nurses laughed gleefully, and now I was forced to straddle her with my cock and balls. She lifted her head, eyes shut, as Goode squeezed my balls tightly and directed my cock between Emma's lips. I did not protest.

'This will teach you to be a disobedient pony,' hissed Cadogan. 'You stumbled and lost the race on purpose!'

Emma had accepted fair punishment for negligence, but opened her mouth to protest at this obvious injustice; her words were stopped as my cock was rammed right to the back of her throat. She gulped and spluttered, but under a new onslaught of sharp strokes on the bare, from the hooded nurse who carried a rattan, she began fervently to suck my hard cock, sliding my peehole and bulging helmet deep in her silky throat as her tongue played on my shaft. Her lips pressed obediently and firmly on my cock, and I felt the pent-up honey well in my balls, which ached to spurt after my long cruel teasing by Matron and Fitzhurst.

In a very short time I spasmed, showering her throat with my spunk with such force that jets of cream spurted from her lips and down her chin over my pumping balls. I groaned in shameful pleasure, and, when I was drained, Emma kissed my peehole! The nurses led me to the operating-table, where the masked girl was strapped face up, her arms and legs splayed, and her cunt gaping open.

I was positioned squatting over the head of the table, my balls above her face, and lowered so that my flaccid cock was stuffed into her mouth, right to the balls, which were prodded between her lips until I thought she would gag on me. Goode said in her haughty county voice that under the pain of 'bangling' she might need something to bite on in her agony, and my cock was to serve as that bit.

I shivered – yet swiftly my cock stirred again and became as hard as rock, to the awe and amusement of the nurses. I shifted and squatted to accommodate my stiff cock and balls in the girl's mouth, which gaped like a young sparrow's. The operation began.

To be bangled meant that her nipples and cunt-lips were pierced and rings inserted. I could see the operation only partially and watched, horrified, as a sharp needle was positioned by her right nipple, the nipple clamped and squeezed so that it thrust upward, monstrously distended, then with a sharp thrust the needle passed right through the nipple's swollen peak.

The girl jerked, and I felt her teeth bite my balls, only a little, but enough to make my eyes moisten. But the procedure seemed painless apart from this first clean jolt, which was repeated three times, and three rings were thankfully inserted with swift efficiency.

The same thing was done to her second nipple, and then the open cunt-lips were attended to. The same clamping device forced them to swell like tomatoes, and the vicious needle passed through, with the girl's teeth now fastening

189

suddenly on the lower shaft of my cock. My erection saved me from too much pain, and I bore her bites in silence as each cunt-lip was pierced and festooned with rings.

I sighed in relief, but the ceremony was not over, for now a welding iron appeared, and, coming within a hair's breadth of her naked skin, was applied to the rings on both nipples and cunt, welding them forever shut and irremovable. Her body shuddered at this prolonged agony, and I winced as her teeth tried frantically not to bite my cock and balls, but with little success, so maddened was she by the nearness of the hot iron.

I felt her teeth and tongue on my sex like so many little birds pecking me with pincer beaks, and to my astonishment and shame the pain made the cream rise again in my emptied balls. I began to moan in this new humiliant pleasure of serving a female and was rewarded with a sharp flogging of four deliberate strokes from the rattan.

The new smarting of my bare bum tipped my pleasure over the edge, and as the canestrokes increased to an angry flurry I spurted again, my spunk still copious enough to dribble over the girl's lips and chin as she herself moaned and swallowed with bobbing pigeon motions of her throat.

At that moment the last clip was welded into place on her cunt-lips, and the nurses set to unfastening her bonds. Her mouth opened, she licked her lips and she gazed shyly at me. Then, suddenly, as the nurses were distracted, she lifted her mask and said, 'Thank you, sir.'

I gazed in shock. I knew her body, her hair, her face – the flogged and now beringed girl was my own sweet Becky, from – it seemed – so long ago in Shoeburyness.

'No, sir,' she said, guessing my thoughts. 'I am Becky's sister Belinda. If you know Becky, as your face tells me, she may have spoken of me, her twin, the first of four sisters, who travelled afar to her destiny across the sea.'

'But – what destiny is this, Miss Belinda!' I stammered. 'I, a mere male, deserve no less than this ruthless torment – I welcome it, in a way I don't expect you to understand, and I bear your sister Becky an eternal love, for it was her whip that first taught me the joy of humiliation and bare flogging. For *male* fesses! But you, the finest flower of a lady – flogged and half-drowned and now seared and ringed with cruel metal! Is there no way to escape?'

'Escape, sir?' she bridled, her eyes flashing.

I saw in her the fire of my Becky, who had introduced me so sweetly to proper chastisement and servitude, but it horrified me that an English lady could be so abused.

'Escape?' she repeated in wonderment. 'I have been ceremonially flogged, bathed and bangled – honours for which I fought hard – and I will thank you, sir, to know that I am now the happiest filly in Masterdale!'

14

Knickers Lowered

Neglecting me for an instant, the nurses ordered Belinda to her knees, and she readily complied.

'Cleansing, filly!' murmured Goode. Belinda smiled.

She pressed her face to the floor as each nurse in turn bared her quim and pissed copiously, bathing her in a hissing golden jet of steaming fluid.

'What about the boy?' asked Cadogan.

'O, we have plenty of time to make more gold for *him*! His bangling will take longer, and he'll squeal well. Miss Bainbridge's orders – though new scum, he is special, and you see why. His cock must not be spared pain.'

'Nor his balls.'

It is not wise to talk loosely in front of servants. I was lower than a servant, and the women chattered gaily as they pissed all over Belinda's naked body, seeming quite to forget my trembling presence as they discussed ways of humiliating me. I could not believe that Miss Bainbridge had ordered such cruelty and knew it must be a lustful deception of the nurses. If only I could get to Miss Bainbridge, *she* would make everything all right.

Light peeped through the hinges of the outside door. As the nurses tapped the last droplets of piss from their gashes, I suddenly made a hobbling run for the light. The doors were unlocked, and I found myself naked and bandaged in a lane covered in snow. I began to run as best I could, with only a few moments' start.

A hundred yards beyond were a few storehouses in a

lane at the edge of the vast open tundra. I made for one of the storehouses, leaving a trail of telltale footprints. I went out the back door of the storehouse, into another just across the lane, leaving the same trail. Then I backtracked, placing my feet in the same footprints, and regained the first storehouse, where I hid myself.

Soon I heard the nurses crying that I was found; they traced my footprints to the second shed, which abutted the busy alleys of the 'town' that surrounded the kremlin of Masterdale, and to my relief I heard their disappointed cries that I must have taken off over the rooftops.

I waited as they dispersed and then set to stripping myself of my bandages. It was very cold, and I was nude; where could I find Miss Bainbridge? The storehouse offered not a scrap of possible clothing, and such was my zeal to enlighten the monitor that I resolved to venture forth quite naked. It would, I reasoned, be assumed that I was a *robotnik* undergoing ordeal.

Extreme cold, however, undoes the power of reason. I wandered naked through the streets of befurred fillies, who warmed themselves by braziers; they hooted with laughter and drove me away with taunts and snowballs if I tried to approach their fires. Some even aimed red-hot coals at my balls. After a while I forgot what I sought and thought only of shelter. The light began to wane, and I knew it would soon be night. I thought of beasts prowling. I could not remember who, or where, I was, only that I must seek warmth. I looped around the busy village, recognising nothing.

I found myself at the slaughterhouse, stinking with meat. I crept in and scavenged a few pieces of filthy offal, which I washed down with melted snow. Then, to my surprise, I saw a fur coat hanging by a peg: a magnificent wrap of black sable. I could not believe my luck but grabbed it and covered my shivering nakedness. But my newfound warmth still gave me no clue as to what I should do. I dimly thought of Miss Bainbridge; the land was a dark blur now, and the twinkling lights of kremlin and village meant little to me.

I trudged aimlessly, weakened by cold and despair, and at last I sank to my knees. I saw the infirmary again – there were bright lights within, and I knew I should be flogged there, or worse, but did not care. I was beside the second isolated building, namely the punishment block. From it I heard the sound of canestrokes and girlish laughter. I tried to rise and return to the known terrors of the nurses, but I was stayed by a hand on my shoulder. I looked up and saw Miss Bainbridge.

'Well, Philip,' she said kindly, 'everyone is looking for you! And stealing a praetorian guard's greatcoat – that belongs to Miss Camilla, whom I think you met before – why, that is a very serious crime. Happily you have come to the punishment block. You'll be safe here.'

Miss Bainbridge lifted me up and unlocked the heavy barred door of the punishment block, then pushed me gently inside. It was huge and smelt like a gymnasium. We were in a deserted changing-room festooned with girls' stockings, knickers, skirts and shoes and all sorts of accoutrements. Miss Bainbridge efficiently scooped an armful of these garments and ushered me into a smaller room which she locked behind us.

'This is my private changing-room,' she said, thrusting the clothing at me, 'so we can make a pretty disguise for you – and then you'll be a filly among fillies, and the praetorians won't know it's you. What sport!'

Bewildered, I began to try on the lovely feminine garb, holding slips and bras and stockings against my naked body and quite forgetting my fears, and the fact that my Mistress Galena had spoken bitterly of Miss Bainbridge's 'betrayal' long ago. My cock, warmed by the hot air, responded to the silky feel of panties and bras still warm and delicately soiled from their owners' bodies, and Miss Bainbridge saw the evidence of my excitement.

She herself took off her leather coat and revealed herself in the uniform of a gymnasium mistress – white pleated skirt so short that it barely covered her panties; tight blouse with a pink strapless bra firmly repressing the massive globes of her teats; pink stockings and suspenders, and, I could see, a sliver of pink silk panties very thin and high stretched over her full swelling mound. I blushed – I wanted to look like her! She understood, and smiled.

'Well, Philip, you are still scum, but you might make a good *robotnik*. I'm not too displeased I captured you. Perhaps I shall need a new slave or two myself soon. A lady must always show her power – the prefects, the drudges who call themselves mistresses, even the praetorian guards, amuse themselves with serfs and slaves, dressing them as they please in female frillies or horrid yokes and making them run errands at their beck and call. And of course rewarding their bums with regular thrashing. Let's see how you bear up.'

At last I was dressed, and as a blushing filly – I begged to see myself in the glass. Smiling, Miss Bainbridge consented and idly flicked her splayed short yellow cane against imaginary dust specks as I gazed at my likeness. I had a white blouse, brassiere very tight over my male breast, and stuffed with two rather soiled panties on each side; suspenders and black cotton stockings, also very tight, and delicious thong panties of pink satin with a frilly black trim: all perfumed with acrid female sweat. My shoes were perilously high, and I teetered awkwardly. The crowning touch was a russet wig that Miss Bainbridge produced with a flourish, coiffing me neatly: it fitted as though made for me. I was the picture of a pretty English schoolgirl.

Miss Bainbridge applied lipstick and face powder and kohl for my eyelashes, and I blushed all the more – she clapped her hands and said I was as pretty as a picture, then lit a cigarette and told me to bend over, lower my panties and touch my toes. I did so, trembling at the beating I expected, but instead I felt her fingers stroke my exposed balls, and she said they must be fixed. I stood and submitted as she wadded my cock and balls in a painfully tight bandage, whose plaster end she affixed to my furrow as a 'gaffe'. She drew up my panties and now it looked as though I were endowed with a very ripe mound.

From the gymnasium, I heard girlish giggles again; then

hush, the patter of running feet, and a sharp crack, a wail, and the sound of giggles again, with hand-clapping. Miss Bainbridge gave me her cigarette to hold and told me to follow her. I obeyed, and we went through the changing-room into an alcove of the gymnasium.

The ceiling was hung with hooks, pulleys and racks; along the walls were clusters of cuffs, chains, branks, shackles and whips. As well, there were the usual fixtures of a gymnasium: bars, horses and so forth, and one of these vaulting horses was positioned at the far end of the gym.

Over this was splayed a filly in school uniform, but with her frilly knickers down, her skirt up to her shoulders, and her buttocks bare. They were white and firm, and sweetly formed like a quivering pear, and already bore pink and red stripes, as the evidence of vigorous lashing.

Along the side of the hall, half a dozen fillies squatted, wearing gym kit like Miss Bainbridge, with rubber tennis shoes, while a tall, rangy figure held a long rattan, trembling in the air above her head, and stood near us, a dozen paces from the flogged wench. She wore a short skirt like a gymslip, that just covered her buttocks and was made of shiny pink latex. So were her boots, and the strapless pink brassiere covering her pert conical breasts, and that was all she wore save for fluffy white socks well dampened with sweat that glistened all down her bare legs and torso. It was Fitzhurst.

'How many was that, Rowena?' she barked.

'Umm . . . eight, I think, Miss,' bleated the whipped girl: Rowena Tushingham, my erstwhile dominatrix in the squalor of the cage and now herself a victim.

Arkwright was among the fillies looking on, and at their head sat Matron and Miss Grant, a distinct frostiness between them; I remembered Matron's distaste at Miss Grant's flogging of Fitzhurst's bottom.

'Gosh,' Rowena cried, 'they're tight! My bum smarts so!'

'Only eight, and she's blubbing!' Fitzhurst sneered. 'Now, girls, see how she's marked: a crisscross pattern, two successive strokes in the same place, for maximum pain, and then shift to another spot, but near enough to allow the cane to graze the first spot as well. Ready, Rowena?'

'Yes, Miss,' whimpered the girl.

'Bum up then, and observe well, girls. I'm going to take her on – but I shan't tell! Let it be a surprise, eh, Rowena, and you'll smart all the more? Eh? Eh?'

'Yes.'

'What?' snapped the prefect.

'Yes, *please*, Miss,' sobbed Rowena.

Fitzhurst raised her cane and started her run-up, padding softly like a tiger, then suddenly sprinting to deliver a savage cut right to the underside of Rowena's spread bare bum that jerked her and had her hopping on tiptoe. Fitzhurst's thrust carried her past the flogging horse and she paused, hands on hips, to look at Rowena's face. She smiled in slow satisfaction.

'Nine,' she said. 'Now – who'll deliver the tenth?'

A volley of hands shot up.

'You, then, Lisa, and remember – pick your spot.'

Lisa, a red-headed freckled girl with long legs and a broad back, her large breasts and bum nestling uncomfortably in her white gym blouse, took the cane and curtsied. She positioned herself at twelve paces, licked her lips and flexed the instrument. Then she began her run-up, just like Fitzhurst, who surveyed approvingly, hands on hips, as the redhead's teats bounced. Lisa delivered her stroke right to the weal on the lower fesse and smiled in triumph as she returned to the applauding fillies, while Rowena's puffy bare buttocks writhed in pain.

Lisa was ordered to deliver two more strokes, and each of her lashes echoed over Rowena's sobs and the enthusiastic applause. 'Who's next?' cried Fitzhurst.

The same hands rose, and one by one the fillies took their turn at caning Rowena, who sobbed and wriggled and said 'please' and 'thank you' at every set of strokes to her quivering bare peach, now purpling horribly. After at least thirty naked strokes of the cane, Fitzhurst stopped the beating and said that the fillies would soon practise on naked males, strapped down, of course, like brutes.

This caused a ripple of excitement.

'Rowena is a crybaby,' sneered Fitzhurst. 'Let us have a stouter volunteer.'

Miss Bainbridge pushed me forward.

'Why, hello, Miss Bainbridge,' said Fitzhurst with false bonhomie; I could sense the malice in her voice.

'This one will do,' said Miss Bainbridge. 'I caught her smoking – a new English whelp called Pippa. I think a mere thirty on bare bum would not be enough for such a dirty offence as smoking. Eh, Pippa?'

I changed my voice to a girlish whisper.

'Yes, Miss,' I said.

'She's a pretty thing!' cried Lisa. 'O, please Miss, let me cane her pretty bum blue!'

'Me! Me!' came the full-blooded cry from half a dozen throats, including the flogged Rowena's, whose eyes shone brightest of all.

She was not seated like her comrades but stood awkwardly, rubbing her buttocks under her skirt. I did not think she recognised me, but her eyes shone with lust to chastise my girl-bottom. If only ladies could be as cruel to willing, submissive males as they are to each other!

Fitzhurst smiled and looked me up and down, not seeming to recognise me – such is the power of powder, paint and ladies' frillies to deceive!

'I am sure there will be instructive pleasure for all you young ladies,' said Miss Bainbridge, tapping my buttocks quite sharply with her splayed yellow cane. 'This one is a hard case – she resisted capture – and needs very firm treatment if she is to wriggle and submit. You are a good class – I am sure I shall enjoy your efforts.'

She nodded to Fitzhurst and told her to carry on; Fitzhurst curtsied, but I could see she resented this intrusion on her domain: she was enjoying her exhibition of power before Matron and Miss Grant, who sat primly but each so ripe and huge of teat that they resembled an array of melons at a fair.

How my cock strained against her thong as I was led on swaying heels to my flogging horse under the eyes of lustful females! I sensed their desire for my humiliation, could almost smell the longing to hear the lash crack against my naked bum-skin. It was a longing quickly fulfilled. I was obliged to bow to Fitzhurst and curtsy before taking position, then kiss the rattan that was to flog me. It was still warm from the other girls' bottoms and I fancied I could smell their scent of fear and pain. Then I took position; frilly knickers shamefully lowered to stretch between my spread thighs, my skirt up, and bum high for my bare caning.

Fitzhurst led the proceedings with a smart dozen that had me sobbing quietly and my bum raw. At each cut she explained her method to her students – touching here, there, this sensitive flesh, that spot unmarked and singled out for two or three in succession, to make my mosaic of welts uniform and pleasing to the eye.

Then the other girls took their turn. My head was lowered behind the cushion, and I scarcely knew who was beating me, feeling only the swipe of the rattan as it bit into my flesh already raw from countless weals. I hopped on tiptoe, squirmed and wriggled in my agony, but nothing could make it abate nor spread the pain evenly; each lash seemed to pin my whole being on that one searing welt. And always I had to remember to sob 'thank you, Miss'.

Rowena had been flogged in threes, but I took eights, and when each girl had her turn, the round began again. My only comfort was the occasional coo that I was a brave girl, and my bum most handsome under her crimson weals. The thought stabbed me through my tears that if I were to be a slave, I should be dressed shamefully as female for my beatings, and my cock stirred violently at the beauty of such humiliance. I was dancing in my agony when at last Miss Bainbridge called a halt. I think I had taken over a hundred with that cruel rattan, the few minutes' pause between beatings only an illusion of relief.

I expected a call to rise, but it did not come. Instead I felt firm hands roll my knickers down my stockinged legs and remove them entirely. It was Matron, for I felt her massive teats brush against my bruised buttocks. Then she

199

applied some ointment to my weals and pronounced me fit for further 'tuition'.

'Miss Grant may care to illustrate the use of the *godemiché*,' said Miss Bainbridge, striking a match on my ridged bum-flesh to light her cigarette.

I breathed the acrid smoke that she blew scornfully over me, wondering what a *godemiché* could be. I peeked, and at the corner of my eye I saw Miss Grant withdraw a giant black rubber dildo, very gnarled and knotted and attached to a ceinture. The dildo had two very large and lifelike balls, like withered apples attached to a branch, and was a horrid facsimile of a male prick, even larger than mine.

Miss Grant smirked at being asked to perform this honour. She apologised for her immodesty and removed her long skirt, revealing her fishnet stockings and garter belt. She placed the ceinture around her waist, just under her suspender belt, and buckled it firmly; then after being permitted to make herself more comfortable she removed her panties and blouse and advanced towards me, her high heels clacking on the polished wooden boards, and her massive titties wobbling in their bra's flimsy restraint.

I lowered my head, my teeth clenched for my ordeal, yet unconsciously parting my cheeks and relaxing my anus. I felt Miss Grant's cool fingers on my croup, spreading me tight, and she fingered my pucker then clucked in approval.

'This, girls, is a service you may feel obliged to perform on unruly males. I am not saying it is inappropriate for females, and indeed it can be most pleasurable, but *buggery* –' she smacked her lips '– can be true humiliation for the male brute, accustomed as most of the filthy creatures are to penetration by a male cock.'

I felt her fingers grease my sphincter with oil, and then the tip of the *godemiché* nuzzled my dilated anus bud. It was rammed in to a depth of two inches or so, and I groaned.

'May I?' murmured Miss Grant. Both Miss Bainbridge and Fitzhurst simultaneously answered: 'Yes.'

I heard Miss Grant take a deep breath, and then my knees buckled as she pushed the enormous dildo right inside my hole, scraping the protesting walls of my bumshaft. The pain was indescribable. I fought to relax my sphincter as she rammed and prodded between my trembling fesses, and suddenly I gasped as my anal passage opened completely and the dildo plunged right to my root, in a fluid, savage thrust that slammed me against the cushion, to Miss Grant's satisfied sigh of 'Aah'.

She withdrew a couple of inches and then thrust again, slamming most vigorously, and repeated her bucking until the shaft slid easily in and out of my squirming bumhole, and she was able to withdraw almost to my pucker before plunging in again with a single mighty thrust, and always jarring against the root of my belly. I groaned and could not help squealing at the dreadful, joyous fullness.

Again, I felt the curious tickling somewhere above my balls, as though my glans were being rubbed, and my pain was increased by the pressure of my swelling cock against the 'gaffe' that bound her tight between my thighs.

Miss Grant buggered me to some hundred thrusts; at each, I felt her haunches slapping the backs of my thighs so vigorously that I was glad my balls were trussed and unexposed. At length I felt a jet of cold fluid wash my root: the 'balls' of the machine were a reservoir of juice, in imitation of manly fluids. Miss Grant withdrew the dildo, leaving my anus with a horrid plopping slither that nevertheless caused me an excruciating tickling. I had but a few moments gasping repose before her place was taken by another.

Each female wished to outdo the last in the stamina and endurance of my buggering, and my arsehole was now as raw as the surface of my caned buttocks. The spurts of fluid into my anus-shaft gave a moment's relief; my sobs and whimpers went unchecked and unchastised, such was the flutter of delight as the ladies watched another lady take dildo in her bumhole. My stirred cock was like a coiled serpent, hard and struggling to rise, and at each thrust of that dildo in my tender bum I felt my cream well again.

I smelt the delicious sweating perfume of Matron's body

straddling me, and my bumhole recoiled from the heavy strength of her loins; my cream longed to spurt. I could not see Matron, Miss Hochhuth, but imagined her powerful blonde body, a German goddess surging from some lair of darkness to bugger my tender English arsehole with all her hideous witch's strength. My cock strained – at each thrust from that supreme nurse my cream surged in my balls.

By the five-hundredth thrust of the monstrous engine, my arsehole felt as wide and slippery as a woman's cunt. My pain was delightful, and I craved more as I squirmed to squeeze the engine with my sphincter muscle. I floated in a swoon of delicious humiliance; suddenly my reverie was broken by a familiar voice close to my ear. It was Rowena Tushingham.

'I thought I recognised that arsehole,' she hissed in her county lady's accent. 'You dirty little worm – dressing as a lady! I bet you wish it were that filthy Denning buggering you, or one of your other male scum friends.'

I suddenly thought of the ugly Tarker, back at Shoeburyness, and wept in the shame that I enjoyed the same filthy pleasure as he and his sort – my only consolation being that it was in submission to ladies.

Her fingers strayed beneath my cleft and poked my trussed balls to verify her finding. Then she finished buggering me and withdrew with a contemptuous twist of the dildo, swivelling her loins to cause it to scrape and hurt my arsehole quite awfully. I panted in pain and feared worse punishment if my disguise were found out. My fears strengthened as I heard Rowena whisper to Fitzhurst.

And it was Fitzhurst who next mounted me, lowering her dildo over her gash-lips so that she could ride me squatting, as though on horseback. This took my bumhole at a different angle, the *godemiché* stabbing sharply upward, and with this new dimension of pain her buggery of me was pure agony. I sobbed and squirmed, and she hissed: 'I said I should have you, whelp! How you'll suffer! That cow Bainbridge, too, for tricking me thus!'

Fitzhurst then resumed position on the floor but continued to stab my root harder than any of the other female sodomites. As she continued to bugger me, she called a further instruction to the eager fillies. They were to jump on to the vaulting horse, and hold on to the handles at each end; then hold themselves in a raised position with their legs stretched and spread and piss in the cleft of my buttocks as Fitzhurst continued to bugger me. There was a scamper of feet and a rush of giggles as they complied, and as the dildo continued to ravish my arsehole I felt powerful jets of torrid girls' piss streaming and splashing down my bare buttocks and into my stockings.

It was too much. Fitzhurst's strokes came like a piston rod, and I could not restrain my spasm. I gasped and moaned as my cream erupted in spurt, and the flow of glistening fluid down my stockings was plain for all to see. Fitzhurst feigned surprise and abruptly ceased her buggery. She ripped my dress and blouse away and tore at my gaffe until I was naked but for bra, spermed stockings and suspender belt, my half-stiff cock swaying like a peapod beneath my wealed buttocks.

'A male! You have brought us a *male* to bugger!' she shrieked at Miss Bainbridge. 'How *dare* you trick me?'

I rose and stood shakily, supporting myself on the flogging horse. The ladies' piss glistened all over my bum and stockings and dripped in a pool at my feet.

'The male is my slave,' retorted Miss Bainbridge drily. 'And I am senior monitor. I can trick whomsoever I like.'

Fitzhurst lashed Miss Bainbridge across the breasts with her rattan, making the monitor's face livid with fury.

'*Your* slave!' cried Fitzhurst. 'He is mine!'

I felt that despite my worship of Fitzhurst's strength, I owed a debt of gratitude to Miss Bainbridge.

'*You* are no stranger to males, nor to a male's cane, Fitzhurst!' I cried in my own voice, to everyone's astonishment. 'It was Denning who signed your big red arse after flogging you – and fucking you, too, I'm sure!'

There was a stunned silence, then the fillies began to babble at once.

'String him up by his balls!' screamed Arkwright.

'Flog him to the bone, hung ten feet high from nipple-hooks!' cried Rowena Tushingham.

Then Miss Grant interjected shrilly that my massive cock was the cause of insult to her Latin class, and that Fitzhurst had been duly chastised for her laxity – by rights my cock and my person belonged to *her*. Matron rose to her full imposing height and, breasts quivering in indignation, said that as senior health officer her needs took precedence and that *she* would have me. She grasped Fitzhurst roughly by the caning arm.

Fitzhurst lunged at her and began to grapple; Miss Bainbridge intervened; Miss Grant lifted her foot and kicked Miss Bainbridge right on her cunt. Miss Bainbridge responded with a savage canestroke to Miss Grant's exposed breasts, ripping off the bra so that the melons flopped out, and Miss Grant was duly thrashed on bare titties. Soon all four ladies were struggling and on the floor, gouging and kicking in vulva and teat and face, scratching and poking and biting in a frenzy of pent-up jealousy and resentment, their clothing and undergarments ripped and scattered and their nude bodies scratched and bruised.

'Ladies! Ladies!' I cried. 'Surely I can be the willing slave of all of you! My body will gladly bear the lashes of four whips! I beg you – it is my heart's desire!'

The combatants paused and looked each other in the eye. And I realised I spoke my true longing.

Suddenly a massive whipcrack lashed the nude bodies of all four ladies. The instrument was a stockwhip, ten feet in length and hideously studded with metal points.

'*What* is the meaning of this?' cried Camilla, the praetorian guard.

Miss Bainbridge was the only one who maintained her dignity. Stiffly she rose to her feet, curtsied and opened her mouth to explain when Camilla cracked the whip again across her cunt-lips and told her to be silent. Miss Bainbridge winced and wiped tears from her eyes.

Camilla was comletely nude, now, her tattoos glowing like her anger. I saw that her shaven pubis had a tattoo of fangs surrounding the beringed cunt-lips. And she wore no helmet: her scalp was indeed completely shorn, and gleamed in its spectral nudity. Her muscles – the powerful thighs, belly slab and pectorals – rippled, as though preparing for combat, and her nude body suddenly seemed familiar to me.

She ordered the audience of fillies, as punishment for witnessing such a degrading scene, to strip naked and proceed at a trot to the marshalling yard, where they were to request the lady marshal to equip them with the heaviest horseshoes and ponies' harnesses. Then they were to trot forty times around the racetrack without stopping, on pain of the knout. The crestfallen fillies curtsied and filed out in sobbing obedience.

'As for *you lot*,' drawled Camilla, 'fighting over a *male* – O, yes, I heard everything. I came for exercise alone – I find that my coat is in your private room, Miss Bainbridge.'

She managed to infuse the word 'male' with all the dripping scorn of a true domina.

'I –' Miss Bainbridge began. 'I mean – it was there by chance, Miss Camilla.'

'No!' I cried. 'I stole it! Punish me, Miss! Punish me – for all my four mistresses!'

Camilla spat on me.

'I have been looking for a reason to humiliate you, high and mighty Miss Bainbridge,' she said coldly, 'ever since I learnt of your behaviour towards a certain Countess Galena, when you were mistress at our cadet establishment in England. Trifling with a lady's affections, like some smutty male – *betrayal* is not too strong a word! And neither is *revenge*. You four will proceed at once to the guardroom dungeon, where you will be chained to await my decision on your separate chastisements.'

The four nude ladies bowed and curtsied sullenly.

'As for you, scum –' she turned to me and smiled the coldest smile I have ever seen grace a lady's lips '– as for you, I shan't punish you at all. No – I have watched you dressed as a girl and buggered with the *godemiché*, a poor thing beside the real item of stiff hot flesh. You shall have your heart's desire! My twin brother Paul is even now chained naked in the same dungeon – while abroad, the fool forgot how to lick my bum properly after commode, and a simple task shall be the price of his release.'

15

The Dungeon

The dungeon of the praetorians was a smaller version of
the infirmary, except that there were no flowers and beds,
just instruments of torment, subtle and abundant: racks,
stools and whipping frames that stood in the passageway
like *robotniks* waiting to be awakened for duty. The walls
were hung with very lifelike drawings depicting the naked
female form, or the bottom alone, grotesquely exaggerated
in size and ripeness, undergoing the most excruciating
torments with whip, pincer, needle or glowing hot iron.
Females were hung by hooks and pincers on, or pierced
through, distended nipples; or even cunt-lips stretched to
pale envelopes of agony. Looking closer, I saw that they
were not drawings but photographs.

There were many depictions of anal penetration, by
dildos so huge that no female anus could possibly take
them, and in two or three a nude praetorian, tattooed and
lustfully leering, had her forearm inside a bound and
squirming slave's anus, right up to the elbow.

The pictures were tantalising, to be sure, but curiously
the male slave – his agony of bare-bum caning with rattan,
or whipping on the penis-shaft or the glans itself, the
tortures of penile suspension and spiked bandaging – was
not thought worthy of depiction.

We passed several small cells, and I heard female voices
from behind the heavy metal doors. The voices screamed,
or whimpered, or cruelly laughed. Camilla, whose bare
tattooed breasts seemed to quiver with pent-up excitement,

thrust us into the last cell, illumined only by moonlight through a thin window slit.

My female garb was torn from me, and I was at once fastened against the dank rock wall by a neck brace, with cuffs for my ankles and wrists, so that I was splayed helpless and naked. Fitzhurst, Matron, Miss Grant and Miss Bainbridge were also made naked, and chained by their necks on leashes about six feet long, one in each corner of the chamber, so that they could not touch. Apart from that they were unfettered.

My eyes grew accustomed to the gloom, and I saw that there was another occupant. At first it had seemed like a supporting colonnade in the centre of the cell, but now I saw a nude male body, suspended by cuffed wrists and standing on tiptoe on the flagstones. His thighs and belly were bound in constricting rubber thongs, and the ankles fastened in shackles set into the floor. His hairless body gleamed in the wan light, and I recognised the face, the rippling musculature and the menace of the flaccid cock. It was Countess Galena's *robotnik*, Paul.

Camilla barked something to him in his own language, and he looked at me and leered. She paused to squat over Miss Bainbridge and pissed on her with a long golden jet, first on the bare fesses then on her face. Miss Bainbridge's face wrinkled and she sobbed in this humiliance, but accepted her bathing.

'Your punishment shall be the worst, *traitor!*' the praetorian spat, her hips writhing to shake the last drops of steaming fluid on Miss Bainbridge's lips.

Then we were left in the freezing dungeon, with no further explanation. I looked uncertainly at Paul, my old comrade, or adversary, in Galena's chains – and now, it seemed, to be the instrument of my utter humiliation. He smiled at me, then, to my astonishment, addressed me in halting French, when I had thought him incapable of civilised speech.

'You are all to be whipped,' he said, 'while the praetorians dine. Miss Bainbridge, I think, will take the worst, for her betrayal of my Mistress Galena. She will endure the extra shame of being whipped by a male – by me! Since my dispatch here by my Mistress, I have been flogged without mercy by my cruel twin, and I thank you, young sir, for delivering me. After the ladies have been whipped, I shall bugger you, and then be released once more into the servitude of my sister. My crime was to linger too long, and take pleasure, in licking my sister's beautiful bum-bud clean of her morning evacuation. A slave must not take pleasure! But I confess I shall take pleasure in my duty of buggering your beautiful arse, English boy.'

I shuddered in disgust at this hideous compliment, and as he spoke his mighty cock stirred and swelled a little, which made the downcast ladies look with eager curiosity.

Miss Grant broke the ice and said it would be shameful to be whipped in front of the praetorians, the wicked minxes, but at least their shame would go no further than praetorian hall, whose proceedings were rigorously secret.

'To think I left Inverness for this –' she sighed, rubbing her bare bum as though anticipating the lash.

'Would you rather be back there?' snapped Miss Bainbridge.

'Why, no,' said Miss Grant, astonished.

'Whipping we can all take,' said Fitzhurst briskly. 'But for the boy to be buggered, and before lustful praetorian eyes! His is the greater shame.'

'Greater than yours, prefect, when the scum Denning whipped and buggered you?' spat Miss Bainbridge.

Fitzhurst's eyes glowed.

'Which of us ladies has not taken cock, has not craved the hard hot meat in our cunts, or the whip of the male caressing our naked bums?' she demanded. 'All ladies crave the same. I – I gave way, that is all. I allowed Denning to whip and sign me, and it was not the first time.'

'This boy did offer to take punishment for all of us,' said Matron, her eyes bright and gazing with some reverence at my dangling member. 'A slave of four mistresses! How quaint the English boy is! We should help him.'

'Do you think a slave can serve four mistresses?' asked Miss Grant, her eyes glinting behind her spectacles.

They all seemed to ponder for a moment, and then Miss Bainbridge said that his four mistresses – begging no further question – must help their slave. If I was to be buggered by Paul, at praetorian command, then my joint slavery would be infringed – it was a point of principle.

Paul addressed me again in broken French, with a shrill snigger, and said there was little use in plotting. The praetorians would dine in an hour, and all the captives would be strung to flogging frames. As the praetorians ate, he, Paul, would wield the cat on Miss Bainbridge's bare back and arse, together with the rattan and the Tunguska tawse, a thong of thick leather split into seven tongues, each with a steel plate at the tip. The other ladies would be whipped by praetorians, and the boy would be flogged too, of course, by his twin Camilla.

Then, over dessert, Paul's sister would give her twin twenty with rattan on bare buttocks, in order to stiffen his penis, if not already erect from the excitement of inflicting pain to the wriggling buttocks of a naked and bound lady. I remembered Countess Galena's screams as I left her railway carriage – even that proud mistress had submitted in thrall to her massively virile *robotnik*.

When his cock stood satisfactorily erect, Paul would attend to the English boy's arsehole, while he was held down in squatting position by his four so-called mistresses, once they had been flogged to utter submission – at which Paul gave another high-pitched snigger. My buggery would obviously be the high point of the entertainment. If he buggered me long and painfully enough, Camilla had promised to take a photograph of my torment for her 'gallery'.

'We have one hour,' said Fitzhurst.

I saw her long muscled legs stretch out, with feet and toes wriggling in the smoky moonlight, towards the trussed body of the slave Paul.

He looked down in alarm as Fitzhurst's toes approached his balls, then both her feet drew back, cupped like eagle's talons, as though she were going to strike him.

'No!' cried Matron. 'We must not damage a male – another lady's property!'

Fitzhurst laughed and said she had no intention of damaging him, only of pleasuring him. With that, her toes cupped the helmet of his penis and clutched it tight, then began to rub vigorously up and down, raising the half-stiff organ to full erection. The other ladies cooed in delight. Miss Grant's toes were the first to reach the underside of Paul's scrotum and tickle his balls while Fitzhurst masturbated him, vigorously rubbing her own clitty.

Miss Grant's hand crept between her open thighs, too, and in full view of us all she began to frot her clitty, matching her pedal stimulation of the slave's balls with her own masturbation, firmer and firmer as the male's cock responded unwillingly to the touch of ladies' artful bare toes. Her gash was spread and pink and shone with streams of love-oil that trickled on her quivering thigh-muscles.

Paul groaned and wriggled in protest, but nothing could stem the pleasure of his foot-frotting, and in a short while he began to moan in ecstasy, then suddenly yelped. His massive stiff cock began to buck, and a jet of sperm spurted from his straining peehole to the height of a good ten inches, splattering the ladies' bare feet as they milked him for spunk. At the same time, Fitzhurst's belly heaved and she moaned long and loud, masturbating her clitty with harsh rapid strokes as she herself climaxed, and shortly afterwards Miss Grant's thumb frigged rapidly on her swollen nubbin so that she gave little jerks and squeals of surprise as her spasm came and her thighs were as wet with her own juices as her foot with Paul's copious sperm.

Paul sobbed, and Fitzhurst withdrew her feet, then to my surprise bent her knees and placed her toes in her mouth and licked the glistening spunk from her toe-skin. She smacked her lips, licked them and swallowed, a satisfied glow on her face.

All the while Miss Grant continued to tickle Paul's balls with teasing toes, until the cock, which had never truly softened, began to stir again, and now Miss Grant took the helmet between her big toe and second toe and began a second, nonchalant masturbation: at the same time recommencing the frotting of her swollen pink nubbin.

The ladies' faces were wreathed in smiles, and each stretched her bare legs to nuzzle the helpless male's balls, playfully tussling for position, as Miss Grant's renewed masturbation of his penis grew harder, and returned him groaning to full erection. The huge bulb of his cock gleamed dark puce as though chastised.

Now all the ladies – my four mistresses – masturbated too, as much to awaken Paul's ardour as for their own satisfaction at this game. My own cock could scarcely fail to respond, and they looked at my erection with mischievous cries of grief that they could not reach me, the bigger and harder of the two males. I blushed happily.

'I admit,' Fitzhurst suddenly gasped, rhythmically rubbing her cunt and with two or three fingers well inside the wet slit, 'that I gave way to temptation when I led the brute Denning alone into his cage. We were alone: naked, that giant cock seemed to mock and tempt me at the same time. I whipped him severely for it, a good fifty on bare, and his cock was as stiff as his grin was wide.

' "I have an arse of old English oak, Miss," he said to mock me as I signed my handiwork on his purpled buttocks.

'I gave him another twenty strokes, but still that cock throbbed, and my cunt was streaming wet and I could resist no more. What lady could? I offered him my bare bum, hoping he would have his will and poke my soaking wet gash. And he had his will – buggered me most shamelessly, and not before giving my bare bum three dozen vicious cuts with my own rattan, and signing with my own pen.

'After he had spurted copiously in my bumhole – I must admit his jet was proud and filled my anus with sticky cream, so that it washed, dribbling, over my bare thighs – he caned me again, only two dozen, but very hard and very painful, with many strokes right on my thigh-tops.

'That made the brute stiffen again, and he took me now in cunt, which was slimy wet for his massive tool, and he fucked me very roughly and spurted again with very fierce and copious cream that had my thighs and stockings sticky

211

and soaked. I spasmed not once but twice, and made pee when his cock was still inside me after his spurt, so that I washed his balls with piss and my stockings were thoroughly drenched by now with piss and cream mingled.

'I was soaking, my thighs wet with my juices, and I begged for more, but he laughed, and said his cock needed a rest, as she would have to satisfy all the other bitches of Masterdale – daring to mock me, a prefect!

'From then on, I resolved that no male or his organ should have the better of me. It has happened so many times before, and was the reason I came to Masterdale – to an empire of women, free of the male yoke! But even here, no lady can truthfully say she is free of the cock's empire.'

All this time her comrades were vigorously rubbing Paul's cock and frotting themselves until the four cunts gleamed in the darkness like so many pools of pink candlelight. Miss Bainbridge's voice trembled as she spoke.

'I, too, have been the slave of lust,' she murmured. 'And that was the reason for my betrayal – shameless, I admit! – of Paul's Mistress Galena. She was a girl –' she pronounced it coyly as 'gel' '– at the junior Masterdale in England, and I the music mistress. I was attracted to her blonde haughty beauty and flogged her bare bum shamelessly and with only the smallest pretext on every possible occasion, somehow realising that the affection was mutual and that she wanted me to admire her bare bum and cane her to stripes. The time came when the tables were turned.

'We were alone in the music room, and I had ordered her two dozen strokes of the cane for a faulty rendition on the spinet – I administered the beating at once to her bare buttocks. I remember her frilly white knickers, soiled from the wearing, and how I decreed four extra strokes for wearing stained panties – a punishment she herself whispered was scarcely sufficient, so I made it eight extra on that luscious squirming bare peach.

'My quim was awash as I applied the cane to her naked buttocks all aquiver like delicious custards. She took it in silence, like a true lady, and when the beating was over we were both panting hoarsely. She put her fingers between her naked cunt-lips and held them up; they were soaking wet. I did not resist as she placed them to my lips and inside my mouth, and my tongue licked them.

' "See what you do to me, Miss," she said softly, fixing me with those green eyes. "I think it is your time –"

'Without a word, I bent over and spread my buttocks in position, lifted my skirts and petticoats and felt her fingers hook the rubber waist of my panties and draw them down ever so slowly across my silk stockings, snagging my suspender belt on the way. When my bum was bare, she took my own cane and gave me the two dozen and eight that I had dealt her, and – and I begged her not to stop!

'The pain was awful, and my bare bum squirmed at each horrid stroke – I thought my legs would buckle, the pain of each lash smarted so on my naked fesses – but I wanted that beating never to end. I think I took over fifty strokes in all, and then we began to meet every week, for mutual caning and – everything else ladies can do for pleasure.

'She came to my room: naked, we would flog each other raw, never less than four dozen, on bare bum and on naked bubbies and nipples, too, an exquisite pain – with a whippy little ashplant I kept under my pillow. Then we would lie entwined in bed, gamahuching in lustful tribadism, my mouth on her gash and her tongue inside my own anus or cunt, and sometimes putting our fingers in our gashes and frotting each other's clitty, or else poking with whole fists in our sopping wet cunts. This went on for several months.

'One day, we had found the seclusion of a stable. We were naked, cuddling in the hay, and giggling because we had just peed on each other, amid all the animal smells. I had just beaten Galena soundly with a tawse – two hundred on bare bum, which she took without flinching, and which raised the most delicious purple welts on her pale peach-skin. It was like our own Tunguska tawse, a much heavier improvement on the Scottish version, and much prized at the junior Masterdale. After I had tawsed her, she tawsed me in return, with only a hundred and fifty, but followed that with fifty of my ashplant, which hurt abominably, so that I had to pee again with Galena watching the stream dribble from my gash.

'My bare was quite blackened and purple, and my fesses glowed with love of her pain; as I pissed, she gave me an extra dozen on my bare nipples, making my love-oil flow with my piss from my swollen cunt-lips, and I could not help frotting my clitty as my nips smarted and my pee and love-juice flowed. I knew I would come. As she caned my breasts, Galena pissed, too, and began to masturbate in time with me. How I loved her!

'Suddenly our frigging was interrupted when Farr the sweeping-boy came in unannounced. He was – well, he was young and brutishly handsome, and he grinned evilly, and winked, and left us. But we both knew our secret was out! Shortly thereafter, Farr accosted me with lewd suggestions, saying he knew I had appetite for cane and should know what a true beating felt like from a man's hand.

'I knew he would tell on me if I refused, so I agreed to an appointment, in the same hayloft. He made me strip to stockings and suspenders and bare my bubbies as well as my bottom, and then he took my own tawse and laid into my bare arse. To my horror, I relished his strokes more than Galena's – I was sopping wet in my cunt – so when after the hundredth stroke I felt a huge hot cock plunge into my squirming bumhole, my protests were mere theatre. Thereafter my trysts with Galena lacked the passion I felt for cock; Farr buggered me expertly and whipped me with such luscious cruelty before fucking my cunt that I always came two or three times. Soon Galena discovered my fresh whipmarks and interrogated me; I wept and confessed, and our affair was over. The wretch Farr blabbed to the headmistress, and both Galena and I were whipped publicly, receiving each thirty strokes of the cane on our bare bottoms, with our best frilly knickers shamefully at our ankles, before the whole school assembly. Galena went down; the headmistress was not unkind, and I was posted here to Masterdale's senior and older establishment, to be free of the disgraceful empire of males. But as Fitzhurst says, we ladies and our cunts can never be free of cock's domain.'

All the while my mistresses gave little gasps and squeals as they masturbated to repeated climaxes.

Suddenly Paul whimpered, and his erect cock began to buck again – and another mighty spurt of sperm splashed on the bare feet of the frotting ladies. From now on he was masturbated cruelly and without pause, spurred by the lustful spectacle of ladies rubbing their bare open cunts, so that he sobbed but could not prevent himself from being milked dry after five or six spurts.

My own cock stood ramrod stiff, and the ladies teased me, with invitations as to the punishment she should receive if they got their hands on me: I should be given full lavage to bursting, then my cock would be bound in wire, my prepuce clamped and my bumhole plugged so that I could not make commode; I would be sheathed in spiked rubber and hung by my balls from the ceiling, with only my bum and cock bare for flogging with many-thonged knout; and so on. My cock throbbed harder at these delicious threats.

All the time the ladies took it in turns to frot the raw cock of the gasping nude slave helpless in their midst. As they frigged themselves, Matron and Miss Grant, too, gasped hints of their past; Miss Grant had left her genteel ladies' academy in Inverness because she longed to see male slaves quiver under her tawse, instead of the endless parade of bare female bottoms she was obliged to chastise. Yet here she had discovered that tanning the female – and baring her own arse – was, after all, her ruling passion.

With Matron it was the obverse: she had forsaken a promising career in the Kaiser's Nursing Corps, under the aegis of her sister, because she longed to discipline the *female* bottom, finding an abundance of males monotonous. Yet all the ladies agreed that while the female being was superior in every way, and especially in physical beauty, at times the infuriating power of the cock overwhelmed the sternest female heart and the proudest cunt.

I felt a certain unease at these stories of girlish submission to male empire – surely it is the cock's duty to worship gash, and the carrier of balls must beg adoringly for a superior lady's heel to crush him under foot.

My four mistresses matched Paul spend for spend, and outstripped him, their howls and sobs of ecstasy from their fingered throbbing clitties growing louder. Paul trembled; his cock was flayed to orgasm again and again, his anguished gasps producing a mere dribble of spunk.

Finally his cock shrivelled and would not stand, while my own throbbed hard, with balls full. At that moment Camilla returned and said it was dinner hour, and time for our collective punishment. We were led upstairs into the vaulted mess-room of the praetorian guard; Paul was a sorry spectacle, trembling and ashen and his once-proud cock shrunk to a wizened peapod.

The mess was comfortable and leathery in the style of a London gentleman's club, with a rosewood dining-table, sumptuously laid for the feast, and around it many lounging armchairs. The walls were hung with draperies of velvet and also with photographs like those in the dungeon corridor, depicting the naked female, and especially the enlarged buttocks, dwelt on in glowing detail in various stages of flogging, piercing and 'cupping' – this meant that the fleshy bum was constrained in an iron collar that was tightened until the buttocks were pumped obscenely large for flogging; the same cupping usually applied to the bubbies also, so that the nipples and areolae stood from the teat-flesh as tight as apples and seemed about to burst under the cane or whip that lashed them.

All around stood pillories, stocks and whipping chairs or frames, and wicked little wooden 'prayer stools' with double prongs in the seat to fit into the squatter's gash and anus. And between the lascivious pictures on the walls hung every variety of rod, whip or birch, with shackles and body sheaths, speculums, chains and cock-harnesses, like fine wines arrayed in a cellar for leisurely selection.

A dozen praetorians greeted our entrance gleefully. All were dressed elegantly, in lace, silk and satin, or else in rubber and leather, spiked brassieres pushing titties out like pinecones, with boned corsets on open view that painfully cinched already tight waists. There were dominants and submissives among the guards, too.

Thighs and bellies and cunts, festooned with spikes or rings, were exposed, and some had beringed titties completely bare, or else wore sumptuous velvet or silk tops with ballooned shoulders, stockings and spiked shoes but no skirt or panties. All had bare shaven heads and were tattooed, though none as much as Camilla.

There were no chairs at table; instead, each guard sat on the rigid back of a crouching serf or filly, naked except for rubber pixie hoods. All these serfs were chained to the table by cruelly distended quim-lips, and some by teat-clamps to their mistress's wrist or gauntlet, with cunt and anus filled with double-pronged plugs, fastened to tight waist cinchers. Their thighs dribbled with the juices of submissive excitement.

The chief guard sat at the table's head, and I recognised her stool; that lush golden body, and the blonde mane cascading under the horribly tight rubber hood. Like the other fillies, she had a naked pubis; only the guards had the privilege of cranial nudity. How long had I dreamt of her sweetness, her cunt's wet velvet – of her delicious transformation from submissive to the harshest dominatrix – and ached for her to make me her willing slave. But the road of a born mistress may twist and turn in many directions, just as her slave's naked buttocks writhe and weal under her implacable canestrokes. The hooded serf was Haralda.

16

Fourfold Slave

The chief guard had high rubber gauntlets almost to her shoulders, and a black collar whose long spikes kept her gleaming shaven head haughtily raised. She wore a skimpy corselet of tight black rubber, which left her heavy and big-nippled left teat naked and slightly drooping. Her legs were sheathed in fishnets, attached to the corselet by rubber garter straps; she had one foot on Haralda's arse-cleft, the long spiked heel embedded in the anus.

This shoe was a surgical boot, with the leg in calipers, and with slab rubber soles a good six inches deep, yet with a spiked domina's heel. A vivid scar just below her stockinged knee suggested some surgical procedure. On her thigh dangled a rubber quirt of over a dozen long tongues.

We captives were eagerly hustled to our flogging frames, steel squares with clamps for neck, wrists and ankles, and movable on wheels for the spectators' convenience. I was strapped naked to a wheeled whipping cart, with a cruel restrainer to clamp my balls and cock, and rubber thongs buckled on ankles and wrists. I was to be wheeled around the table by a naked serf wearing an ankle ball and chain that snaked through pierced cunt-lips and nipples to a steel collar, and I was to be caned by each guard in turn.

The maids in attendance were female serfs and wore a pastiche of a French maid's outfit, with flounced little rubber bonnets, skirtlets of black rubber, and white rubber aprons and blouses; these were cut away to reveal both the naked titties, the buttocks – lividly striped – and the shaven cunt-lips. All had their hair in pigtails, and their nipples and quim-lips were tightly clamped in buckled pincers. From these dangled lumps of quartzite, so that their teats and cunt-lips were pulled well down, and, with heavy titties and swelling gash-flaps, they moved painfully with jagged rocks scratching their bellies and thighs.

The guards gleefully quaffed wine or vodka, and clapped as my mistresses were tightly braced into their flogging frames, and myself thonged to my stool with my buttocks well spread by my cock-clamp. The dinner itself was carried by a succession of nude serfs who clambered on to the table and crawled awkwardly round with delicacies of oyster, herring or shrimp carried in their quims! They would squat before a guard's plate and emit a portion from their filled gashes, being caned if the seafood was not deposited neatly; they had sauces in their bumholes, and squirted the fish with brown or yellow liquids.

Paul was given a long cat, the thongs a good six feet, but he took it shakily, his face pale and his hand trembling. I saw frowns at his shrivelled cock, and accusing looks at Camilla, who had evidently boasted of her twin's virility and bugger's prowess. The ladies murmured complaints in the refined accents of Bath or Cheltenham.

Camilla was to cane Matron and Miss Grant with a long rattan, almost as long as the metal-studded cat, and with a tip splayed into three six-inch tongues. My shackled drudge wheeled me to the chief's chair, and I found my face inches from Haralda's hood; I breathed the smell of her latex. The chief lifted her rubber whip, which was studded with sharp nuggets of quartz all along the length of the thongs, and dealt me four vicious strokes across my bare bum, which made my cart jolt as I repressed a scream.

'Haralda!' I sobbed. 'Haralda! It's me, Philip!'

'I do not know you!' she hissed through the rubber mask that covered her lips and allowed only the thinnest of apertures at her mouth. 'By privilege, I am a serf!'

I looked at the magnificent globes of her arse, now cruelly welted and striped by flogging: between her cheeks, forcing the rim of her rectum as wide as a plum, was stuck

219

an anus-plug, attached to a cord held by the chief. Seeing her serf turn her head, she tugged this and Haralda jerked in pain. The arse-plug snaked across her perineum and grew to a larger plug studded with sharp stones that filled her slit, linked by chain to a hobble-bar cuffing her ankles.

My bum shivered again as another vicious cut from the rubber quirt lashed me, followed by three more in quick succession, which left me squirming and breathless. Haralda's own arse was now visited by the chief's vengeful whip, which fell on her bare peach a full seven times, adding to her livid stripes and making her whistle.

'I'll get you,' she hissed, sobbing, 'you'll pay –'

I then received a further five cuts from the whip, whose stone nuggets made my bare flesh smart horribly. The chief cackled, as if her cruelty avenged her own malformation. At her signal, the next guard brandished a thin, whippy willow before me. I saw Camilla applying energetic strokes to the bare bums of Matron and Miss Grant, whose faces were contorted in pain. But Paul seemed scarcely able to lift the cat: the buttocks of Miss Bainbridge and Fitzhurst were merely pink from his feeble strokes.

My buttocks were seared once more, a flurry of over a dozen from the thin cane, which raised peals of laughter from the company. Then there was a cry of 'Borscht!'

One of the maids was upended on the tablecloth, and with her bare bum quivering like jellies a surgical speculum was inserted – the instrument used by women doctors to hold the cunt open for intimate inspection. It was a ring which clamped on the labia, with springed prongs that were pushed right to the womb-neck. The maid took this with tears streaming on her cheeks, and then a tureen full of steaming beetroot porridge was poured and wadded into her open cunt. Then a second speculum was forced into her anus, holding the hole open until it seemed ready to burst, and her spread bumhole was packed with white sour cream.

Like this, with upturned buttocks carefully spread, she crawled round the table, dispensing dollops of the hot borscht from parted cunt-flaps on to the diners' plates, and topping it with a gobbet of the cream from her arsehole. She served the chief last, who pushed away her plate, delivered a vicious hand-spanking to the proffered bare buttocks, and when they were reddened she pressed her nose between the livid bum-cheeks. Her teeth fastened on the cunt and bit the lips before sucking food from them, and then she kissed the arse-bud, slurping greedily as she drained the dregs of food from the girl's stretched holes.

Under Camilla's rattan, Matron had started to wail, and Miss Grant's spectacles had slipped to the end of her nose, slippery wet with tears. Both ladies were shuddering in their tight bonds, their naked bodies and braced necks splayed in an X, the loins weaving and dancing as though to avoid the pitiless rod that struck both bare arses with an almost simultaneous vip! vip!

Camilla did not stint in caning very low and very high, and the tops of both arses were as raw and red as the cherries on a cake, while their upper thighs were wealed brightly like spilt jam; the full central globes of the naked buttocks spectacularly crisscrossed with deft welts, as Camilla dealt strokes time and time again right in the trench of a recent weal. Yet both ladies had trickles of juice from their quims glistening on their thighs, and beneath Matron's bare arse was a golden pool where she had pissed, belly uncontrolled in her agony.

Another maid crouched on the table, again with her bare bum held high and with speculums already inserted into gash and rectum. Toasts were proposed by the boisterous guards, with a choice of pepper vodka or lemon vodka, the first dispensed in artful squirts from the girl's anus, the second from her brimming slit. The company began to look at me. By this time I had taken over fifty welts from various canes or quirts, and my bare arse smarted awfully. At each cut I shuddered against my sharp metal trolley and made it ring – to the amusement of all – but squirming in my thongs and cock-restrainer, all I could do was sob.

Then they scrutinised the flogging in process, after ordering the positions to be changed. Miss Grant's and Matron's scarlet faces were masks of agony; Miss

Bainbridge wore an expression of lofty scorn as the cat feebly slapped her bum, and Fitzhurst actually wore a smirk. Paul was dripping with sweat: normally the sight of a naked brute like him flogging two naked women would thrill any lady, but the diners murmured displeasure. They clamoured to see me buggered; the dread moment had come.

Camilla was told sharply by the chief that her twin had better buck up his performance and deliver a proper buggery, or Camilla herself would be deemed unsound. Unsound! There was a ripple of shock, and I knew this was the most dreaded word in the English public-school lexicon.

Sweating profusely, Paul approached my trolley, which was placed beneath Miss Bainbridge's feet. I groaned in shame and from the smarting of my wealed bottom as I felt the naked male slump directly on top of me, his soft cock in my own furrow! Never had I imagined such shame, and my pain was nothing to my horrified humiliance as I felt his giant body lurch against me under the impact of the rattan wielded by his twin Camilla on his own bare bum.

He took twenty in rapid succession, enough to harden the cock of any submissive male, yet his cock was as soft as a raspberry by the flogging's end. There were jeers and slow hand-claps, and Camilla in desperation made Paul stand, knelt before him and took his flaccid cock and balls fully into her gaping mouth, her lips and tongue working furiously to bring his cock to hardness. It did not work.

'Buggery! Bugger the boy!' cried the assembled guards, sucking vodka from the pumping holes of their serfs.

Their consumption of drink was such that they had frequent occasion to make commode; cane on naked rump brought the girl to her knees, mouth open like a sparrow, and casually the guard pissed into her open lips.

Camilla looked distraught. I saw the chief bend her shaven skull to Haralda's hooded head and heard a whisper. Haralda was released from her position and hobbled towards me in her shackles, her pale nudity gleaming with sweat and well striped on nipples, thigh and bare fesses

Her eyes gleamed savagely as she took position behind me, and I saw she held a steel speculum! I sobbed and groaned as I felt the vicious metal prongs inserted roughly into my anus, then expand to spread my hole wide, to my unspeakable agony. The rim was clipped to the folds of skin of my lower fesses, and then I felt one of Haralda's fingers probe my open bumhole. There followed a second finger, a third, the nails sharp as knives on my tender bum-wall, and they pushed steadily towards my root.

My anus screamed with the pain, and I writhed helplessly in my cock-vice; Haralda got her whole hand inside my spread arsehole, balling it into a fist, and began a vicious buggery that thrust her arm into my bumhole right to my root, and with half her forearm inside me. My cock was rock hard in this humiliant agony and scraped the metal wall of her restrainer as the excruciating tickle of buggered pleasure flooded me.

Haralda fisted me most brutally, to uproarious cheering, punching my root with her fist, my buggery far harder than before, when my hole was dildoed in the gymnasium. I looked up at Miss Bainbridge for sympathy but saw her smile in satisfaction, her face bright red and a stream of shiny love-juice flowing on her trembling naked thighs. Through my tears I saw her belly flutter, and she panted. A droplet glistened at her swollen fat cunt-lips, then another – she was trying to hold back, but in vain, and soon a golden shower of her piss splattered my face.

Suddenly I could no longer resist. Haralda's powerful fist-fucking in my stretched anus had my balls churning with cream that begged to be released, and when she unballed her fist and pinched the root of my anus, tweaking me very tightly between two fingers, my agony and humiliance was so excruciating that my balls gave up their load of sperm, which squirted from the edges of my restrainer like the cascade from a garden watering can.

'O . . . O . . .,' Miss Bainbridge sighed, and then cried out sharply, and I knew the sight of my spunk cascading made her come to orgasm.

The guards, too, were busy at increasingly fervid

embraces, frotting and even kissing one another on nipple, mouth or clitty at the spectacle of my buggery. Only Paul seemed forgotten, slumped in his sister's arms, and embarrassing her by his failure. No sooner had I spurted than Camilla herself was seized, and Paul thrust down with his face on the table. Then Camilla, after five resounding lashes of the chief's quirt on her tattooed bum-skin, was obliged to ball her own fist and bugger the hulking male, her twin, just as Haralda had fist-fucked me.

He writhed and screamed, and Camilla, grinning despite her striped nates, worked fiercely to rouse his flaccid cock with hard punches inside his strained rectum. Fitzhurst winked at me, and my heart swelled with gratitude to my four new mistresses – their draining of Paul's scrotum had saved me from a hideous, shameful fate.

But a further task awaited. Haralda withdrew her fist from my anus and removed the speculum, which she thrust into the gibbering Paul's mouth to silence him. Then, it was the work of a moment for her to bring my sticky cock to full erection again with two dozen stingers on bare bum, from the chief's heavy rubber quirt. Released, I knelt and covered her feet with kisses, aching in worship, but two guards pulled me away and placed me behind the pumping Camilla, red with exertion and shame at her failed promise.

I was to bugger her for her own punishment! We must have made a curious spectacle as I pushed my stiff cock quite roughly – vengefully, I must admit – into the red little honeysuckle of her bumhole and thrust my shaft until the glans touched root. She cried out in shame and pain as I fucked her very hard and to great applause – pleasing even to a slave's ego – for my balls were well drained and I knew I could fuck indefinitely without risk of spurt.

Gradually I became aware of a pair of eyes surveying the scene from the slightly open door. They watched me for a long time as I fucked, and with (I hope pardonable) male vanity I put on a good performance, gratified that I brought the squirming Camilla to orgasm after vigorously spanking her bare buttocks with my palms a good hundred or so times. As my cock slammed hard into her tight slimy bum-gash, she groaned in pleasure and vigorously fist-fucked her twin, but still his spread arse and flaccid balls hid the merest pimple of a once-mighty cock.

Emboldened, I reached down and put my fingers in Camilla's cunt, then began to tweak her boatman until he was stiff and throbbing again, and she howled in angry pleasured shame as I made her come a second time, this time her spend accompanied by a generous flood of piss that slopped her feet and mine and steamed in a golden pool.

There was the sound of two hands clapping at the doorway and a gorgeous figure entered, flanked by two tattooed praetorians, nude but for gleaming metal corsets, and wearing purple, not pink, helmet plumes. She herself was nude under a billowing, semi-transparent veil. All three women wore high spiked boots and at their crotch a belt from which dangled an enormous black dildo and balls. The veiled mistress carried a long whip with a jewelled hilt and four jewelled black thongs, which she cracked lazily in the air. There was an instant hush. The guards ceased their gamahuching, and in haste fell to their knees.

'Mistress Dushanka!' gasped the chief guard with an obsequious smile, tangling her whip in her surgical boot.

'Why, girls, carry on your sport,' said Mistress Dushanka in a melodious English voice that was the twin of her sister Galena's. 'The male *robotnik* – how virile! Enough, it seems, to serve four mistresses at once! When he has proved himself thus, he may be fit to serve *me*.'

My life for the next four months at Masterdale was the dream of any submissive male: to serve *four* mistresses! I had what every submissive longs for, and thus wanted for nothing, except the exquisite pleasure of longing.

To a true submissive, fucking is secondary to the supreme joy of pain and humiliance: a spurt can never rival a flogging, for who can remember orgasm? But every submissive remembers with relish his welts and degradation: the curl of scorn on the lips of a demanding mistress as she flogs his bare bottom while he licks her boots spotless for the third time in a bright sunlit morning.

After the flagellant praetorian dinner, my mistresses resumed their normal roles within the hierarchy of Masterdale, addressing each other with exquisite formality; the proceedings of the praetorians were not mentioned. I lost track of my former comrades in servitude: Denning, Rowena and even my beloved Haralda. I hoped that Haralda had found her niche with the praetorians, whether as slave or guard or bizarre combination of both. I glimpsed Denning once or twice, a sullen drudge much whipped in slaughterhouse, tannery or goldsmith's.

At first, I should serve each mistress on alternate days. Soon it became clear that some of the tasks and punishments allotted me would be more efficient for my humiliation if spread over two or three days – for example, the enforced wearing of chafing and humiliating restraints, or female clothing or enforced nudity. Now each mistress should have me for a week, during which another mistress was to treat me like any other *robotnik* and flog me no more but no less severely. When I was hers again, she was free to devise the most intricate and painful humiliations.

Miss Bainbridge was the most regal, liking to chain me naked by a dog-leash while I licked her parquet floor clean, or her boots. She insisted that her household be spotless and I was kept busy, under threat of constant lashings with the riding crop which was her favoured tool. For maid's housework, she dressed me as a filly, in a French maid's uniform, or a parlourmaid's apron, always bewigged and with face painted.

It also pleased her to send me to classes, dressed as a girl – males being unworthy of instruction – and in Miss Grant's class we both pretended that she knew me only distantly, among the hundreds of Masterdale fillies, and when she frequently caned my bare bum in front of the class she was always careful to draw my knickers down only partly, so as to hide my manhood.

The scholarly Miss Grant also kept me nude for my work, as she thought it more efficient. I had to help her sort papers and books and to take dictation for a book she herself was writing on the Scottish arts of correction. She thought the English lacking in seriousness and reverence for the flogged posterior and devoted many pages to ingenious instruments such as the tawse, or the 'Highland tail', or the 'crofter's cudgel', which was a baton of solid granite, about three feet by three inches in width. My naked bottom tasted them all.

The tawse was designed for long, humiliating flogging, and two hundred strokes on bare was quite normal, while fifty rounds with the cruel weight of the crofter's cudgel made me stiff and sore for days, to my unspoken delight. The Highland tail was a bull's tail dried and pickled, with the beast's pizzle or cock stitched to the tip, and weighted with metal studs. This, too, caused unbearable agony, and I never took less than five dozen, the strokes divided between back and buttocks. For back-stripes I was obliged to stand on tiptoe with my fingertips touching the wall, like a seaman flogged at the mast.

Matron's approach was more surgical. Naturally I had to help in the wards, helping to hold down or even whip the naked arse of an errant filly. I also had to administer lavage to squirming arseholes and became quite expert at that, since I took the treatment regularly myself. Matron liked to beat my buttocks with a rubber hosepipe, a very heavy instrument that hurts abominably, especially on wet buttocks; frequently she would administer it under lavage with my bumhole plugged, and these strokes were torment.

Fitzhurst was the most athletic of the four. Her small apartment was surprisingly scruffy, like a boy's, and wanted little cleaning. But she liked to saddle me and ride me around the rooms like a pony, energetically lashing my thighs with sharp English spurs and beating my buttocks with a short quirt of ten studded thongs.

She also introduced me to pony-racing. I would be bridled, shod and harnessed, with blinkers, and tethered to a chariot, from which she would flog me with a long horsewhip to race round the track in competition with other male and female slaves. Drivers as well as ponies were nude, and drivers were permitted to strike their opponents with their whips, so that frequently Fitzhurst's nude bottom and back ended the race as scarred as my own.

Though blinkered, I was sometimes able to espy my competitors. Twice I saw Haralda, driven by a praetorian, and on both occasions she won, my defeat earning me a vicious flogging in Fitzhurst's apartment. She would truss me in leg-irons and a woman's tight corset, gag me with her own sopping, soiled panties, and flog my bum raw with rattan or quirt, while she masturbated to orgasm, cursing the stiffness of my cock under my – delicious! – beating.

Even after coming, she would spit on me and kick me and then squat over my face to piss; then take my stiff cock right into her spread anus, and bugger herself, riding me anew while she masturbated to a fresh moaning climax.

None of my mistresses could manage to ignore the constant stiffness of my cock in humiliance. Matron liked to be fucked in her anus, before her own lavage, which I administered deep between her squirming melons. Miss Bainbridge would permit me to take her from behind, but in cunt, while I dusted or cleaned, wearing full maid's frillies, and she pretended to write a letter.

Miss Grant would busy herself with papers, using me as a stool, and make me arch my back, naked, supporting myself on my elbows and knees, and impale her cunt on my cock while she frequently took off her glasses to wipe them, all the while churning my penis and tickling my balls, until her churning became bouncing, and her love-juice cascaded over my belly and she would spill her papers in signal of a noisy climax.

One day, after a tumultuous orgasm, she bit her lip and said that naughty Scottish girls must be spanked, and she was a naughty Scottish girl. I put her over my knee and obliged with a bare-bum spanking of thirty or so, which had my palm quite sore.

'No,' she gasped somewhat irritably, 'that won't do.'

I fetched a tawse and gave her bare bottom a hundred and fifty hard, slow strokes, while she masturbated herself to two more climaxes. It seemed that was enough – for the moment.

Shortly after, Miss Bainbridge admitted me to her chambers entirely nude. I feigned not to notice and donned my girl's frillies as usual, and instead of a feather duster she handed me her rattan.

17

Family of the Knout

'I have forgotten what it is like to feel a good tanning,' she said haughtily, 'and forgetfulness is imperfect, so for that, maid, you shall beat me on bare.'

Naturally I obeyed, and raised delicious red welts with a good forty strokes of the rattan, which had her squirming violently as she stood on tiptoe, bent over her chairback. Without shifting from her place, she then loftily ordered me to fuck her in the anus. I saw that her thighs dripped with gash-oil and used it to lubricate her bumhole. She frigged her clit as I buggered her and came very rapidly.

'There!' she said with a smile as she rose, rubbing her sore bum. 'I don't think I shall be forgetful any more – not with frequent reminders from my slave.'

Fitzhurst, too, began to make me fuck her without any preamble or games: she would birch me naked – she said Miss Bainbridge had given her a supply – then, at first to my astonishment, invite me to birch her own bottom. She, too, was nude and insisted on more strokes than I had taken, as though to prove herself: if I took forty, she would have fifty.

My cock throbbed at her delicious hard arse writhing naked and purpled under the crackle of the birch; afterwards she cursed my erection, fastening her lips around my glans and sucking eagerly, wetting me with her tears while her cunt-juices flowed to her floor matting. When she had sucked my cock and licked my balls, she would spit on them and direct my glans to her anus bud, spreading her cheeks and crouching with her face to the floor.

I buggered that wealed and bony croup with genuine enthusiasm. Sometimes she would make me come in her anus, then birch me again until I was hard, and make me take her in gash, lying on her back and locking her long muscled thighs around my neck as I pumped to spurt in her wet cunt.

I think Fitzhurst was my favourite mistress, with her raw savagery and resentment, as though in whipping me she was whipping herself; when I beat her she genuinely wanted to be hurt. With the other ladies, tasting my cock, or having me beat their naked bums, was more a natural task, like a chamber pot wiped clean, distasteful but necessary, and occasioning relief when it was over. But Fitzhurst revelled in my humiliation and her own.

One day she strapped on a huge black dildo, like that in which Mistress Dushanka had briefly appeared. She grinned evilly as she birched my arse in preparation for buggery, for I knew that only Mistress Dushanka and her personal praetorians were permitted this daunting luxury. Fitzhurst buggered me hard and long until I sobbed for mercy, but she showed none, raining blows from her short quirt on my naked buttocks as they clenched in agony under that fearful dildo's penetration of my deepest innards. She asked me dreamily if I had ever been buggered by a black man, and when I indignantly said no she said it was the loveliest thing on earth.

'But this is nothing to what you'll get when the Mistress calls a whipping-feast!' she would taunt me as she bum-fucked me.

She said this almost wistfully, and more and more I sensed that Fitzhurst alone of my mistresses was pleading to be a male and to submit to be flogged as one.

At last, a whipping-feast was announced! By tradition, in the vaulted kremlin hall, the staff and fillies sat in tiers below Dushanka's throne, according to rank; all the *robotniks* and serfs were below, naked in pillories. Throughout the meal, they were whipped with the knout,

231

by praetorians expert in orchestrating their screams in a symphony for Dushanka's pleasure. There followed debauched scenes that Fitzhurst only hinted at.

I sensed that my mistresses exchanged confidences about me: their modesty dissolved at the same pace. Furthermore, as they demanded harsher beatings from me, my own lashings became more perfunctory. I began to see them together, and on weeks off two or three of my mistresses would gather for a pooled session of discipline, which usually ended with all of us naked, and the ladies caning or gamahuching each other while I wielded the cane or stood while my erect penis was sucked by eager lips, or else fucked one lady after another in anus or cunt; always with perfect mistress's decorum. Yet my mistresses seemed to worship the size and stiffness of my cock, and I felt uneasy: I, the submissive, should grovel at *their* feet.

For my sleeping arrangements, Misses Grant and Bainbridge provided me with hard planks, to which I was chained by neck or ankle, with my cock usually in a restrainer. Matron liked to truss me in splints, which I hated, and wrap me in a hospital bed, with my bum and prepuce clamped, so that I was unable to make commode until morning. Fitzhurst carelessly chained my cock on her bedpost and made me sleep on her rush-matting floor, but after a while she took me into her bed and practised *soixante-neuf* with me as though I were another female.

I fucked her only in daytime and out of bed, but at night she gushed with a copious flow of love-juice for my swallowing, as she writhed with the full weight of her huge arse suffocating my face and her fingers masturbating the swollen knob of her clitty against my eager tongue and nose. She enjoyed pissing noisily on my face while she came.

Miss Bainbridge, I knew, had other slaves – all fillies, a degree higher than serfs. Miss Grant announced that sharing me would not do and that she needed a full-time slave: Emma Porritt was shyly introduced to my disciplinary sessions, and my cock and flogging arm were further strained. Matron, of course, had her nurses;

Fitzhurst said I was to meet an 'old friend' – her new slave was Belinda! I looked in awe at her whip-scarred body, the rings that tightly clamped her pierced cunt-lips and nipples, and wished I, too, could possess such beauty, to submit so proudly.

Belinda proved an adept and true submissive, especially with witnesses. Fucking her beringed cunt was a new and thrilling sensation, and she took hard bare caning with only the sweetest gasps of pain at the writhing of her puffy welted bottom. She liked golden downpour, being pissed on by all of us at once, and all the ladies enjoyed seeing my stiff cock spout her narrow jet straight up, like a fountain.

Matron made showering games a regular feature in her infirmary, and the ladies performed quite casually or unannounced, this surprise being part of the fun as they washed each other's bare bums with hearty golden jets of piss. Emma Porritt appeared, stripped for her caning, and she, too, bore the rings. And Matron brought Rowena Tushingham, at whose aspect I brightened, for I remembered her haughty viciousness and looked forward to a thorough thrashing from her. But no – she, too, shyly showed a single cunt-ring and a thin ring pierced in each nipple, through holes designed to accommodate far more.

Rowena excelled at taking enemas, and she had a further ring pierced right through her anus bud which made her jet spray like a hosepipe. Sometimes she brought Arkwright, who excelled at cunnilingus and anal penetration with fingers, and the two would gamahuche or fist-fuck as my mistresses masturbated each other's clitties and sopping gashes.

Emma and Belinda demanded to be anally ringed too. Such marks of slavery were forbidden to seniors, but I saw Fitzhurst stroking and licking the rings in the girls' cunts and bumholes, as their bare bums were prettily lined up for chastisement, as though she longed to exchange her prefecture for slavery she had once known as a filly.

I noted that no further male slaves were introduced and began to feel isolated. The elements of surprise and fear, so essential to a slave, were somehow lacking. I thought fondly of my mistress Galena and my delicious imprisonment in dread of her capricious power. I even thought longingly of my dear Becky – the enchantment of discovering that her cosy Essex cottage harboured an expert dominatrix.

Belinda was a cruel reminder of Becky, since, like me, she was not dominant but truly submissive. She loved being fucked by Fitzhurst's massive dildo almost as much as by my cock, especially when my cock filled her anus and the dildo her cunt. But always I felt myself distant, my virility an icon, while the ladies writhed under each other's whips and tongues and indulged in every luscious tribadism, using my cock as a key to unleash their real lesbic lusts.

I felt I was taken for granted! My only consolation was their increasing delight in robing me as a female, without which no male submission is true: the silky feel of stockings rolled up the shaven leg (I, too, was completely shaven now, apart from my cropped head); the bite of panties in anus and furrow as they are pulled up tight; the stretch and stiff caress of brassiere and corset; and the feathery touch of the wig as powder and paint are applied by mischievous female fingers. Then the pouting and preening in the mirror, just like a girl, though the cock throbs stiff to bursting when the 'girlie' is upturned for a vigorous caning or spanking on 'her' bare, the panties so lovingly rolled up now ripped mercilessly down, and the buttocks spread to receive the hard dildo thrust right to the root of 'her' anus for a hard buggering: in short, the joy of being robed *as* a lady *by* ladies, and fucked as one.

Still, I yearned for more! When Fitzhurst told me that the next week would see a whipping-feast, I was thrilled.

The great hall of the kremlin was decked as sumptuously as any Caesar's palace. The complement of Masterdale, nearly a thousand souls, wore the most luxurious finery, or the most chilling dominant uniforms, or else nothing at all.

The dining-area was tiered like the entry to an ancient Greek temple, with each tier containing a long dining-table, and at the top, the place of Mistress Dushanka herself, and her two acolytes, the senior praetorians. Below stood an array of pillories, a good six feet tall, half with anal prongs standing cruelly high, and half with prongs for both anus and cunt.

We male slaves were the first to enter, and were thrust into our pillories, our wrists strapped, and the prongs thrust into our bumholes. Then the females entered chained, and were fastened to their own twin-pronged poles. The company of praetorians, all nude, took position, each with a real knout, and in charge of flogging a row of a dozen bare bodies. We watched as the fillies entered in their school uniforms, then the prefects, the monitors and mistresses, and then Mistress Dushanka herself, gorgeous in a sequinned silk corselet with a gauze veil over shoulder and sleeve, and leaving her stockinged legs bare – the suspender straps on full view – to show the massive dildo between her thighs, not dangling now but erect like a penis.

On a double leash, she led two naked pets on studded collars: Camilla and her twin Paul. Her two acolytes followed her, carrying black whips and nude except for the same erect organs. I recognised one of them, despite her cruel, shiny shaven head – it was Haralda. Dushanka's blonde mane was full, and my heart ached, for she was the image of her sister, my adored Countess Galena.

At a signal from Mistress Dushanka, the praetorians raised their whips and in unison lashed the bare backs of the first in the line of pillories. There was a piercing shriek, as though from violins. The next crack came, and the next, bass voices screaming now with shrill treble females, until the music of our pain enlivened the diners and the meal commenced. I was at the end of my line of pillories; the cock-prong was agony in my raw bumhole, but nothing compared with the lash of the knout across my naked shoulders.

I wriggled and screamed like all the others: a long studded knout can have no other effect. Then, the trembling wait for the next stroke as my screams ebbed to a sob and my fellow sufferers pierced the air with their own yells. The strokes were given alternately to back and buttocks; only a few from the knout and the flesh is wealed deep and ugly purple. Many times I felt about to faint, and those who did, male or female (the same strength of knout was used on both), were crudely roused with a bucket of ice-crusted water.

The assembled ladies were merry with the music of our flogging. Each filly, prefect and monitor in turn was permitted to ascend the steps and kiss Dushanka's foot, while her acolytes gave ten strokes each on the bared buttocks. Also, certain male and female slaves were detached from their pillories to wrestle naked, daubed in grease, on a raised platform. The victor in these contests was ordered to bugger (or dildo) the loser on pain of returning to the pillory. I was matched – by design, I know – against Denning. I used every unfair trick and made him submit, and the brute grinned and spread his arse for my cock, but I refused him this satisfaction and we were both sent back to the knout. I saw Mistress Dushanka eyeing our combat with particular interest and applauding my decision.

By the end of the banquet only a dozen or so male cocks stood stiff under that flogging. Most of the females had pissed themselves, but some bore streams of cunt-juice. They, and we erect males, were the true submissives. We were paraded like victors of our hideous ordeal, to the applause of the company; our prize, or penalty, was to bugger or be buggered by the male or female of our choice.

First, we were led up to Mistress Dushanka's throne; kissed her boots while we received ten extra strokes from each praetorian, which I hardly felt, and then had to bare our fesses for Dushanka and each of her guards to bugger us in turn, male and female. As prologue to the spectacle, Paul thrust his cock in his twin sister's cunt and slowly fucked her hard, in doggy fashion, with orders not to spurt.

I was buggered gently until it was Haralda's turn, then almost spurted, so hard was her shafting! Though she was lost to me and could never be my mistress, I loved her and wanted her to fuck my bumhole raw. But her buggery was nothing beside Dushanka's. She was a consummate mistress. Her dildo had the force of a living thing as it poked and slammed and prodded in my anus until my agony was perfect, and I knew she was Galena's sister. She fucked my anus for fifteen minutes until we had to choose our sodomic partners.

Rowena Tushingham, her thighs streaming with piss and cunt-juice, was chosen by Denning, while Crocker took Emma Porritt. When my turn came, I looked again and saw only the image of my adored mistress. Haralda stared at me, and for the first time her lips creased in a smile of invitation.

I chose to bugger Mistress Dushanka herself.

My voice was greeted with shocked silence, then uproar, stilled by a wave of Dushanka's hand.

'The male may choose to bugger any female,' she said. 'He is smarter and braver than the rest of you. He may have me – *after he has been bangled.*'

I have described Belinda's painful bangling – my own humiliance was beyond pain. I was tattooed on my wealed buttocks, my breasts and penis-shaft, and on my glans itself. My tattoos represented the nude female cunt, or buttocks, or the breasts themselves, so that forever after I would wear a cruel mockery of my manhood. I wore a silver ring pierced right through my glans, called an 'Albert'; a half-dozen rings at my perineum, between my balls and anus, and called 'guiches'; three rings pierced through each orb of my ball-sac and a ring sewn through the stretched lips of my arse-bud itself. All were welded fast by scalding iron, so that I could never remove them: I was marked for life.

Dushanka knelt and bared her buttocks, spreading them so that I saw she wore the cunt-rings and guiches, and a larger guiche through her anus, big enough for my erect cock.

I buggered her hard but briefly, for her elastic anus milked my cock so deftly and her writhing peach-globes bewitched me so that I spurted copiously and fast, my sperm

237

spilling over her anal guiche and on to her thighs. She shuddered in orgasm! And then shortly after she gasped that I must leave Masterdale, and return to the eastbound train, as though the preceding four months had not happened.

'Your virility disturbs our family of girls,' she said. 'I hear more about you than I wish. My sister Galena may relish female gash, but her true love is humiliating males. *My* academy is not for male correction. We allow males to be submissive because we cannot really be bothered to make them anything else. We esteem the lesbic pleasures, and cock is a spice, not a substitute, for cunt. We all have an occasional appetite for buggery or fucking by male, much as one eats an ice-cream occasionally on a hot day: but it must remain occasional. That cock of yours, Philip, is *not* occasional. You are, by your own endowment, surplus to requirements.'

I was numb with distress, but a lady had given her command.

'Thank you, Mistress,' I said, kissing her boots. 'It is my duty to obey.'

I could not but help admire the lady who shared my first-class compartment as the train rolled across the Siberian plains, now a vast carpet of spring flowers. She sat next to the closed window, feet on the banquette opposite, with a book and a sheaf of documents, and her skirts and petticoats drawn up for her ease, so much that I saw her purple suspenders and frilly knickers.

Her stockings were of the purest white silk, her thin petticoat apparently of mille-feuille black latex, and her boots of clinging leather with steel spikes for heels and toecaps. Her face and corn-yellow hair were veiled under a large black bonnet, so I did not distinguish her features. Outside in the corridor there was quite a bustle, and I saw a blue naval uniform just like my own pass back and forth and peer quickly inside.

She ignored my presence until she suddenly said: 'Boy, open the window. I wish to smell the flowers.'

238

I had to clamber across her legs to do so but obeyed a lady's command. I saw the title of her leather-bound book: *Divers Instructions for the Discipline and Chastysement of Errant Males by Stricte Mistresses.*

She did not thank me but continued reading, until she threw the book to the floor and said: 'Bah! Not much new in that. Take a look, boy, perhaps *you* will learn something.'

I got to my knees and reached for the book under the banquette. I could somehow sense her eyes inspecting my bottom. As I read, I recalled all my fond memories, which I had been trying to suppress in my sadness at leaving Masterdale. Woodcut illustrations showed naked young males flogged, racked and pilloried, and all manner of whips and rods used to chastise their bare buttocks, with detailed instructions to the corrective ladies, who were very skimpily attired, or in dominas' costumes, or nude: surprisingly for such an antique book, but stern mistresses are timeless.

'I dare say a whelp like *you* knows nothing of such matters,' she snapped, her voice as firm and fluted and English as any lady of Masterdale.

I blurted out my whole story! She said nothing, but nodded and pursed her lips.

'Going to sea, eh?' she sneered. 'You know what Dr Johnson said: "No man would take a ship who could get a prison, for a ship is but a prison with the risk of drowning." Let me see your bare bum, boy.'

I was taken aback at her extraordinary command! But it was a lady's order, and I obeyed without question. Cool fingers ran along the ridges of my many painful welts.

'Hmmph!' she said. 'Perhaps the whelp is not *quite* green. *I* run a prison – a *kind* of prison – for unruly males. Masterdale is just for *gels* – although we do have some correspondence, and Dushie sends me some of her more promising ones.'

She scanned her papers.

'Let's see ... Bainbridge ... Haralda ... Fitzhurst ... somebody called Demesne ... who knows, they might

239

prove useful. In my establishment there is none of this soppy nonsense about gels with gels. My women are there for one thing only: to flog and enslave and inflict as much pain on naked male bodies as the serfs can possibly endure – and that is only the *beginning* of their discipline. I have plenty of money, so my pleasure in discipline is its own end: total chastisement and humiliation of the male, without mercy.'

She looked at my crotch and saw I was erect.

'I have need of extra slaves,' she drawled, throwing off her veil; her blonde mane cascaded over her breast.

I gasped; she was the image of Dushanka – of Mistress Galena herself.

'Well?' she snapped. 'We are nearly at Irkutsk, and I can use an extra pony or two to pull my droshky.'

'I – I am supposed to go to sea, Mistress,' I stammered, 'on the Royal Stavanger Line.'

'Bah!' she snorted. 'I *own* the Royal Stavanger Line. Consider yourself dismissed this instant. Anyway, there will be a war soon, and all the ships will be sunk, while my sister Galena makes a fortune from her munitions and bandages. *You*, worm, can be safe as a slave of women.'

She looked into my eyes and touched my throbbing cock.

'I am Princess Irena Volchuk,' she said, 'and am addressed as Mistress. But as a slave you will never be allowed to address me at all, on pain of a naked flogging.'

At that moment the door slid open and the blue uniform I had seen before seated itself beside me. I looked in amazement, for it was the same uniform Haralda had worn, but the handsome face beneath the cropped dark hair and the peaked seaman's cap was not Haralda's.

'I could not let you leave me,' she whispered.

'Fitzhurst!' I cried, overjoyed.

'Pardon me for the intrusion, Mistress,' said Fitzhurst, 'but I could not help overhearing. You need extra ponies to pull your droshky – perhaps I might be of service?'

She paused, her lips trembling, obviously longing to beg for more. Princess Irena scrutinised her with distaste.

240

'I do *not* pardon the intrusion,' she said, 'and you may expect to be punished for it as long as I possess a knout. You too,' she added, with the hint of a grin, '*Mister* Demesne. I take it, then, that you both accept my dominion?'

I embraced Fitzhurst and with hands clasped we sank to our knees before her.

'Yes, Mistress!' we cried in unison, thus earning a naked flogging.

'I supposed you would,' Princess Irena sighed. 'In Russia, we are such a large family.'

NEW BOOKS

Coming up from Nexus, Sapphire and Black Lace

Nexus

Giselle by Jean Aveline

October 1999   £5.99   ISBN: 0 352 33440 1

Aside from her extreme beauty, Giselle appears to be an ordinary country girl when the English photographer Charles discovers her in Northern France. Yet when he takes her to Paris to recreate her as a model, he discovers that she has a history. On an island in a flooded quarry in Avignon, boys and men have already reached her and corrupted her. All Charles can do is feed her appetite for perverse sex, and the higher she rises in the world of fashion the lower she falls in her sexual games with strangers.

House Rules by G.C. Scott

October 1999   £5.99   ISBN: 0 352 33441 X

When Richard meets Helena in Hamburg's red light district, he isn't prepared for either the forwardness with which she seduces him or his imminent involvement in her curious business dealings. For Helena is a designer of fetish clothing, and her colleagues have very forceful ideas about how a man should be treated.

Bound to Serve by Amanda Ware

October 1999   £5.99   ISBN: 0 352 33457 6

Caroline West is facing up to the absence of her master, Liam, as he battles to save himself from bankruptcy. When the cruel and manipulative Clive offers her a means of helping him, on condition that she becomes his slave for three weeks, she does not hesitate, and is soon signed over to him. She is then handed over to Lynne, her former mistress for further, more severe training – treatment which Caroline soon finds is more and more to her liking. A Nexus Classic.

In For a Penny by Penny Birch

November 1999   £5.99   ISBN: 0 352 33449 5

Penny Birch is back, as naughty as ever. *In for a Penny* continues the story of her outrageous sex life and also the equally rude behaviour of her friends. From stories of old-fashioned spankings, through strip-wrestling in baked beans, to a girl with six breasts, it's all there. Each scene is described in loving detail, with no holding back and a level of realism that comes from a great deal of practical experience.

Maiden by Aishling Morgan

November 1999   £5.99   ISBN: 0 352 33466 5

When Elethrine, Princess Talithea and their maid, Aisla, threaten to spank the sorceress Ea, they are punished by being transported to a distant part of their world. *Maiden* charts their journey home through a series of erotic indignities and humiliations, throughout all of which Elethrine is determined to retain her virginity. What she doesn't realise is that this will involve far more humiliating encounters for her than for her companions.

Bound to Submit by Amanda Ware

November 1999   £5.99   ISBN: 0 352 33451 7

The beautiful and submissive Caroline is married to her new master and the love of her life, James, at a bizarre fetishistic ceremony in the USA. He is keen to turn his new wife into a star of explicit movies and Caroline is auditioned without delay for a film of bondage and domination. Little do they know that the project is being financed by James' business rival and Caroline's former master, the cruel Clive. Clive intends to fulfil a long-held desire – to permanently mark Caroline as his property. Can her husband save her from his mesmeric influence? A Nexus Classic.

A new imprint of lesbian fiction

Getaway by Suzanne Blaylock
October 1999   Price £6.99   ISBN: 0 352 33443 6
Brilliantly talented Polly Sayers had made two big life shifts concurrently. She's had her first affair with a woman, and she's also stolen the code of an important new piece of software and made her break, doing a runner all the way to a seemingly peaceful coastal community. But things aren't as tranquil as they appear in the haven, as Polly becomes immersed in an insular group of mysterious but very attractive women.

No Angel by Marian Malone
November 1999   £6.99   ISBN 0 352 33462 2
Sally longs to test her limits and sample forbidden pleasures, yet she's frightened by the depth of her yearnings. Her journey of self-discovery begins in the fetish clubs of Brighton and ultimately leads to an encounter with an enigmatic female stranger. And now that she's tasted freedom, there's no way she's going back.

B L A C K
l a c e

The Ties That Bind by Tesni Morgan
October 1999   Price £5.99   ISBN: 0 352 33438 X
When Kim meets devilish stanger Jack Loring at a fancy-dress party, her comfortable world turns upside down. For a start, Jack might have some family ties to Kim, which only makes their mutual attraction all the more problematic. As he demonstrates some kinky new ways of loving her, she's torn between his amoral lust for life and her love for her husband – which will she choose?

In the Dark by Zoe le Verdier
October 1999   Price £5.99   ISBN: 0 352 33439 8
Zoe le Verdier's first collection of stunning short stories, *Insomnia*, pushed the boundaries of women's erotica – but this collection looks set to be even hotter. The author's never been afraid to explore the most explicit female fantasies, from kinky fetishism to sex with a stranger, and her unashamed, powerfully erotic style shows these situations as you've never seen them before.

Bound by Contract by Helena Ravenscroft
November 1999   Price £5.99   ISBN: 0 352 33447 9
Samantha and Ross have been an illicit item for years – rivals as children, and passionate lovers as adults. When Ross becomes involved with the submissive Dr Louisa Richmond, Sam senses his waning interest in her own dominating ways. Reading the classic *Venus in Furs* inspires her to sign a contract to be Ross's slave for a month. She imagines it will rekindle the spark in their relationship – but it becomes altogether more erotic, and totally out of her control.

Velvet Glove by Emma Holly
November 1999   Price £5.99   ISBN: 0 352 33448 7
At the ripe young age of 22, Audrey is an SM Goldilocks in search of the perfect master. Her first candidate, an icy-eyed international banker, is far too hard. Her second, a childhood playmate, is far too soft. A charismatic bar owner seems just right, especially when he saves her from a watcher the bank has set on her trail. But can Audrey trust the man behind the charm? Or will Patrick drag her deeper into submission than even she would care to go?

Nexus

NEXUS BACKLIST

All books are priced £5.99 unless another price is given. If a date is supplied, the book in question will not be available until that month in 1999.

CONTEMPORARY EROTICA

THE ACADEMY	Arabella Knight	
AMANDA IN THE PRIVATE HOUSE	Esme Ombreux	
BAD PENNY	Penny Birch	
THE BLACK MASQUE	Lisette Ashton	
THE BLACK WIDOW	Lisette Ashton	
BOUND TO OBEY	Amanda Ware	
BRAT	Penny Birch	
DANCE OF SUBMISSION	Lisette Ashton	Nov
DARK DELIGHTS	Maria del Rey	
DARK DESIRES	Maria del Rey	
DARLINE DOMINANT	Tania d'Alanis	
DISCIPLES OF SHAME	Stephanie Calvin	
THE DISCIPLINE OF NURSE RIDING	Yolanda Celbridge	
DISPLAYS OF INNOCENTS	Lucy Golden	
EMMA'S SECRET DOMINATION	Hilary James	
EXPOSING LOUISA	Jean Aveline	
FAIRGROUND ATTRACTIONS	Lisette Ashton	
GISELLE	Jean Aveline	Oct
HEART OF DESIRE	Maria del Rey	
HOUSE RULES	G.C. Scott	Oct
IN FOR A PENNY	Penny Birch	Nov
JULIE AT THE REFORMATORY	Angela Elgar	
LINGERING LESSONS	Sarah Veitch	

ANCIENT & FANTASY SETTINGS

EDWARDIAN, VICTORIAN & OLDER EROTICA

THE GOVERNESS AT ST AGATHA'S	Yolanda Celbridge	
THE MASTER OF CASTLELEIGH	Jacqueline Bellevois	Aug
PRIVATE MEMOIRS OF A KENTISH HEADMISTRESS	Yolanda Celbridge £4.99	
THE RAKE	Aishling Morgan	Sep
THE TRAINING OF AN ENGLISH GENTLEMAN	Yolanda Celbridge	

SAMPLERS & COLLECTIONS

EROTICON 4	Various	
THE FIESTA LETTERS	ed. Chris Lloyd £4.99	
NEW EROTICA 3		
NEW EROTICA 4	Various	
A DOZEN STROKES	Various	Aug

NEXUS CLASSICS
A new imprint dedicated to putting the finest works of erotic fiction back in print

THE IMAGE	Jean de Berg	
CHOOSING LOVERS FOR JUSTINE	Aran Ashe	
THE INSTITUTE	Maria del Rey	
AGONY AUNT	G. C. Scott	
THE HANDMAIDENS	Aran Ashe	
OBSESSION	Maria del Rey	
HIS MASTER'S VOICE	G.C. Scott	Aug
CITADEL OF SERVITUDE	Aran Ashe	Sep
BOUND TO SERVE	Amanda Ware	Oct
BOUND TO SUBMIT	Amanda Ware	Nov
SISTERHOOD OF THE INSTITUTE	Maria del Rey	Dec

Please send me the books I have ticked above.

Name ....

Address ....

....

....

.... Post code........................

Send to: **Cash Sales, Nexus Books, Thames Wharf Studios, Rainville Road, London W6 9HT**

US customers: for prices and details of how to order books for delivery by mail, call 1-800-805-1083.

Please enclose a cheque or postal order, made payable to **Nexus Books**, to the value of the books you have ordered plus postage and packing costs as follows:

UK and BFPO – £1.00 for the first book, 50p for the second book and 30p for each subsequent book to a maximum of £3.00;

Overseas (including Republic of Ireland) – £2.00 for the first book, £1.00 for the second book and 50p for each subsequent book.

We accept all major credit cards, including VISA, ACCESS/ MASTERCARD, AMEX, DINERS CLUB, SWITCH, SOLO, and DELTA. Please write your card number and expiry date here:

....

Please allow up to 28 days for delivery.

Signature ....